哈福

Financial Accounting English QR Code 版

財務會計英語
看這本就夠了！

- **Revenue and Expenses** (收入與支出)
- **Debits and Credits** (借方與貸方)
- **Cash Flow Statement** (現金流量表)
- **Assets and Liabilities** (資產與負債)

百萬高薪族最佳跳板

附QR碼線上音檔
行動學習・即刷即聽

張瑪麗 ◎編著

哈福

[前言]

同步學會英語 & 財會觀念
快速成為百萬高薪族

● ● ● ● ● --------------------------------

　　在外商會計師事務所上班，年薪動輒百萬、千萬，是屬於令人欣羨的高薪族，資深者甚至有可能成為分公司的股東，賺取更多的公司分配利潤，還可以繞著地球跑，和全球頂尖企業家往來，所以，為了創造美好的人生，非學好財務會計英語不可，我有個朋友在 4 大會計師事務所之一上班，她就是一個鮮明的例子。

本書可幫助您：
   1. 迅速提升英語能力
   2. 打好財務會計觀念
   3. 快速學會財務管理訣竅

本書分二部份：

Part 1 財務會計英語入門

　　本書是一本主題特別的英語學習書籍！它的功能也是多面向的！作者希望藉由編纂英語會話，同時傳遞財務會計的專業概念，使讀者能提昇英語能力、打好財務會計觀念、快速學會財務管理訣竅，三者同步精進，迅速累積知識，一舉多得。

　　本書專為學生、一般大眾、企業人士、中小企業經營者、財務會計相關工作者學習英語而寫。對於已有財會概念者，本書引導你的英語能力結合專業更上層樓；不懂財務或初學財會概念的讀者，可以學習英語、吸收財會觀念兩者同時並進。擁有靈活的英語會話，又有正確的財會概念，將使你比別人更有競爭力，對工作發展當然更是莫大的助力。

　　作者以主題式的學習設計為主軸，使讀者悠游在有趣、有情境的語言學習氛圍裡，這樣的學習效果更好、收穫更豐富。本書設定幾種常見的財務對話情境，藉由口語化的英語交談，討論有關會計工作的話題。

　　在此你會了解到會計師的簡要工作內涵、基本的會計流程、了解何為收入支出、認識現金法、應記法、資產或負債等名詞代表的意義。這些專業的討論都以英語會話或例句呈現，協助你在很短的時間內，就能用流利英語洽談財會相關事宜，成功表達無障礙。

　　新時代的競爭無所不在，既要允文允武，速度上更要不落人後；優良的英語能力只是基礎，更強的是在各項專業領域也有所涉獵。尤其在財經方面，更要有基本認知，才能與人侃侃而談。認識財務會計觀念，幫助你規畫未來的人生與發展，發掘自己的財務天賦，這是現代人不可或缺的知識背景。

財會英語範圍廣闊，專業領域的語言學習是必經的過程。大部分的人，都是碰到問題了才想學，這樣顯得被動。若能主動學習，在專業領域上即能勝人一籌，在競爭激烈的時代，不怕沒機會，只怕沒準備，讓財務會計英語成為自己的強項，不但對工作有幫助，也讓自己對理財更有概念。

Part 2財務會計英語會話

第二部份是一本生活化的英語會話學習書籍，作者希望藉由編纂英語會話，同時傳遞財務會計的專業概念，使讀者能提昇英語會話能力以及吸收財務會計觀念，迅速累積知識，一舉數得。

作者以一家會計師事務所同事之間生活化的英語會話，討論有關會計工作的話題，使讀者沉浸在有趣、有情境的語言學習氛圍裡，學習的效果也更佳、收穫更豐富。本書設定幾種常見的會計對話情境，在此你會了解到會計師的相關工作內涵與英語專有名詞，這些專業的討論都以英語會話呈現，協助你了解會計師的工作與生活，學習到運用英語與人就會計相關主題暢談、交換意見。

在每個情境英語會話中，介紹簡要的會計工作內容、基本的會計概念與流程，例如借方/貸方、總分類帳、支票、收據、日記帳、應收／應付帳款、資產或負債、損益表、未付清帳款的發票、收益表、折舊、現金流量表、現金法、應記法、零用金、結帳等專有名詞。

對於已學過財務會計者，本書引導你的英語能力結合專業更上層樓；不懂或初學財務會計概念的讀者，可以學習財會英語、吸收財會觀念兩者同時並進。促進英語會話能力，又加強會計概念，將使你比別人更有競爭力，對工作發展當然更是莫大的助力。

本書內容深入淺出，讓您在短時間內，熟悉財經英語，舉止、言談輕鬆、流暢，用英語與人溝通，一點也不費力。不論您是業務行銷人士、企業主管、各級經理人員，或是有心尋求昇遷的上班族，都能讓您在一陣唇槍舌戰中，完成任務，達到雙贏的局面。

● ● ● ● ● ----------------------------

這是大家的第一本財務會計英語學習書：‧專為想學財務會計英語者編寫，

‧學校、企業人士、財務會計相關工作皆適用！

‧Step by step，學好財務會計管理英語，

‧快速學會財務會計專業英語會話，

‧短時間，流利開口說財務會計英語，

‧外商會計師事務所上班必備英語。

在每個情境英語會話中，介紹簡要的會計工作內涵、基本的會計概念與流程，例如借方／貸方、總分類帳、支票、收據、日記帳、應收／應付帳款、資產或負債、損益表、未付清帳款的發票、收益表、折舊、現金流量表、現金法、應記法、零用金、結帳等專有名詞和常用會話。

本書內容特色

1. 原汁原味・美語會話

特聘請財會英語專家撰寫，內容自然生活化，故事輕鬆有趣，情境逼真，實用美語，讓您想一口氣看完，實力馬上突飛猛進！

2. 對話簡潔・方便套用

藉由故事中角色輕鬆的對話討論財經話題，讀完可以馬上跟英語同好沙盤演練一番，英語口說聽力絕對一把罩！

3. 嚴謹編撰・專業錄音

由美籍專業人士精心錄製的精質線上 MP3，發音純正標準，腔調自然符合情境，讓您在實況會話的帶領下，快速學會道地美式發音，搭配學習，效果加倍！

4. 實況對話・生動流利

特地營造出最佳英語環境，把英語帶進生活圈，做個聽、說皆棒的「國際人」。本書讓您時時說英語，日日皆進步。與人對答如流，實力大躍進。

Contents

Part 2 財務會計英語實用會話

Chapter 1 Overworked 工作過度

Part 1 財務會計英語入門

Chapter 1

The People
人

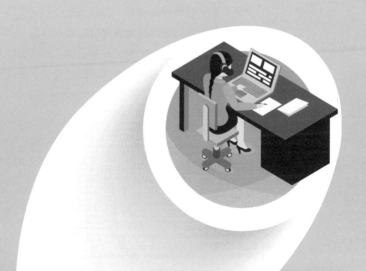

Unit 1 Choosing an Accountant
選擇一個會計師

`MP3-2`

Choosing an **accountant** to work in your business or on your business should not be taken lightly. Ask the accountant you are interested in for **references** from other **clients**. Make sure that you like this person and trust them. They will be *in charge of* your company's money. That's why you want to choose wisely when you choose an accountant. Some accounting people work right in the company if it's a large company. Some accounting people work for an **accounting firm**. They may have several different businesses as clients. Either way, the person must be **trustworthy**.

> **提示**　選擇一位會計師不應該掉以輕心。要求你有興趣的會計師提供其他客戶的推薦。確定你喜歡這個人，並且信任他們。他們將管理你公司的金錢。這是為什麼你要明智地選擇會計師的原因。如果是一家大公司，一些會計人員會直接在那間公司裡上班；一些會計人員在會計師事務所上班。他們的客戶可能是數家不同的公司。總之，這個人都必須值得信任。

Dialogue 1

A　We need a new accountant. Our accountant is moving out of the country.

B   We could use a different accountant from the same firm.

A   No. I don't like that firm. I think they **charge** too much.

B   Yes. I know what you mean. We could shop around for a better **rate**.

A   Good stuff. I'll grab the phone book. We'll start by looking in the yellow pages.

中譯 ··

A: 我們需要一位新的會計師。我們的會計師要搬到國外去住。

B: 我們可以用來自同間事務所的另一位會計師。

A: 不，我不喜歡那家公司，我認為他們收費太高了。

B: 是啊，我知道你的意思，我們可以到處找找有沒有比較好的價錢。

A: 好主意。我去拿電話簿，我們從黃頁開始看。

Dialogue 2

A   Excuse me. I have just opened up a business and my bank account is at this bank.

B   Yes? What can I do for you today?

A   I don't know who to ask. I need an accountant. There are so many to choose from.

B   Don't worry. Because we are a bank we get asked about accountants all the time.

A   There are so many. How do I choose? What do I need to know?

中譯 ··

A: 抱歉打擾。我剛開了一家公司，我的銀行帳戶在這家銀行。

B: 是嗎？我今天可以幫你什麼忙？

A: 我不知道該問誰，我需要一位會計師，但是有太多選擇可以選。

B: 別擔心。因為我們是一家銀行，經常有人問會計師的問題。

A: 有這麼多，我應該怎麼選擇？我需要知道什麼事？

Dialogue 3

A　We're thinking of having your firm do our accounting. We aren't happy right now.

B　I'm **flattered** that you are thinking of using our services. We would take care of you.

A　Has your firm worked with a business of this size? We are a very large company.

B　I know. Yes, we have. We have several clients that are as large as your company.

A　We need to know your rates. Since we are such a big company, we expect a good rate.

中譯

A:　我們在考慮請你們公司處理我們的會計事宜。我們對於現況不太滿意。

B:　對於您考慮讓我們服務,我感到很榮幸。我們會照顧您們的。

A:　你們公司曾服務過這種規模的公司嗎?我們是一家很大的公司。

B:　我知道。是的,我們有這樣的經驗。我們有好幾個客戶跟你們一樣是大間的公司。

A:　我們需要知道你們的收費標準。因為我們是這樣大的一個公司,所以我們希望得到好價錢。

Dialogue 4

A　Thank you for agreeing to see me on such short notice.

B　It's not a problem. That's what I'm here for. What did you want to see me about?

A　I am a **massage therapist**. I work out of my home. My home business is new.

B　Let me guess. You want to find an accountant to do your accounting. Am I right?

A　That's why I'm here. Will you be able to help me? Have I come to the right place?

中譯 ....

A: 謝謝你同意馬上就與我會面。

B: 這沒問題，本來就是我的工作。你來見我有什麼事？

A: 我是一個按摩治療師，我在外頭工作，我的家庭事業是新成立的。

B: 讓我猜猜！你想要找一個會計師幫你作帳。我說對了嗎？

A: 我就是因為這件事才到這裡來。你能幫助我嗎？我找對地方了嗎？

Dialogue 5

A　How long have you been an accountant? Do you have a lot of experience?

B　I have been an accountant for over thirty years. I know accounting very well.

A　You must like it. I was never very good with numbers. I didn't do well in math.

B　It's important to like money. It's also important to like people. I like both.

A　You sound like a nice lady. I'm new to town. I need an accountant.

A: 你擔任會計師的工作有多久了？你很有經驗嗎？

B: 我做會計師已經三十年了，我非常了解會計。

A: 你一定很喜歡這個工作。我一向對數字不在行。我的數學不好。

B: 喜歡錢很重要，喜歡人也很重要，我兩者都喜歡。

A: 你聽起來是一個不錯的女士，我剛到這個城市，我需要一位會計師。

Dialogue 6

A　My family has just moved to town. We are thinking about buying a clothing store.

B　What clothing store are you thinking of buying? I

didn't know there was one for sale.

A   There is a store on Main Street. It's called Fred's Fashions. Do you know it?

B   Yes. It's a good store. My husband buys his business suits there.

A   Before we make a decision, we need to have an accountant look at the books.

中譯

A: 我家剛剛搬進城裡來。我們考慮買下一間服飾店。

B: 你們考慮買什麼樣的服飾店？我不知道有任何店面在賣。

A: 在大街上有一家店，名字叫做佛雷德時尚。你知道這家店嗎？

B: 是的，那是一家不錯的店，我的丈夫都在那裡買西裝。

A: 在我們做決定之前，我們需要一位會計師來看看帳本。

Dialogue 7

A   We need to have someone on our staff to do our accounting full time.

B   I agree. Our **bills** from the accounting firm we're using are too expensive.

A   It would be more **cost effective** to have some on the **payroll** and in the office.

B   Yes. We could save this company a lot of money that way.

A   We need to **advertise** for the **position**. We'll put an ad in the paper next week.

中譯

A: 我們需要一個員工，全職地做我們的會計工作。

B: 我同意。我們所用的會計師事務所的帳單金額太高了。

A: 在辦公室裡雇一個在職人員會比較有經濟效益。

B: 對。這樣我們可以為公司省下很多錢。

A: 我們需要登廣告找人來擔任這個職位，我們會在下週的報紙裡登一則廣告。

There are several accounting firms listed in the phone book for us to choose from.	在電話簿裡有列出好幾家會計師事務所，可以供我們選擇。
How many accountants are there working in your firm?	你的公司裡有幾位會計師？
We must choose an accounting firm that has cost effective rates.	我們必須選擇一家收費標準最具有經濟效益的會計師事務所。
Will you place an ad in the local newspaper for an accountant who can do payroll?	你會在地方報紙上登一則廣告，請一位會計師來核算薪水嗎？
We're thinking of having your firm do our accounting	我們在考慮請你的公司來幫我們作帳。
We need to have someone on our staff full time to do our accounting.	我們需要請一位全職的在職人員來做我們的會計工作。
Has your firm has worked with a business of this size? We are a very large company.	你們公司曾服務過這種規模的公司嗎？我們是一家很大的公司。

Vocabulary 字彙

accountant	*n.*	會計師
client	*n.*	客戶

reference	*n.*	推薦
accounting firm	*n.*	會計師事務所
trustworthy	*adj.*	值得信任
charge	*v.*	收費
rate	*n.*	價錢
flattered	*adj.*	榮幸
massage therapist	*n.*	按摩治療師
bills	*n.*	帳單
cost effective	*n.*	經濟效益
payroll	*n.*	在職人員
advertise	*v.*	登廣告
position	*n.*	職位

Useful Phrases 實用片語

In charge of 負責、管理

This means to be in control of or responsible for.

例句 I'm in charge of doing the payroll for this accounting firm.
我在這個會計師事務所裡負責核算薪水。

Good stuff 真好

This is an expression that means something is good or the speaker agrees.

例句 You're done checking his references? Good stuff. We'll make a decision tomorrow.
你已經查過他的推薦人了？真好。我們明天就做決定。

Short notice 馬上、臨時

This means something is occurring without much warning.

例句 I'm sorry to do this to you on short notice but we have to cancel your appointment.
我很抱歉臨時這樣做，但是我們必須取消你的預約。

Unit 2 A Career in Accounting
會計事業

MP3-3

Accountants aren't the only people who do work in accounting for a living. There are lots of people who have different training and different titles who work in this field. In order to be called an accountant the person must have a university degree in accounting. The person would attend the college of commerce at a university to get an accounting degree.

提示 會計師並不是唯一以會計維生的人，還有許多接受不同訓練，擁有不同頭銜的人在這個領域裡工作。被稱為會計師的人必須擁有會計的大學學位，這個人在大學裡必須上商學院才能拿到會計學位。

Dialogue 1

A You're almost done school. Soon you'll go to

university. What do you want to take?

B I've been thinking about that. I like math. I think I'll study accounting.

A If you take accounting, you can become an accountant. There are lots of jobs.

B I know. Every business needs someone who knows how to do accounting.

A You will be able to work any place where there's money coming in and going out.

中譯 ....

A: 你高中快要念完了，很快就要升上大學。你想要讀哪一科？

B: 我一直在考慮那件事，我喜歡數學，我想我會攻讀會計。

A: 如果你讀會計，你可以成為一位會計師，有很多工作機會。

B: 我知道。每間公司都需要一個知道如何做會計的人。

A: 你可以在任何有錢進出的地方工作。

Dialogue 2

A I can't **afford** to go to university. It would take me four years to get a degree.

B You would *end up* with a lot of **debt**. It's not good to owe money.

A There is a **career college** in this city. They offer an accounting **diploma**.

B What can you do with a diploma in accounting? It's not the same as a degree.

A No, it isn't but I can still work in accounting. I would be an **accounting technician**.

中譯 ....

A: 我無法負擔上大學的費用，我要花四年才可以得到一個學位。

B: 你最後會有很多負債，欠錢不太好。

A: 這座城市裡有一個職業學院，他們有提供會計證書的課程。

B: 你修一個會計證書有什麼用？它跟學位又不一樣。

A: 是不一樣，但是我仍然可以在會計界工作，我可以做一個會計技術員。

Dialogue 3

A　We are looking to hire an accountant. What did you take in university?

B　I have a degree. I studied finance and management in the college of commerce.

A　That sounds very interesting. Please tell me more about your education.

B　In my program I studied management accounting for future managers.

A　That's good. We hope to hire an accountant who can become a **partner** in the firm.

中譯

A:　我們想雇用一位會計師，你在大學裡修什麼科目？

B:　我有學位，我在商學院裡讀財務與管理。

A:　那聽起來很有趣，請多告訴我一些關於你教育的事。

B:　在我的課程中，我學習為未來的經理管理會計事務。

A:　那很好。我們希望雇用一個能在公司裡變成合夥人的會計師。

Dialogue 4

A　It's nice to meet you, Steve. I'm glad you came to the party. What do you do?

B　I'm a **certified financial analyst**. This is a nice party. Thank you for inviting me.

A　Oh, my goodness. What a long title you have. What does it mean?

B　It means I have a degree in commerce and I majored in finance. What do you do?

A　I have a bakery not too far from here. We've never used a financial analyst.

中譯

A:　史提夫，很高興認識你，我很高興你來參加派對。你的工作是什麼？

B: 我是一個有證照的財務分析師。這是個不錯的派對。謝謝你邀請我。

A: 喔，我的天啊，你的頭銜真長，它的意思是什麼？

B: 它的意思是我擁有商業學位，主修財務。你的工作是什麼？

A: 我在這附近開了一家麵包店，我們從來沒用過財務分析師。

Dialogue 5

A　Hello, Mrs. Smith. Thank you for coming. Let me introduce you to our team.

B　Great. I want to meet all of the people in your firm. They'll be working hard for me.

A　There is Sandra. She is an **investment manager**. She will advise you on saving.

B　Good. Do you have a **quality manager** on staff? That'd be good for my company.

A　Yes, we do. His name is Ken. He's very good and he's been with us for a long time.

中譯

A: 史密斯先生，您好。謝謝你跑一趟，讓我來介紹我們的團隊。

B: 很好。我想要認識你公司裡所有的人，他們都會為我努力的工作。

A: 這是珊卓。她是投資經理，她會在存款上給您建議。

B: 很好。你們有品管經理嗎？這會對我們的公司很好。

A: 我們有。他的名字是肯，他很不錯，在我們公司裡很久了。

Dialogue 6

A　Hello, Janet. It's nice to finally meet you. Tommy has told me so much about you.

B　Our boys *get along* so well. They are very good friends. Where do you work?

A　I work at Anderson Accounting. I'm an accountant. I've been there for two years.

B　Are you a **certified management accountant**? My brother does that.

A　No. I'm a **certified general accountant**. That's different from what your brother does.

中譯

A: 珍納你好。很高興終於能見到你，湯米告訴我很多關於你的事。

B: 我們的孩子相處得很好，他們是好朋友。你在哪裡工作？

A: 我在安德生會計事務所工作，我是一位會計師，我在那裡兩年了。

B: 你是一位有證照的管理會計師嗎？我的哥哥是。

A: 不，我是一個有證照的一般會計師。跟你哥哥的工作不一樣。

Dialogue 7

A　There has been a crime committed. We think that someone has stolen money.

B　If there has been money stolen from the company that's not good. What do we do?

A　We'll call the police. They have people with accounting backgrounds who can help.

B　Who do the police know that could help us find out who has stolen money?

A　They will send a **certified forensic investigator** and a **certified fraud investigator**.

中譯

A: 有人犯罪了，我們認為有人偷了錢。

B: 如果公司裡有錢被偷走那就不好了，我們怎麼辦？

A: 我們可以叫警察，他們會有具會計背景的人可以幫忙。

B: 警察知道誰能幫我們找到偷錢的人嗎？

A: 他們會派一個有證照的鑑識調查員與有證照的詐欺調查員來。

Sentence Structure 重點句型

The people who can afford to get a university degree get to introduce themselves by long titles.	能負擔去大學讀書拿學位的人，就可以用長長的頭銜介紹自己。
I'll go into debt if my son goes in the college of commerce.	如果我的兒子去讀商學院，我就會負債了。
My son would go to a career college to get a diploma but he has been hired by a bakery.	我的兒子本來要去專業學院修一個證書，但他被一家麵包店雇用了。
I introduced that accounting technician to a person who majored in finance in university.	我把那位會計技術員介紹給一位在大學攻讀財務的人。
It's good to check our employees' backgrounds to see if they have committed a crime.	調查我們員工的背景，看看他們是否曾犯罪，這是不錯的。
There are lots of people who have different training and titles who work accounting.	有許多接受不同訓練，擁有不同頭銜的人在會計領域裡工作。
Every business needs someone who can do their accounting.	每個公司都需要會處理會計事務的人。

| You'll be able to work anywhere there's money coming in and going out. | 你可以在任何有錢進出的地方工作。 |

Vocabulary 字彙

title	n.	頭銜
field	n.	領域
university degree	n.	大學學位
college of commerce	n.	商學院
afford	v.	負擔
debt	n.	負債
career college	n.	職業學院
diploma	n.	證書
accounting technician	n.	會計技術員
partner	n.	合夥人
certified financial analyst	n.	有證照的財務分析師
investment manager	n.	投資經理
quality manager	n.	品管經理
certified management accountant	n.	有證照的管理會計師
certified general accountant	n.	有證照的一般會計師
certified forensic investigator	n.	有證照的鑑識調查員
certified fraud investigator	n.	有證照的詐欺調查員

Useful Phrases 實用片語

End up 結果、結束

This means to arrive at or to finish at.

例句 I'm going to end up becoming an accounting technician because I can't afford university.
因為我負擔不起大學的費用，我最後會成為一個會計技術員。

That's good 那很好

This is an expression that shows approval.

例句 You're going to become a certified forensic investigator? That's good.
你將成為一個有證照的鑑識調查員。那很好。

Nice to meet you 很高興見到你

This is an expression that's almost always said when two people meet.

例句 Fred, this is Wilma. We work together. Wilma, I want you to meet my good friend Fred.
佛瑞德，這是威瑪。我們一起工作。威瑪，我要你見見我的好朋友佛瑞德。

It's nice to meet you, Wilma.
很高興見到你，威瑪。

Nice to meet you too, Fred.
很高興見到你，佛瑞德。

Oh, my goodness 喔，我的老天啊

This is an expression that shows surprise.

例句 You want to become a certified management accountant? Oh, my goodness. What a title.
你想要變成一位有證照的管理會計師？喔，我的老天啊。真是個了不起的頭銜。

Team 團隊

This word is taken from sports and is often used instead of the word "staff".

例句 Donna, I want you to meet your new team of salespeople. They're ready to work hard.
堂娜，我要你見見你的新團隊裡的銷售人員。他們已經準備好要努力工作了。

Get along 相處

This means to work well with someone or to enjoy being with them.

例句 Our certified general accountant gets along well with the quality manager.
我們有證照的一般會計師與品管經理相處融洽。

Unit 3 The Clients
客戶

MP3-4

Most clients of accountants are businesses or companies. Some people get accountants to take care of their personal finances but most do this by themselves. Accountants can help anyone who has money whether it's lots or just a little. They help all types of businesses whether they're big or small.

提示　會計師的多數客戶都是企業或公司，有些人找會計師來掌管他們的個人財務，但大多數人自己管財務。會計師可以幫助任何有錢的人，不管是有很多錢還是只有一點錢。他們幫助各種類型的公司，不管是大公司還是小公司。

Dialogue 1

A　I'm a business person. I have a small business **downtown**. Are you an accountant?

B　Yes. I work with all different sizes of business. Do you have an accountant?

A　I do, but I'm not happy with his work. He's very busy and I feel like he has no time.

B　You feel **neglected**. It's not good for a client to feel that way. Maybe I can help.

A　Let's talk about your services and how you can help me. I might give you my work.

中譯

A：　我是一個生意人。我在市中心鬧區有一個小公司。你是一位會計師嗎？

B：　是，我是。我為各種不同大小的公司工作。你有會計師嗎？

A：　我有，但我對他的工作不滿意。他很忙，我覺得他沒有時間。

B：　你覺得被忽略了，讓客戶有這種感覺是不好的，或許我能幫忙。

A：　我們談談你的服務以及你能夠如何幫助我，我或許會給你工作。

Dialogue 2

A　Our biggest client is coming in this afternoon. I want you to treat them very well.

B　I will. What is the name of the company? Who

will I be talking to?

A   It's a **chain** of clothing stores. It's the largest in the country. Martha is coming.

B   Will I be **dealing** with Martha all by herself? Will someone else be coming with her?

A   Martha will have some **advisors** with her. They go with her wherever she goes.

中譯

A: 我們最大的客戶今天下午要來，我要你好好款待他們。

B: 我會的。（他們）公司的名稱是什麼？我會與誰交談？

A: 那是一個服飾連鎖店。它是國內最大的（連鎖店）。瑪莎要來。

B: 我會一個人招待瑪莎嗎？還是有其他人會跟她一起來？

A: 瑪莎會帶一些顧問一起來。她到什麼地方，他們都會隨行。

Dialogue 3

A   You've just started your own **consulting** business. It's a **home based** business right?

B   That's correct. I officially opened for business less than a year ago.

A   You'll need an accountant soon. Your **year end** is coming. You'll need help.

B   I think I can manage. There isn't much to do. I don't have many customers yet.

A   Please take my business card. Please call me when you decide you do need someone.

中譯

A: 你才剛開始自己的顧問公司。它是一個在家經營的公司，對吧？

B: 沒錯。我正式開始營業是一年不到之前。

A: 你不久就會需要一個會計師，你的年底結算快到了，你會需要幫忙。

B: 我想我可以應付，沒有太多事可以做，我還沒有許多客戶。

A: 請收下我的名片。當你決定自己確實需要某人的時候，請打電話給我。

Dialogue 4

A　Jennifer is a very famous movie star. She wants our firm to do her accounting.

B　Doesn't she have an accountant already? Why would she need us?

A　She did have some people in charge of her finances but they stole from her.

B　I hope she fired them. That kind of person gives the good ones like us a bad name.

A　She did fire them. Now she needs help. That's why she wants to hire us.

中譯

A：珍妮佛是個非常有名的電影明星，她要我們的事務所幫她做會計工作。

B：她不是已經有一位會計師了嗎？為什麼她會需要我們？

A：的確有人在管理她的財務，但是他們偷她的錢。

B：我希望她把他們開除，這種人讓我們這些好人的名聲大壞。

A：她是把他們炒魷魚了。現在，她需要幫忙。這是為什麼她要雇用我們的原因。

Dialogue 5

A　I don't know how to do my **income tax return**. Will you help me?

B　I'll tell you a secret. I don't know how to do them either. I use an accountant.

A　An accountant? Wouldn't that be expensive? You are just one person.

B　It doesn't cost that much. Besides, I know it's done right. It doesn't take long.

A　Tell me about your accountant. If you think she does a good job I might go to her.

中譯

A: 我不知道怎樣辦我的所得稅申報，你能幫我嗎？

B: 我要告訴你一個秘密，我也不知道要怎麼申報，我雇用一個會計師。

A: 會計師？那不會很貴嗎？你只有一個人。

B: 它不會很花錢。除此之外，我知道事情都做對了，而且不花很久的時間。

A: 告訴我你的會計師是誰。如果你認為她做得不錯，我或許會找她。

Dialogue 6

A My husband always used to do our taxes. Now that we have split up I need help.

B I can show you how to do them. Then you can do them all by yourself.

A I don't want to do them. I was never any good at math. Maybe you'd do them.

B You should do your own taxes. That's best. Besides, I don't have time.

A Maybe I'll go see an accountant. Then I won't need to know how to do taxes.

中譯

A: 我的丈夫總是習慣報我們的稅。現在，我們離婚了，我需要幫忙。

B: 我可以教你報稅的方法。然後，你就可以自己報了。

A: 我不要自己報，我數學向來不行，或許你可以幫我報。

B: 你應該自己報稅，這樣最好了。此外，我沒有時間。

A: 或許我應該去見會計師。那我就不需要知道如何報稅了。

Dialogue 7

A You have a small store and your wife is a **real estate agent**. Is that right?

B　Yes. We also have one daughter in university and a son who is **disabled**.

A　You **definitely** need the help of an accountant to do all of your taxes.

B　Can you do the taxes for everyone in the family? That would be good.

A　That's the best thing we can do. We'll do everyone's taxes for you all at once.

中譯

A:　你有一間小店，你的太太是一個房地產經紀人，這樣對嗎？

B:　是的。我們也有一個女兒在讀大學，還有一個殘障的兒子。

A:　你肯定需要一個會計師來幫你報所有的稅。

B:　你能幫家裡的每一個人報稅嗎？這樣會很好。

A:　這是我們所能做最好的事了，我們會一次幫你們所有人報稅。

Sentence Structure　重點句型

My personal advisor wants to know whether or not I want my business to be home based.	我的個人顧問想知道，我是不是要在家經營生意。
He neglected to tell me about the types of chain stores that I could invest in.	他忽略了告訴我，我可以投資哪一種連鎖店。
I'm in consulting and my year end is officially two weeks from now.	我是做顧問諮詢的，而我的年底結算正式來說是兩個星期以後。
My real estate agent is famous for handing in her income tax return late.	我的房地產經紀人是以遲交所得稅申報著稱的。

I definitely think where he gets his accounting done is a secret.	我肯定地認為，關於他的會計事務在哪裡做是個秘密。
Most clients of accountants are businesses or companies.	會計師大部分的客戶都是企業或公司。
I'm an accountant. Take my business card and call me when you need someone.	我是一位會計師。拿我的名片並在你需要人的時候打電話給我。

Vocabulary 字彙

downtown	n.	市中心鬧區
neglect	v.	忽略
chain	n.	連鎖店
deal		招待
advisor	n.	顧問
consulting	adj.	顧問的
home based	adj.	在家經營
year end	n.	年底
income tax return	n.	所得稅申報
real estate agent	n.	房地產經紀人
disabled	adj.	殘障的
definitely	adv.	肯定地

Useful Phrases 實用片語

Movie Star 電影明星

This phrase refers to an actor who is well known or famous.

例句 There are lots of movie stars who live in Hollywood, in America.
有許多電影明星住在美國的好萊塢。

Split up 分手、離婚

This means a couple has divorced or ended their relationship with each other.

例句 After his sister Janet split up with her husband Ted, he didn't see Ted any more.
在他姊姊珍納與她丈夫泰德離婚後，他就再也沒有見過泰德了。

Chapter 2

The Basics
基本規則

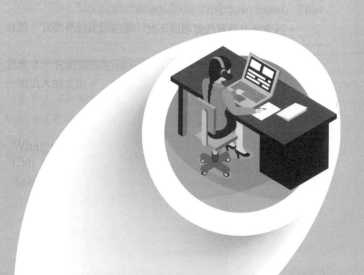

Unit 1 Keeping Good Records
把記錄保存好

MP3-5

Accountants need to keep good records. Businesses and companies need to keep good records for their accountants. A good suggestion is to keep a filing cabinet that is just to be used for accounting and bookkeeping records and papers. Keeping all financial records and documents separate from other things will help the business to keep good records.

提示　　會計師需要將記錄保存好。企業與公司需要為他們的會計師將記錄保存好。一個好建議是留一個檔案櫃只放會計與簿記記錄和文件。將所有的財務記錄與文件與其他東西分開，有助於一家公司將記錄保存好。

Dialogue 1

A　Good morning. I'm your new accountant. We need to talk about your records.

B　Do you mean my accounting records? I'll be glad to hear what you have to say.

A　You need to keep better records. Your financial records aren't very good.

B　I know. That's because I don't know what to keep and how to keep it.

A　Keep your papers well organized and separate from all other types of documents.

中譯

A:　早安。我是你的新會計師。我們需要跟你談一談你的記錄。

B: 你是說我的會計記錄嗎？我會很高興聽你想要說的事情。

A: 你需要把記錄保存得更好，你的財務記錄不是很好。

B: 我知道。這是因為我不知道什麼要保存以及如何保存。

A: 將你的文件組織好，並將其他種類的文件分開。

Dialogue 2

A Our accountant loves you. She says you make her work easier. What's your secret?

B I **keep track** of all the money coming in and money going out of our business.

A That's what I thought. I've never paid attention. How do you do that?

B You need to be an organized person and everything needs to be documented.

A If you're recording all **transactions** in our business you're keeping good records.

中譯

A: 我們的會計師喜歡你。她說你讓她的工作較容易。你的秘訣是什麼？

B: 我記錄所有進出我們公司的錢。

A: 我也是這麼想。我從來不注意。你怎麼做的？

B: 你必須做個有組織的人，每一件事都必須記錄下來。

A: 如果你記錄我們公司所有的交易，你的記錄就保存得很好。

Dialogue 3

A Thank you for agreeing to let us interview you for the accounting position.

B I'm the one who should be thanking you for this chance at a job with your firm.

A As you know, we are an accounting firm. We need people who keep good records.

B You will find that I'm well organized and I document everything.

A　You will also have to **sort** through the poor records that most of our clients keep.

中譯 ....

A: 謝謝你同意接受我們為會計這個職位所舉行的面試。

B: 我才是應該謝謝你們給我這個機會，為你們公司工作。

A: 正如你所知，我們是一個會計師事務所，我們需要會保存良好記錄的人。

B: 你會發現我是一個很有組織的人，我每件事情都記下來。

A: 你也必須整理我們大多數客戶所保存的雜亂記錄。。

Dialogue 4

A　Thank you for coming. We're setting up our new office and need your input.

B　It's no problem. I'm glad to help. What do you need to know?

A　You're our accountant. You'll know best. How should we keep our records for you?

B　I suggest you have a filing cabinet that's just for financial documents.

A　That's where we'll keep all the files on different **vendors** and **purchasers**.

中譯 ....

A: 謝謝你來。我們正在設立新的辦公室，需要你的投入。

B: 這沒有問題，我很高興可以幫忙。你需要知道些什麼？

A: 你是我們的會計師，你最清楚，我們應該如何為你保存我們的記錄？

B: 我建議你專為財務文件準備一個檔案櫃。

A: 我們會在那裡保存所有不同賣主與買主的檔案。

Dialogue 5

A　Since I'm the new secretary I need to know where everything goes in the office.

B Do you see this top **drawer** in the filing cabinet? This is where all our **suppliers** go.

A Okay. Files for suppliers go in the top drawer. What goes in the bottom drawer?

B That's where all the files on our customers go. The people we supply to.

A Files on money going out go in the top drawer. Money coming in goes in the bottom.

中譯

A: 因為我是新秘書，我需要知道所有東西在這間辦公室裡的位置。

B: 你看到這個檔案櫃頂端的抽屜嗎？這是我們供應商資料的位置。

A: 好。供應商的檔案放在頂端抽屜，什麼資料放在底部抽屜？

B: 那是我們放所有客戶檔案的地方，我們提供產品的對象。

A: 金錢流出的檔案放在頂端的抽屜，金錢流進來的檔案放在底部抽屜。

Dialogue 6

A What are you doing? Is that the **receipt book** you're writing in?

B Yes. I'm writing a receipt.

A But that lady who just paid us said she didn't need a receipt.

B I know but we need to record that **payment** some how so we can keep good records.

A I see. There have been three times that I've taken a payment and not recorded it.

中譯

A: 你在做什麼？你在寫的是收據本嗎？

B: 對。我正在寫一張收據。

A: 但是，剛剛付錢給我們的女士說她不要收據。

B: 我知道，我們需要以某種方式記錄這筆款項，這樣我們才能保存記錄。

A: 我懂了。我已經收了三次款卻沒有記下來。

Dialogue 7

A This receipt book is full now. We need another one. Should I throw this one away?

B *Are you crazy?* Just because it's full doesn't mean that it's garbage. Give it to me.

A What are you going to do with it? Are you going to keep it?

B It goes in the financial records now. It has information in it for our accountant.

A That's good to know. I won't throw the next one out when it gets full.

中譯

A: 這個收據本現在已經寫滿了，我們需要另外一本，我應該把這本丟掉嗎？

B: 你瘋了嗎？只因為它被寫滿了，並不表示它就是垃圾。把它拿給我。

A: 你要拿它做什麼？你打算把它保存下來嗎？

B: 它現在要歸入財務記錄中，它裡面有要給我們會計師的資料。

A: 知道這件事很好。當下一本被寫滿時，我就不會把它丟了。

Sentence Structure 重點句型

She suggested we keep our bookkeeping records and documents in a filing cabinet.	她建議我們將簿記記錄與文件保存在檔案櫃裡。
The secretary put the files on our suppliers in the drawer with the old receipt books.	秘書把我們供應商的檔案與舊的收據本放在這個抽屜裡。

I agreed to be interviewed for the position. It was my chance to give them some input.	我同意接受這個職位的面試。這是我給他們一些資訊的機會。
We need to keep track of and pay attention to our transactions with all purchasers.	我們需要記錄並注意我們與所有買主的交易。
Keep a filing cabinet that is just used for accounting and bookkeeping records and papers.	留存一個檔案櫃只放會計與簿記記錄和文件。
Keeping financial documents separate will help the business to keep good records.	將所有的財務記錄與文件與其他東西分開，有助於一家公司將記錄保存好。

Vocabulary 字彙

record	n.	記錄
filing cabinet	n.	檔案櫃
bookkeeping	n.	簿記
keep track		記錄
transaction	n.	交易
sort	v.	整理
vendors	n.	賣主
purchasers	n.	買主
drawer	n.	抽屜
suppliers	n.	供應商
receipt book	n.	收據本

payment   *n.*   款項

Useful Phrases 實用片語

Loves 喜歡

can mean "likes very much" or "is impressed with"

例句 My boss loves when I bring in cookies on Friday afternoons.
我的老闆喜歡我星期五下午帶餅乾進辦公室。

Are you crazy? 你瘋了嗎？

This expression means that the speaker doesn't agree at all.

例句 You threw the information and records on the vendors in the garbage? Are you crazy?
你將賣家的資料與記錄丟在垃圾裡？你瘋了嗎？

Unit 2 Debits and Credits
借方與貸方   MP3-6

Debits and credits are the fundamentals of accounting. The idea of debits and credits must be understood before anything else can be learned. Making a debit or a credit is easy. However, any mistakes made with a debit or a credit can become bigger and bigger.

This is why it's important to pay attention when making a debit or a credit.

提示   借方與貸方是會計的基本原則。必須先了解借方與貸方的觀念，才可以學習其他的東西。標示借貸很簡單。然而，在借方或貸方上一出錯，錯誤會變得愈來愈大。這就是為什麼在標示借貸時要專心是很重要的。

Dialogue 1

A   Okay. Remember that our clients do not understand accounting. They don't like it.

B   I don't know why anyone wouldn't like accounting. It's very simple.

A   It's very simple when you understand it. Our clients don't. They think it's difficult.

B   I know. It's our job to make it easy. All they need to know is debits and credits.

A   It's a little more **complicated** than that but debits and credits are the basics, yes.

中譯

A: 好。記得我們的客戶不了解會計，他們不喜歡它。

B: 我不懂為什麼有人不喜歡會計，它非常簡單。

A: 當你了解它時，它就很簡單。我們的客戶不了解，他們認為它是困難的。

B: 我知道。我們的工作就是讓它變得簡單，他們所需要知道的就是借方與貸方。

A: 比那要複雜一些，但是借方與貸方是基本的，對。

Dialogue 2

A   The financial information we give to our clients helps them to run their businesses.

B　Why don't people just use computers to do their accounting themselves?

A　People are **intimidated** by numbers. They don't understand debits and credits.

B　A debit is simply an entry made in the **general ledger**. That's all a credit is too.

A　I know that and you know that but lots of people don't. They think it's yucky.

中譯 ....

A:　我們給客戶的財務資料可以幫助他們管理自己的公司。

B:　為什麼人們不使用電腦做自己的會計事務？

A:　人們對數字感到害怕，他們不了解借方與貸方。

B:　借方只是在總帳裡記上的一條帳目，貸方也是這樣。

A:　我知道，你也知道，但很多人不知道。他們認為它很討人厭。

Dialogue 3

A　Have you **posted** all the debits to the general ledger?

B　I have. There were lots to record because I haven't done the books in days.

A　Have you recorded all of the credits as well?

B　Yes. It took longer than the debits did. That's good. Credits mean money for us.

A　Yes. I like to see very few debits and lots of credits. It means we're making money.

中譯 ....

A:　你把所有的借方都記入總帳中嗎？

B:　我有。有許多的記錄，因為我已經好幾天沒有記帳了。

A:　你是不是連所有的貸方都有記錄？

B:　對。它比借方更花時間，這樣很好，貸方是給我們的錢。

A:　是。我樂見非常少的借方帳目，但有許多的貸方帳目。這就表示我們在賺錢。

Dialogue 4

A   I'm glad to be taking this accounting **course**. Please explain **balancing** again.

B   Okay. I'll start by telling you about debits and credits again.

A   I know. They are the most important part of accounting.

B   That's right. There's a thing that is called the general ledger.

A   Yes. Every entry you make in the general ledger must have a debit and a credit.

中譯

A: 我很高興去上這個會計課程，請再一次解釋收支平衡。

B: 好。我就從告訴你借貸方再開始一次。

A: 我知道。它們是會計中最重要的部分。

B: 沒錯。還有稱為總帳的東西。

A: 對。你在總帳裡記入的每一筆帳目都必須有借方與貸方。

Dialogue 5

A   When you do one you always do the other. That's the rule with debits and credits.

B   Whenever I record a credit I must record a debit. I see. That's how you balance.

A   That's right. The books must always balance. All debits must equal all credits.

B   If they don't equal each other, it means the books are not balancing.

A   Out of balance entries mean that the whole record system is out of balance.

中譯

A: 當你記其中一個時，你總是要同時記另外一個。這就是借方與貸方的規則。

B: 每當我記錄一個貸方時，我必須同時記下一個借方。我懂了，這就是你使收支平衡的方式。

A: 沒錯。帳冊裡永遠必須平衡,所有的借方必須與貸方相等。

B: 如果它們彼此不相等,那就表示帳冊收支不平衡。

A: 不平衡的帳目記錄表示整個記錄系統都不平衡。

Dialogue 6

A A way of **explaining** accounting is that it's a record of the finances of a business.

B We help clients to have good records of the finances of their businesses.

A We make that record by making entries in a general ledger for each client.

B Our entries are debits and credits. Whenever we do one, we do the other.

A This is so the books balance. Our goal is to always have the books balance.

中譯

A: 解釋會計的一個方式是,它是一個公司的財務記錄。

B: 我們幫助客戶的公司保存良好的財務記錄。

A: 我們利用在總帳中記入帳目,為每個客戶製作記錄。

B: 我們的帳目就是借方與貸方。每當我們記下一個,我們(同時)記下另外一個。

A: 這樣帳冊才會收支平衡。我們的目標總是使帳冊收支平衡。

Dialogue 7

A This book that I record entries in is called the general ledger.

B Yes. I have seen books that look like that one before.

A All of the entries that I make in this book are either a debit or a credit.

B A debit is a record of money that will leave your business and **bank account**.

A　Yes. A credit is a record of money that will come into the business and bank account.

中譯

A:　我用來記錄帳目的這本帳冊稱為總帳。

B:　是。我以前看過跟這本相像的帳冊。

A:　我在這本帳冊中記錄的所有帳目，不是借方就是貸方。

B:　借方是會離開你的公司與銀行帳戶的金錢記錄。

A:　是。貸方就是會進入公司與銀行帳戶的金錢記錄。

Sentence Structure　重點句型

The fundamental rule of the accounting system is that all debits must equal all credits.	會計系統的基本規則是所有的借方與所有的貸方必須相等。
It's easy to understand posting to the general ledger. It's not difficult or complicated.	將帳目記入總帳中是很容易了解的，它並不困難或複雜。
Don't feel intimidated if you make mistakes while you're learning how to post entries.	當你在學習如何記入帳目時如果犯錯，不要覺得害怕。
This course will explain the ideas and rules of accounting things, like balancing.	這個課程會解釋會計事務的概念與規則，例如收支平衡。
Debits and credits are the fundamentals of accounting.	借方與貸方是會計的基本原則。

| I like to see very few debits and lots of credits. It means we're making money. | 我樂見非常少的借方帳目，但有許多的貸方帳目。這就表示我們在賺錢。 |
| People are intimidated by numbers. They don't understand debits and credits. | 人們對數字感到害怕。他們不了解借方與貸方。 |

Vocabulary 字彙

debits	n.	借方
credits	n.	貸方
fundamentals	n.	基本原則
complicated	adj.	複雜的
intimidated	adj.	感到害怕
general ledger		總帳
post	v.	記入
course	n.	課程
balancing	n.	收支平衡
explain	v.	解釋
bank account		銀行帳戶

Useful Phrases 實用片語

Yucky 討人厭的

This means something is not nice or is unpleasant.

例句 I don't want to take a course on accounting. I think accounting is yucky.
我不要上會計的課程。我認為會計很討人厭。

Unit 3 Cash or Accrual
現金或應計

MP3-7

There are two different methods of accounting. One is called the cash method and the other is called the accrual method of accounting. These are the two different ways of accounting for business. It is up to each business to decide which of these two methods are best for it. Businesses that have a lot of products should use the accrual method. Businesses that sell a service rather than a product can think about using the cash method.

提示　做會計有兩種不同的方式，一種是現金法，另一種是會計的應計法，這就是公司使用的兩種不同的會計方式。由每個公司自己決定兩種中哪一種最適合他們，擁有許多產品的公司應該使用應計法，提供服務而非產品的公司可以考慮使用現金法。

Dialogue 1

A　If I'm going to be a good accountant, I need to review the methods of accounting.

B　Okay. There are two methods. They are called cash and accrual.

A　These are the two different ways that accounting can be done.

B　Yes. I want you to tell me what you know about the cash method of accounting first.

A   Okay. I know that you only record **income** when you get paid.

中譯 ....

A: 如果我打算做一個好的會計師，我需要複習會計方法。

B: 好。有兩種方法，他們叫做現金與應計。

A: 會計的作法有兩種不同的方式。

B: 是的。我要你先告訴我，你對現金法了解多少。

A: 好。我知道當你收到錢時，你才記錄營收。

Dialogue 2

A   You're doing that wrong. You're forgetting the difference between cash and accrual.

B   Oh, I forgot. I only record income when I **receive** payment from a customer.

A   That's if you're using the cash method of accounting.

B   Yes. And I only record an **expense** when I make a payment to someone else.

A   Again, that's if you're doing the cash method. You need to make up your mind.

中譯 ....

A: 你這樣做錯了。你忘了現金與應計之間的不同。

B: 喔，我忘了。當我收到顧客的付款時，我才記錄營收。

A: 那是當你使用會計的現金法時才這麼做。

B: 是。當我付款給其他人時，我才記錄支出。

A: 再說一次，這是你在用現金法時才這樣做。你需要做決定。

Dialogue 3

A   The problem I have with the cash method is if you do a lot of **invoicing**.

B   Exactly. The problem is it's hard to know what's **in stock** all the time.

A　That's because stock has left the store but you didn't record the sale.

B　And I didn't record the sale because the customer did not pay me yet.

A　Do you see why I'm concerned? I think we should do the accrual method.

中譯

A: 我用現金法所遇到的問題是，如果你要開很多的發票的時候。

B: 沒錯。問題是，很難隨時知道庫存的情況。

A: 這是因為庫存品已經離開店舖了，但你沒有記錄這筆銷售。

B: 而我不記下這筆銷售是因為客戶還沒有付錢給我。

A: 你看得出來我為什麼擔心了吧？我想我們應該用應計法。

Dialogue 4

A　Now what about accrual? Can you tell me how accrual accounting works?

B　Sure. With accrual, you record the income at the time of sale not when you get paid.

A　That means you record the expense when you get your stuff, not when you pay for it.

B　That's right. This is more work but it makes for better bookkeeping.

A　I can see that you'd have better records this way.

中譯

A: 那應計法呢？你能告訴我應計法是怎麼做的？

B: 沒問題。用應計法，你在銷售發生的當時就記錄營收，而不是在你收款的時候。

A: 這表示當你收到東西時，你就記下支出，而不是在你要付錢時才記。

B: 沒錯。這樣工作比較多，但簿記會比較清楚。

A: 我看得出，用這種方法記錄會比較清楚。

Dialogue 5

A　We need to decide which accounting method we'll use in our new store.

B　Since we sell product, I think we should use the accrual method.

A　Then we would always know **exactly** what we have left on the shelves.

B　Yes. It's a great way to keep track of product.

A　If we were a service business, we could think about doing cash accounting instead.

中譯..

A：　我們需要決定在新店裡將用哪種會計方法。

B：　既然我們賣產品，我想我們應該用應計法。

A：　然後，我們就永遠都能知道我們在架子上確切地剩下哪些東西。

B：　對。這是追蹤產品的好方法。

A：　如果我們是服務公司，我們可能要考慮用現金會計法。

Dialogue 6

A　You're my new accountant. I need your advice. We've been using the cash method.

B　You have been using the cash method of accounting? That's not a good choice.

A　I wondered about that. Do you think we should switch over to the accrual method?

B　Yes. It's a little bit more work but it makes for more **accurate** records.

A　And since we are a store with lots of product it'll help us track the product better.

中譯..

A：　你是我的新會計師，我需要你的建議，我們一直用現金法。

B：　你們一直用現金會計法？這不是個很好的選擇。

A:　我也對那感到懷疑。你認為我們應該改用應計法嗎？

B:　對。它是工作比較多，但它的記錄會更正確。

A:　而且，既然我們是擁有很多產品的商店，它會幫助我們追蹤
　　產品。

Dialogue 7

A　It's nice to talk with other business owners. What accounting method do you use?

B　I do my own accounting because my company is small. I do the cash style.

A　Do you? I thought that wasn't as good as the accrual style of accounting.

B　It depends on the type of business you have. I'm a consultant. I provide a service.

A　That's why the cash method will work fine for you. I sell farm **machinery**.

中譯

A:　能跟其他公司的老闆談談真不錯。你用什麼會計方法？

B:　我處理自己的會計事宜，因為我的公司很小。我使用現金法。

A:　是嗎？我以為它沒有應計會計法來得好。

B:　這端看你的公司是哪一種的。我是一個顧問，我提供服務。

A:　這就是為什麼現金法在你那裡運作沒有問題。我賣農場的機
　　具。

Sentence Structure　重點句型

The accrual method of accounting helps you keep track of product.	應計會計法幫助你追蹤產品。
Let's review the different expenses you have and the income you're been receiving.	讓我們來回顧你所有的不同支出與你所收到的營收。

I'll do the invoicing and I'll keep track of what's in stock.	我會開發票並且我會記錄庫存。
You need to get some advice on what is the best choice of bookkeeping styles for us.	你需要得到一些關於選擇哪種簿記種類對我們最好的建議。
There are two ways of accounting. One is the cash method. The other is called accrual.	做會計有兩種不同的方式。一種是現金法,另一種叫做應計法。
With accrual, you record the income at the time of sale, not when you get paid.	用應計法,你在銷售發生的當時就記錄營收,而不是在你收款的時候。

Vocabulary 字彙

cash method		現金法
accrual method		應計法
income	*n.*	營收
receive	*v.*	收到
expense	*n.*	支出
invoice	*v.*	開發票
in stock		庫存
exactly	*adv.*	確切地
accurate	*adj.*	正確的
machinery	*n.*	機具

Useful Phrases 實用片語

Make up your mind 請你做決定

The speaker of this expression is asking that a decision be made.

例句 Do you want me to use the cash method or the accrual method? Make up your mind.
你要我用現金法還是應計法？請你做決定。

Stuff 東西

This word means "things".

例句 Come by the office tomorrow and pick up your stuff.
明天順道到辦公室來，把你的東西拿走。

Chapter 3

Money Coming in and going out
資金進出

Unit 1 Assets and Liabilities
資產與負債

MP3-8

Assets are things of worth and **liabilities** are things that cost. The more assets a company has, the more that company is worth. The more liabilities a company has, the more it costs and expenses it has.

提示　　資產是有價值的東西，負債則是會支出成本的東西。一家公司擁有愈多資產，這家公司的價值就愈高。一家公司的負債愈多，它就有愈多的成本與支出。

Dialogue 1

A　How is our newest accountant working out? Did we do well with hiring her?

B　Yes. I've been showing her some basics. I want to *start her off* slow.

A　A review is always a good idea. What have you been going over with her?

B　We've been looking at different kinds of accounts.

A　What kind of accounts? Are you talking about assets and liabilities?

中譯

A:　我們最新的會計師做得如何？我們雇用她做得對吧？

B:　對。我已經告訴她一些基本的東西，我要慢慢讓她開始。

A:　回顧總是不錯的辦法。你跟她談到哪些東西了？

B:　我們看過不同種類的帳戶。

A:　哪種帳戶？你講的是資產與負債嗎？

Dialogue 2

A   That last client that just left your office looked happy. What did you tell him?

B   He wanted a better understanding of what assets and liabilities mean.

A   What did you tell him?

B   I told him the more assets the better and the less liabilities the better.

A   I'd say that's the name of the game. Spend very little and **invest** and save lots.

中譯

A: 最後一個離開你辦公室的客戶看起來很高興，你跟他說了什麼？

B: 他想要更了解資產與負債的意義。

A: 你告訴他什麼？

B: 我告訴他資產愈多愈好，負債愈少愈好。

A: 我會說那是最重要的事。少花錢，投資並存很多錢。

Dialogue 3

A   I've been looking over your books. You have a lot of assets in this company.

B   Yes, I do. I've invested a lot into this business.

A   You also have very few liabilities. This is a good position to be in.

B   I had a lot of debt when I started this business but I paid it off as fast as I could.

A   Lots of assets and very few liabilities means a business that is worth lots of money.

中譯

A: 我看過你的帳冊了，你在這家公司裡有許多資產。

B: 是，我是有很多，我在這家公司上投資了很多。

A: 你還擁有極少數的負債，這是一個很好的處境。

B:　當我開始這家公司時，我有很多債務，但我盡可能快速地將它償還了。

A:　許多的資產與少數的負債代表這個公司值很多錢。

Dialogue 4

A　I'm **retiring** and I need some money. I wonder if I should sell my business.

B　It depends on how much money you'd get for the business if you sold it.

A　I have lots of debt and very few assets. What do you think?

B　Debt is a liability. You should keep the business until you **get rid of** some of that.

A　That's what my wife said. She's so smart. She used to work in an accounting firm.

中譯

A:　我即將退休，並需要一些錢。我在想我是否該賣掉我的公司。

B:　這要看如果你把公司賣掉，你能從這裡拿到多少錢。

A:　我有大量債務與少數的資產。你認為如何？

B:　債務是一種負債。你應該留著你的公司，直到你擺脫一些債務為止。

A:　我太太也是這麼說，她很聰明，她以前在會計師事務所工作。

Dialogue 5

A　I don't understand this whole asset and liability thing. Can you explain it?

B　Assets and liabilities can change. If a company owns a company car, it's an asset.

A　But it's not an asset if the company owes money on it right?

B　In that case that car is thought of as a liability.

A　The building my business is in is a good thing because we own it and it's paid off.

中譯 ....

A: 我不懂資產與負債這整個東西。你可以解釋一下嗎？

B: 資產與負債可以改變。如果一家公司擁有一部公司車，它就是資產。

A: 但是，如果公司因為它而欠錢，那它就不是資產，對吧？

B: 這樣的話，這部車就被認為是負債。

A: 我公司所在的這棟建築物是很好的東西，因為我們擁有它，款項都付清了。

Dialogue 6

A My company is thinking about investing in your company.

B That's great. Your company would be making a good investment.

A It depends how well your company is doing. Having high sales isn't everything.

B What else could be as important as that? We are very **popular** and we have big sales.

A Does your company own anything? Does it have a lot of debt?

中譯 ....

A: 我的公司正在考慮投資你的公司。

B: 那很棒。你的公司會有很好的投資。

A: 這要看你公司營運的狀況有多好，銷售狀況很好並不代表一切。

B: 還有什麼東西能跟它一樣重要？我們非常受人歡迎，而且我們賣得很好。

A: 你的公司擁有任何東西嗎？它有許多債務嗎？

Dialogue 7

A Our new accountant is great. She's been teaching me about assets.

B　You are just the secretary. Why do you want to know about assets?

A　I want to own a business one day.

B　So, tell me. What is an asset?

A　An asset is anything of value a company owns. A company car would be an asset.

中譯

A:　我們的新會計師很棒，她在教我關於資產的事情。

B:　你只是個秘書，你為什麼想知道關於資產的事？

A:　有一天我想擁有自己的公司。

B:　那你告訴我，什麼是資產？

A:　資產是一家公司所擁有任何有價值的東西，一部公司車就會是一項資產。

Sentence Structure 重點句型

Investing in assets is popular because it brings you money one day.	投資在資產上很受人歡迎，因為它有一天會為你帶來財富。
You should get rid of as many liabilities and of as much debt as you can before retiring.	在你退休之前，你應該盡可能擺脫多一點負債與債務。
Assets are things of worth and liabilities are costs or expenses.	資產是有價值的東西，負債則是成本與支出。
The more assets a company has, the more that company is worth.	一家公司擁有愈多資產，這家公司的價值就愈高。

The more liabilities a company has, the more costs and expenses it has.	一家公司的負債愈多，它就有愈多的成本與支出。
Lots of assets and very few liabilities mean a business that is worth lots of money.	大量資產與少數負債代表這家公司值很多錢。
I told him the more assets the better and the less liabilities the better.	我告訴他，資產愈多愈好，負債愈少愈好。

Vocabulary 字彙

asset	n.	資產
liability	n.	負債
invest	v.	投資
retire	v.	退休
get rid of		擺脫
popular	adj.	受人歡迎的

Useful Phrases 實用片語

Do well 做得對

This means that something is a good or a smart thing to do.

例句 You would do well to pay off your debt.
你將債務付清的事做得對。

Start her off 讓她開始

This means to begin with.

例句 I'll start him off with the basics of accounting.
我會讓他從會計的基本開始。

Going over 談到、看

This means to look at or to talk about something.

例句 We're going to go over the books with the new accountant this week.
這個星期，我們會跟這個新的會計師從帳冊開始看起。

That's the name of the game 那是最重要的事

This means "that's what it's all about."

例句 Getting lots of assets and getting rid of liabilities is the name of the game.
得到許多資產並擺脫負債就是最重要的事。

Unit 2 Revenue and Expenses
收入與支出

MP3-9

Revenue is the proper name for any kind of money that comes into a company. Expense is the correct name for any kind of money that goes out of a company. The more revenue a company has and the fewer expenses it has, the more money it makes.

提示 收入是用來稱呼進入一家公司的任何款項的適當名稱。支出是流出一家公司的款項的正確名稱。一家公司的收入愈多、支出愈少，它賺的錢就愈多。

Dialogue 1

A　Revenue is good. It's like an asset. Our job is to **generate** revenue.

B　Expenses aren't bad. They're **necessary**. But it's good to keep them down.

A　Keeping expenses down is part of the manager's job.

B　A business needs to spend money. You just don't want to waste it.

A　The more money coming in, the better. That's why I'm glad I'm in sales.

中譯 ....

A: 收入是好的,它就像資產一樣,而我們的工作就是創造收入。

B: 支出不是不好,它們是必要的,但將支出維持低水準是好的。

A: 經理的部分工作是使支出維持低水準。

B: 一家公司需要花錢,你只是不希望浪費了錢。

A: 進來的錢愈多愈好,這就是為什麼我很高興自己是做銷售業的。

Dialogue 2

A　I need to do an **assignment** for my high school accounting class.

B　What is the assignment? I'm taking accounting at college. I might be able to help.

A　I need to find out what revenue is.

B　Revenue is any money that a business makes. It's any money a business brings in.

A　I also need to find out about expenses but I think I know what those are already.

中譯 ....

A: 我需要做我高中會計課的一項作業。

B: 這項作業是什麼？我在學院裡修會計，我或許可以幫忙。

A: 我需要找出收入是什麼。

B: 收入是一家公司所創造的金錢，它是一家公司賺進來的任何金錢。

A: 我也需要知道支出，但我想我已經知道那是什麼了。

Dialogue 3

A How are things going with your **tutor**? Are you getting better marks?

B Yes. My grades have **improved**. We're working on expenses.

A How do you define an expense?

B An expense is anything a business spends money on. **Staff** is an expense.

A If you were a business one of your expenses would be your tutor.

中譯

A: 你的家教如何？你的成績有改善嗎？

B: 有。我的成績已經改善，我們正繼續在複習支出。

A: 你如何定義支出？

B: 支出是一家公司任何需要花錢的東西。員工就是一項支出。

A: 如果你是一家公司，你的一項支出就是家教費。

Dialogue 4

A I've been looking over the financial records. There's something I don't get.

B What's that? Does something seem out of place?

A Yes. You have some **spa treatments** listed as an expense.

B My spa treatments are a business expense. I have to look good for my work.

A But you are in radio. You're a **radio announcer**. In your work no one sees you.

中譯

A: 我有仔細檢查財務記錄，裡面有我不懂的事情。

B: 是什麼事？有什麼事看起來不對勁嗎？

A: 是。你有一些溫泉水療費用掛在支出上。

B: 我的溫泉水療費用是一筆生意的支出，我為了工作必須很體面。

A: 但是，你是做廣播的，你是一個播音員。你在工作時，沒有人會看見你。

Dialogue 5

A　We need to go over the books. We don't seem to be making any money.

B　The books will be able to show us what our revenues and expenses are.

A　I think we're spending more than we're making. I don't know what we're buying.

B　We did just buy two new pieces of **equipment**. Are you forgetting that?

A　I forgot. They haven't arrived yet. That's why I forgot. They're a big expense.

中譯

A: 我們需要看一遍帳冊，我們似乎沒有賺什麼錢。

B: 帳冊能告訴我們收入與支出有哪些。

A: 我想，我們花的比賺的多，我不知道我們買些什麼東西。

B: 我們確實剛買了兩部新設備，你忘了嗎？

A: 我忘了，它們還沒送到，這是我之所以忘記的原因，他們是一項很大的支出。

Dialogue 6

A　What were our revenues in the last four weeks? Can you tell me?

B　**According to** the books, we brought in a million dollars in the last four weeks.

A   That's great. I can't believe we made that much money. We're going to be rich.

B   There's a problem. You need to know that we spent almost as much in that time.

A   If we are spending almost as much as we bring in our expenses are out of control.

中譯 ....

A: 過去這四個星期來我們的收入如何？你能告訴我嗎？

B: 根據帳冊，我們過去這四個星期賺進了一百萬元。

A: 這很不錯。我不敢相信我們賺了那麼多錢，我們會變得有錢。

B: 有一個問題。你需要知道，我們在那段時間幾乎花掉了同樣金額的錢。

A: 如果我們花的幾乎跟我們賺的一樣多，那我們的支出就是失去控制了。

Dialogue 7

A   I have some concerns. Tell me if popcorn seems like a normal business expense.

B   Yes. Are there other expenses that you don't understand? Tell me.

A   You're spending lots and lots of money on pop. Is that a **justifiable** expense?

B   We're a movie theatre. Of course, we need to buy popcorn and *soda*.

A   Oh. I thought you published a newspaper. How did I get so confused?

中譯 ....

A: 我有一些擔憂。你告訴我，爆米花看起來是否是一項正常的生意支出。

B: 是。其他還有你不懂的支出嗎？告訴我。

A: 你花許多錢在汽水上，這是一項有道理的花費嗎？

B: 我們是一間電影戲院，我們當然需要買爆米花與汽水。

A: 喔。我以為你出版一份報紙。我怎麼會搞混了？

Sentence Structure 重點句型

It's necessary that we generate more revenue.	我們製造更多收入是必要的。
We can't waste money. All expenses must be justifiable.	我們不能浪費錢。所有的支出必須是有道理的。
The radio announcer needs some new sound equipment.	這個播音員需要一些新的音響設備。
It's not normal to buy spa treatments for your staff every month.	每個月為你的員工付 spa 的錢並不正常。
Revenue is the name for any kind of money that comes into a company.	收入是用來稱呼進入一家公司的任何款項的名稱。
Expense is the name for any kind of money that goes out of a company.	支出是用來稱呼流出一家公司的款項的名稱。
Revenue is good. It's like an asset. Our job is to generate revenue.	收入是好的，它就像資產一樣。我們的工作就是創造收入。

Vocabulary 字彙

revenue	n.	收入
proper	adj.	適當的
generate	v.	創造
necessary	adj.	必要的
assignment	n.	作業

tutor	*n.*	家教
improve	*v.*	改善
staff	*n.*	員工
spa treatments		溫泉水療
radio announcer		播音員
equipment	*n.*	設備
according to		根據
justifiable	*adj.*	有道理的

Sentence Structure 重點句型

Out of control 失去控制

If something is out of control, it's not good. It needs to be fixed.

例句 Your grades at school are out of control. You need a tutor to help with your assignments.
你在學校的成績已經失去控制,你需要一位家教幫助你的功課。

Pop 汽水

a short term for soda pop

例句 I'm thirsty. Do you have any pop?
我很渴,你有汽水嗎?

Soda 汽水

a short term for soda pop

例句 I'm thirsty. Can we go get a soda?
我很渴,我們可以去買罐汽水嗎?

Unit 3 Posting to Ledgers
記入分類帳
MP3-10

A ledger is a group of accounts. Posting to a ledger means making or recording entries in the ledger. This is an essential part of good record keeping. Entries must always be recorded regularly and accurately.

提示　一本分類帳就是一群帳戶。記入分類帳表示在分類帳中標註或記錄一個帳目。這是保存良好記錄必要的一部份。帳目總是需要定期並正確地記錄。

Dialogue 1

A　Our accounting assistant is a big help. He learns so quickly.

B　What have you been having him do lately?

A　We've been talking about ledgers. I've started explaining them to him.

B　Did you tell him about the general ledger yet? That's important for him to know about.

A　I want to take it slow. Ledgers are a big step from doing the filing and making coffee.

中譯

A:　我們的會計助理幫了很大的忙，他學習得很快。

B:　你最近要他做些什麼？

A:　我們談到了分類帳。我開始對他解釋分類帳。

B:　你有告訴他關於總帳的事了嗎？這是重要的事，他需要知道。

A:　我想要慢慢來。要從做歸檔與泡咖啡進到分類帳是很大的一步。

Dialogue 2

A   Tell me what I need to know about ledgers if I am to keep my own records.

B   All right. A ledger is a group of accounts.

A   I don't need to know that part. Tell me about the general ledger.

B   If it has all the financial statements accounts it's called the general ledger.

A   I don't care about **definitions**. I just want to know what I do with it for my records.

中譯

A: 請告訴我如果要自己保存記錄，我需要知道哪些關於分類帳的事情。

B: 好。一本分類帳就是一群帳戶。

A: 我不需要知道那個部分，告訴我關於總帳的事情。

B: 如果它擁有所有財務報表的帳戶，它就稱為總帳。

A: 我不在意定義。我只想知道我怎樣用它來做記錄。

Dialogue 3

A   Have you seen the **chart of accounts**? I can't find it anywhere.

B   I'm new here. It's my first day. What's a chart of accounts?

A   It's a list of account titles. It has account titles and account numbers.

B   I don't know where that might be. I did write down a phone message on this paper.

A   That's the chart of accounts. It's not supposed to be used like a piece of **scrap paper**.

中譯

A: 你見過那個會計科目表嗎？我到處都找不到它。

B: 我是新來的，這是我第一天上班。什麼是會計科目表？

A:　它是一張帳戶名稱的列表。上頭有帳戶名稱與帳戶編號。

B:　我不知道那會在哪裡。我有把一個電話留言寫在這張紙上。

A:　這就是會計科目表。它不應該被當作一張廢紙用。

Dialogue 4

A　Are you posting to the general ledger right now? I'd like to have it.

B　It'll be a while. There's lots of **catching up** to do. I'll tell you when I'm done.

A　I need to look at our financials. I want to get a head start on year end.

B　You're talking about year end while I'm trying to get caught up. Be patient.

A　Maybe you could do year end for me when you're finished catching up.

中譯

A:　你現在正在把帳目記到總帳裡嗎？我現在想看看。

B:　還要一會兒，還有很多要趕工。當我做完時，我會告訴你。

A:　我需要看一下我們的財務狀況，我想盡早開始做年底結算。

B:　你講的是年底結算，而我正試著要趕工，有耐心點。

A:　當你趕工完時，或許你能幫我做年底結算。

Dialogue 5

A　How much work goes in to doing the accounting here? It's a small business.

B　Even a small business needs detailed records and those take time to do well.

A　But it's easy, isn't it? How hard can it be? It's just numbers.

B　It's not really hard but it is work that requires **concentration** and focus.

A　How often do you post to the general ledger? Once every six months? Once a week?

中譯

A: 這裡的會計需要做多少工？這是一家小公司。

B: 即使是一家小公司也需要仔細的記錄，而那些要花時間。

A: 但是，它很簡單，不是嗎？能有多難？它只是數字而已。

B: 它並不是真的很難，但是它是需要專注與專心的工作。

A: 你多久過一次總帳？每六個月一次？一個星期一次？

Dialogue 6

A　That lady sitting in that office is Anne Smith. She does our accounting.

B　How long has she been on your staff?

A　Anne's been with us for five years now. She's very good and we're glad to have her.

B　She looks like she's working very hard. What's she doing?

A　It looks like she's posting to the general ledger. She takes pride in her work.

中譯

A: 坐在那個辦公室裡的那位女士是安‧史密斯。她處理我們的會計事宜。

B: 她成為你們的員工有多久了？

A: 安妮目前已經為我們工作五年了。她很棒，我們很高興能有她在。

B: 她看起來像是正在非常賣力地工作著。她現在在做什麼？

A: 看起來她像在記總帳，她對自己的工作非常自豪。

Dialogue 7

A　I thought we were going out for lunch. You don't have your coat on. Hurry up.

B　I don't think I can go now. I found some errors in one of my client's records.

A　What is it? Maybe I can help. Is it one of the

journals?

B　No. It's the **daily summary of sales**. But I have to go through some ledgers also.

A　You have a busy afternoon. Do you want me to bring something back for you?

中譯

A:　我以為我們要出去吃午餐，你還沒穿外套，趕快。

B:　我想我現在不能去了，我在自己的一個客戶記錄中發現一些錯誤。

A:　是什麼？或許我可以幫忙，是其中一本日記帳嗎？

B:　不是。是每日銷售摘要。但是，我也必須查一些分類帳。

A:　你會有一個忙碌的下午，你要我為你帶一些東西回來嗎？

Sentence Structure　重點句型

It's essential that we have a chart of accounts.	我們要有一張會計科目表是很必要的。
The daily summary of sales must be done regularly.	每日銷售摘要必須定期地做。
She takes pride in her work. She keeps detailed records and updates them regularly.	她對自己的工作感到自豪。她保存詳細的記錄，並定期地做更新。
This work requires my concentration. Can you be quiet so I can focus?	我需要專心地去做這個工作。你能安靜些，好讓我集中精神嗎？
A ledger is a group of accounts. There are different types of ledgers.	一本分類帳就是一群帳戶，有不同種類的分類帳。

| If it has all the financial statement accounts it's called the general ledger. | 如果它擁有所有財務報表的帳戶，它就稱為總帳。 |
| Posting to a ledger means making or recording entries in the ledger. | 記入分類帳表示在分類帳中標註或記錄一筆帳目。 |

Vocabulary 字彙

essential	*adj.*	必要的
regularly	*adv.*	定期地
definition	*n.*	定義
chart of account		會計科目表
scrap paper		廢紙
catching up		趕工
concentration	*n.*	專注
daily summary of sales		每日銷售摘要

Useful Phrases 實用片語

Get a head start 盡早開始

This means to start something as soon as possible

例句 I need to go to work early tomorrow to get a head start on the accounting.
我明天需要早一點去上班，我想盡早開始做帳。

Hurry up 快點

This is used when asking someone to hurry.

例句 Hurry up or we're going to be late.
快點，我們要遲到了。

Chapter 4

Annual Report
年度報告

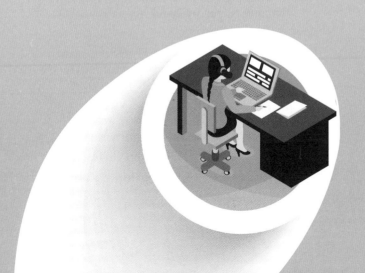

Unit 1 Balance Sheet
資產負債表

MP3-11

A **balance sheet** is a financial **snapshot** of how a business is doing at the moment. It includes a **summary** of assets and liabilities. From it a person can tell what the business is worth at that time. A balance sheet has important information for the people running the company. Most people want a balance sheet done every month.

提示　　資產負債表是一家公司當下營運狀況的財務概要。它包含了資產與負債的摘要。一個人可以從它裡面看出一家公司在當時的價值是多少。對經營該公司的人來說，一張資產負債表上有重要的資訊。大部分的人每個月都要做好一張資產負債表。

Dialogue 1

A　I've got great news. You don't have to prepare the balance sheet **by hand** anymore.

B　Are we going to get computers? Are we finally stepping into the **modern age**?

A　Yes. I have this wonderful software that will generate a balance sheet for you.

B　How **thoughtful** of you. What kind of software is it?

A　It's a **spreadsheet.** Just like what you have been doing by hand. It'll be much faster.

中譯 ....

A:　我有很棒的消息，你再也不用手寫準備資產負債表了。

B: 我們打算買電腦了嗎？我們真的要踏進現代了嗎？

A: 是啊。我有一個很棒的軟體，能為你做出資產負債表。

B: 你真是體貼。是什麼樣的軟體？

A: 它是一張試算表，就像你用手寫的一樣，而且它會快很多。

Dialogue 2

A I have this new **template** that I would like to try. It's for balance sheets.

B What's wrong with the old template you've been using?

A I haven't been using it and it's not that old. You bought it yesterday.

B Fine. But I still want to know what's wrong with it. We have to watch our money.

A Yes. We have to watch our money correctly. The template you bought is wrong.

中譯

A: 我有這個自己想試試看的新範本，這是要做資產負債表的。

B: 你以前用的舊範本有什麼問題？

A: 我沒有在用，而且它沒有這麼舊，你昨天才買的。

B: 好。但我仍想知道它有什麼問題，我們必須看緊荷包。

A: 對。我們必須正確地看緊荷包，你買的這個範本不對。

Dialogue 3

A I want to see a balance sheet. I've been asking you for one to two months.

B *Keep your pants on.* What's the **rush**? It's not your year end yet.

A You are the **rudest** accountant I have ever dealt with. I pay you. You do what I say.

B *You're not the boss of me.* You can't talk to me like that.

A Give me all my records. I'm taking my business

somewhere else.

中譯

A: 我想要看資產負債表。我一到兩個月前就一直找你要。

B: 耐心點。這麼緊張做什麼？還不到你的年底結算。

A: 你是我遇過最無禮的會計師，我付錢給你，你做我交待的事。

B: 你不是我的老闆，你不能這樣對我講話。

A: 給我所有我的記錄，我要把我公司的會計給別人做。

Dialogue 4

A　I want to know how my business is doing. I need to buy some new equipment.

B　I have just completed a balance sheet for you. I was going to fax it to you.

A　That's great. This will help me get an idea of how we're doing.

B　It has all of your assets and liabilities on there as well as your **equity**.

A　This is great. Can I get this once a month from you please? It's useful information.

中譯

A: 我要知道我的公司情況如何，我需要買一些新的設備。

B: 我才剛為你完成一張資產負債表，我正打算傳真給你。

A: 那太好了，這會幫助我對情況有概念。

B: 它上頭有你所有的資產與負債，還有你的業主權益。

A: 這真的很棒。我能不能請你一個月給我一次這個東西？它是很有用的資料。

Dialogue 5

A　Honey, we need to do up a balance sheet. The bank will want to see that.

B　They need to see that if they are going to give us a loan?

A   Yes. Can you do that up for me? You're so much quicker at the books than I am.

B   Okay. I'll do it. But it'll take some time. You'll have to be patient.

A   Great. While you're at it, will you do up an **income statement**? They'll want that too.

中譯

A: 蜜糖，我們需要做一張資產負債表。銀行要看那個東西。

B: 他們需要看那個東西，以決定是否要給我們貸款嗎？

A: 對。你能為我做一張嗎？你做帳冊比我快得多了。

B: 好，我會做。但這要花點時間，你必須要有耐心。

A: 太好了。當你在做時，可不可以也做一張收益表？他們也會要那個。

Dialogue 6

A   I've been looking over this balance sheet. I see something that concerns me.

B   What is it? Did I add something up wrong? I was in a bit of a rush.

A   There's a lot of money owed to the business for purchases made by customers.

B   You're talking about the accounts receivables. Everyone will pay when they can.

A   This is my money we're talking about. You work for me. I need you to collect.

中譯

A: 我一直在看這張資產負債表。我看到讓我擔心的事。

B: 是什麼呢？我有什麼東西加錯了嗎？我當時有一點趕。

A: 客戶在購買東西時，欠了公司很多錢。

B: 你在講的是應收帳款。當客戶付得出的時候，每個人都會付錢的。

A: 我們在談的是我的錢。你為我工作，我要你把錢收回來。

Dialogue 7

A How much money do we have readily **available**? Will the last balance sheet tell me?

B Yes. What kind of money are you talking about? Do you mean in **short term** assets?

A Yes. I need to know what kind of money we have in the **checking account**.

B The balance sheet will tell you that but that balance sheet is three weeks old.

A Is there another one coming out soon? I need to see our accountant about this.

中譯

A: 我們手上可用的錢有多少？我能從上一張資產負債表看出來嗎？

B: 可以。你講的是哪一種錢？你的意思是短期資產嗎？

A: 是的。我需要知道我們在支票存款帳戶有多少錢。

B: 資產負債表能告訴你這些事，但是那張資產負債表是三個星期前的。

A: 是不是有另外一張就快出來了？我必須與我們的會計師談談。

Sentence Structure 重點句型

The balance sheet will give us a snapshot of how the business is doing.	資產負債表能讓我們知道這家公司當下營運狀況的概要。
The balance sheet gives you a summary of the assets and liabilities.	資產負債表給你資產與負債的摘要。
I prepare the spreadsheets by hand using this template.	我利用這個範本手寫準備了這張試算表。

Will an income statement show me what equity I have in the company?	收益表能顯示出我在這間公司裡有多少業主權益嗎？
A balance sheet is a financial summary of how a business is doing at a certain time.	資產負債表是一家公司在某個特定時期的財務概要。
It includes a summary of all the assets and liabilities.	它包含了所有資產與負債的摘要。

Vocabulary 字彙

balance sheet		資產負債表
snapshot	*n.*	概要
summary	*n.*	摘要
by hand		手寫
modern age		現代
thoughtful	*adj.*	體貼的
spreadsheet	*n.*	試算表
template	*n.*	範本
rush	*n.*	緊張、匆促
rudest	*adj.*	最無禮的
equity	*n.*	業主權益
income statement		收益表
available	*adj.*	可用的
short term		短期
checking account		支票存款帳戶

Useful Phrases 實用片語

Keep your pants on 耐心點、別緊張

This is a rude expression that means "be patient" or "calm down"

例句 I need to leave right now. My job interview is in five minutes.
我現在就要離開,我的工作面試再五分鐘就要開始了。

Keep your pants on.
別緊張。

You're not the boss of me 你不是我的老闆

People might say this if they feel pushed around

例句 You shouldn't be eating that cookie. You should watch your weight.
你不應該吃那個餅乾,你應該注意體重了。

You're not the boss of me.
你不是我的老闆。

Honey 蜜糖

a term of endearment used with loved ones.

例句 Honey, come to bed. It's late.
蜜糖,來睡吧。很晚了。

Unit 2 Income Statement
收益表

The income statement is created to show the revenue and expenses for the business. These are usually done once a month. They are also sometimes referred to as profit and loss statements. Some businesses don't do them every month but it's a good idea to have it done that often. Like the balance sheet, an income statement gives a person an idea of what the business did that month. It's good information that helps a person to run the business efficiently.

提示　製作收益表是要顯示一家公司的收益與支出,這些通常一個月做一次,有時候也被稱為損益表。一些公司沒有每個月都做,但經常製作是一個好點子。和資產負債表一樣,收益表可以讓人知道公司的當月表現。它是很好的資訊,幫助人更有效率地經營公司。

Dialogue 1

A　George, I'm glad you're back. I've been looking all over for you.

B　Sorry. I'm back a little late from lunch. My order at the restaurant got *screwed up*.

A　You've got to stop going to that place next door. They're disorganized.

B　I know. Why did you want to see me? Is something wrong?

A　I **shredded** the income statement by accident. Can you **print off** another copy?

中譯

A: 喬治，我很高興你回來了，我到處在找你。

B: 對不起，我去吃午餐回來晚了。我在餐廳的點餐被弄錯了。

A: 你不要去隔壁的那個地方了，它們很亂。

B: 我知道。你為什麼要見我？有什麼問題嗎？

A: 我不小心把收益表用碎紙機裁掉了。你可以再印另一份出來嗎？

Dialogue 2

A   Here is the balance sheet you asked me for yesterday. I got it done this morning.

B   Bill, do you remember us talking about how you don't listen very well?

A   Not really. Why were we talking about that?

B   Because you don't listen very well, Bill. I asked you for an income statement.

A   Did you? Are you sure? I could have **sworn** you asked me for the balance sheet.

中譯

A: 這是你昨天向我要的資產負債表。我今天早上完成了。

B: 比爾，你記不記得我們談過，你聽話聽得不清楚嗎？

A: 不記得。我們為什麼會談到那件事？

B: 比爾，因為你沒有聽清楚。我跟你要的是收益表。

A: 真的嗎？你確定？我可以發誓你跟我要的是資產負債表。

Dialogue 2

A   What does a balance sheet show you?

B   It shows assets and liabilities. These are broken down into long term and short term.

A   Very good. You're catching on quickly. What does an income statement show you?

B   It shows **profit** and **loss**. It shows you the revenues and expenses for a month.

A　Very good. I think you'll easily pass the accounting exam that's coming up.

中譯

A: 資產負債表告訴你什麼？

B: 它顯示資產與負債，這些都分成長期與短期。

A: 很好，你很快就學會了。收益表告訴你些什麼？

B: 它顯示出營利與虧損。它告訴你一個月內的收益與支出。

A: 很好。我想你很容易就能通過即將到來的會計考試。

Dialogue 3

A　Have you seen the profit and loss statement for this past month yet?

B　No, I haven't. How does it look? How's the company doing?

A　Not good. Our revenues were way down and our expenses were way up.

B　You're right. We can't have that. That's not good at all. What are you going to do?

A　First I'm going to talk to the sales staff and tell them to get their sales back up.

中譯

A: 你看了過去這個月的損益表了嗎？

B: 沒有，我還沒看。它看起來怎麼樣？公司的狀況如何？

A: 不太好。我們的收益過低，而我們的支出過高。

B: 你是對的。我們不能容忍這種事。這一點都不好。你打算怎麼做呢？

A: 首先，我要與銷售人員談一談，告訴他們把銷售量提高。

Dialogue 4

A　If you are going to do accounting for a living, you'll have to do a lot of paperwork.

B　I thought accounting people were *numbers people*. What paperwork do they do?

A　They do lots of paperwork. They do things like income statements.

B　I don't like paperwork even if it's about numbers instead of words.

A　Then don't go into accounting for a living. Think of some other career to try.

中譯

A：　如果你打算靠做會計維生，你就必須做很多文書工作。

B：　我以為會計人員是與數字為伍的人，他們做什麼樣的文書工作？

A：　他們做很多文書工作，他們做像收益表之類的東西。

B：　我不喜歡文書工作，即使是關於數字，而不是文字。

A：　那就不要以會計維生，考慮試試其他的職業。

Dialogue 5

A　I've decided to start saving the income statement each month.

B　That's a great idea. That way you can look back at months past to compare.

A　That's what I thought. The income statement is valuable information.

B　I'll let you in on a little secret. We already do keep them. They're in a **binder**.

A　I'm **embarrassed**. I didn't know that. Where is this binder you're talking about?

中譯

A：　我已經決定將每個月的收益表保存起來。

B：　這是一個好主意，這樣你可以回顧過去的月份來做比較。

A：　我也這麼想，收益表是很有價值的資料。

B：　我讓你知道一個小秘密，我們已經保留它們了，他們在活頁夾裡。

A：　好尷尬。我不知道這件事。你說的活頁夾在哪裡？

Dialogue 6

A Will you phone our accountant for me? Find out where our income statement is.

B Is he late with it? How long ago was it supposed to be here?

A He usually faxes it by the end of the first week of the month. We're a week past that.

B I don't want to scare you but it's not ringing. It says the number is out of service.

A I don't like the sounds of that. I think I'll go down to his office in person.

中譯

A: 你能幫我打電話給我們的會計師嗎？查出我們的收益表在哪裡。

B: 他遲交了嗎？它多久之前應該到這裡來？

A: 他通常在一個月的第一週結束前傳真過來，已經遲了一個星期。

B: 我不想嚇你，不過電話沒有響。它說，這個號碼暫停服務。

A: 聽起來不妙。我想我會親自到他的辦公室去。

Sentence Structure 重點句型

I usually make a copy of the profit and loss statement.	我通常會將損益表影印一份下來。
She shredded the contents of that binder.	她把那個活頁夾裡的東西用碎紙機裁掉了。
You did that work very efficiently.	你很有效率地完成了那個工作。
The income statement is created to show the revenue and expenses for the business.	製作收益表是要顯示一家公司的收益與支出。

| They're done once a month and are sometimes referred to as profit and loss statements. | 這些通常一個月製作一次，有時候也被稱為損益表。 |
| It shows assets and liabilities. These are broken down into long term and short term. | 它標示出資產與負債，這些被分成長期與短期。 |

Vocabulary 字彙

efficiently	adv.	有效率地
shred	v.	用碎紙機裁掉
print off		印
swear	v.	發誓
profit	n.	營利
loss	n.	虧損
binder	n.	活頁夾
embarrassed	adj.	尷尬的

Useful Phrases 實用片語

Screwed up 弄錯

means to have made a mistake

例句 I screwed up and shredded that paper instead of copying it.
我弄錯了，我沒有影印那張紙，反而把它裁掉了。

Numbers people 與數字為伍的人

refers to people who like math, accounting, and working with money

例句 Bank jobs and accounting jobs are good for numbers people.

對與數字為伍的人來說，銀行與會計的工作很不錯。

Unit 3 Cash Flow Statement
現金流量表
MP3-13

A cash flow statement shows what cash is available in a business and when more cash will be coming in. It enables the operators of a business to look at past performance to plan for the future. When the cash flow statement is done along with a balance sheet and an income statement, it's called a pro-forma financial projection.

A cash flow statement is another important document that helps a company run effectively.

提示 現金流量表顯示一間公司有哪些可用的現金，以及何時有現金會進來。它使一家公司的經營者可以看過去的表現來規劃未來。 當現金流量表與資產負債表、收益表一起製作，這被稱為「預估財務預測」。

現金流量表是另一個有助公司有效運作的重要文件。

Dialogue 1

A   Things around here have to change. We just haven't been making enough money.

B　I agree with you. We need to do some **restructuring** and some **budgeting**.

A　Why don't you get the balance sheet done. I'll do the income statements.

B　I'll get our third partner to do the cash flow statement.

A　Once we have all of that done the three of us can do some planning for the future.

中譯

A: 這裡的事情必須改變，我們賺的錢不夠。

B: 我同意你的話。我們需要一些重整動作與預算安排。

A: 你為什麼不把資產負債表做好？我會做收益表。

B: 我會要我們第三位合夥人做現金流量表。

A: 我們一旦做好了，我們三個人就可以為未來做一些計畫。

Dialogue 2

A　We've been doing a cash flow statement once a year. The boss wants it every month.

B　Why does she want it every month now? She must want to make some changes.

A　She said we need to do more financial planning. She wants to redo the budget also.

B　I'm glad I'm one of the accounting staff. If there are **cutbacks** I'll get to stay.

A　Probably. A person who knows numbers is crucial to a successful business.

中譯

A: 我們一直一年做一次現金流量表，老闆要每個月一張。

B: 她現在為什麼要每個月一張？她一定是要做一些改變。

A: 她說，我們需要做更多的財務規劃，她也要重新安排預算。

B: 我很高興我是會計部的一員。如果有縮減，我會留下來。

A: 大概是。一個懂得數字的人對一個成功的企業很重要。

Dialogue 3

A   In preparing for your accounting exam, we've reviewed cash flow statements.

B   No, we haven't. We've reviewed the balance sheet and the income statement.

A   Oh. I'm getting ahead of myself. Today we'll talk about cash flow statements.

B   I know that they are often used along with the balance sheet and income statement.

A   Yes, you have that right. All three together are important for the future of a business.

中譯 ....

A: 為了幫你準備會計考試，我們已經複習了現金流量表。

B: 不，我們沒有。我們複習了資產負債表與收益表。

A: 喔，我超前了。今天，我們要談談現金流量表。

B: 我知道它們經常與資產負債表與收益表一起使用。

A: 對，你說對了。三個文件全部都對一家公司的未來很重要。

Dialogue 4

A   Cash flow statements are used to **analyze** cash **inflows** and **outflows**.

B   That means where the money came from and went to during a certain period of time.

A   Remember that there are three parts of cash flow.

B   I know. They are the business **operations**, investments and financing.

A   Good job. I think you are well prepared for your interview with the accounting firm.

中譯 ....

A: 現金流量表被用來分析現金的流入與流出。

B: 這表示在某一段特定的時間裡，錢從哪裡進出。

A: 記住，現金流量有三個部分。

B: 我知道。它們是公司運作、投資與融資。

A: 做得好。我想你已經充分準備，可以參加會計師事務所的面試。

Dialogue 5

A　A cash flow statement can show you things that the income statement cannot.

B　It's just too much paperwork for me to read. I don't have time.

A　Without the cash flow statement, you don't have an accurate picture of your business.

B　I told you already. I'm too busy to read all this paperwork you send me.

A　I'm only the bookkeeper and yet I think I care more about this business than you do.

中譯

A: 現金流量表可以讓你看到收益表上所沒有的東西。

B: 只是有太多文件要我看了，我沒有時間。

A: 你沒有現金流量表，你就無法準確地知道自己公司的情況。

B: 我已經告訴過你了。我太忙，無法看你給我的所有文件。

A: 我只是個簿記員，但是我認為我自己對這家公司比你還關心。

Dialogue 6

A　Where's my accountant? He's not in his office. We had an **appointment** today.

B　I'm sorry, sir. Dave had an accident. He's in the hospital. He'll be out for weeks.

A　That's terrible. I'm sorry to hear that. I needed him to do my pro-forma papers.

B　Someone else will help you while Dave is away. Let me get my manager.

A　He sent me a balance sheet and an income statement. I need the cash flow statement.

中譯

A: 我的會計師在哪裡？他不在他的辦公室，我們今天有約。

B: 我很抱歉，先生。大衛發生意外了，他現在在醫院，他有好幾個星期都不會在。

A: 真是糟糕。很抱歉聽到這個消息，我需要他幫我做預估 的文件。

B: 大衛不在時，其他人會幫你。我把我的經理找過來。

A: 他已經送資產負債表與收益表給我了，我需要現金流量表。

Dialogue 7

A   I want to do some **projections** for the future. We might need to restructure.

B   Okay. Let me get the accounting staff on it. We'll need the right documents.

A   We'll need the balance sheet and income statement. Tell them to do those up.

B   I'll also tell them to do up the cash flow statement for you.

A   Oh right. I almost forgot the most important part. We'll need that for sure.

中譯

A: 我想為將來做一些預測，我們或許需要重組。

B: 好，讓我們找會計人員來做，我們需要正確的文件。

A: 我們需要資產負債表與收益表，告訴他們把這些做好。

B: 我也會告訴他們為你把現金流量表做好。

A: 喔，好。我幾乎忘記了最重要的部分，我們肯定會需要那個的。

Sentence Structure 重點句型

A cash flow statement enables the operator of a business to plan for future performance.	現金流量表使一家公司的經營者可以規劃未來的表現。
Pro-forma financial projections can help us to plan for restructuring and budgeting.	預估財務預測可以幫助我們為重整與安排預算做計畫。

By analyzing the inflows and outflows of money he can see we need to make cutbacks.	利用分析錢的流出與流進，他可以看出我們需要做一些削減。
A cash flow statement shows what cash is available and when more is coming.	現金流量表顯示出可用的現金有哪些，以及什麼時候會有更多進來。
It allows the business owners to look at past performance to plan for the future.	它使得公司老闆能看到過去的表現，計畫未來。
A cash flow statement, a balance sheet, and an income statement is called a pro-forma financial projection.	現金流量表、資產負債表與收益表被稱為預估財務預測。

Vocabulary 字彙

cash flow statement		現金流量表
operators	n.	經營者
pro-forma financial projection		預估財務預測
restructure	v.	重整
budget	v.	預算安排
cutbacks	n.	縮減
analyze	v.	分析
inflow	n.	流入
outflow	n.	流出
operations	n.	運作
appointment	n.	約
projections	n.	預測

Chapter 5

Journals
日記帳

Unit 1 Daily Summary of Sales
每日銷售摘要

MP3-14

The daily summary of sales is how a business can compare receipts against cash received. It's how a business can keep track of daily sales. The daily cash summary is made up of three different parts: the cash receipts, the cash on hand, and the total sales. The daily summary of sales is also called the daily summary of cash receipts. This is a good way to make sure you have all the money you should have at the end of the day in a store. It will also show you how much money is owed for purchases already made on that day.

提示　每日銷售摘要是一家公司比較收據，與收到現金的方法。它是一個公司追蹤每日銷售的方法。每日現金摘要由三個部分組成：現金收據、手上有的現金與全部的銷售量。每日銷售摘要又被稱為每日現金收據報告，這是一個確定你在每天結束時，店裡有所有應該在的錢，它也會顯示出當天銷售出去的欠款。

Dialogue 1

A　The manager is away this afternoon. I need you to close up the store.

B　I'll be glad to. Just tell me what all needs to be done. I've never closed before.

A　It's simple. The most important thing is to make

sure, the doors are locked.

B That's **obvious**. What do I do with the money from the cash register?

A Fill out this form. It's the daily summary of cash receipts. It's quite simple.

中譯

A: 今天下午經理不在，我需要你來關店。

B: 我很樂意，只要告訴我需要做什麼事，我以前從來沒有關過店。

A: 它很簡單，最重要的事是確定門鎖上了。

B: 這是當然的，收銀機裡的錢我要怎麼辦呢？

A: 把這張表格填好，這是每日現金收據報告。它很簡單。

Dialogue 2

A Today I'm going to teach you how to do the daily summary of sales.

B Will that be another one of my duties as the new **assistant** manager?

A You'll do it if I'm not here to do it myself. See this form? You need to fill it out.

B Okay. I have to write down how much money we brought in today.

A You also have to record the cash on hand. That includes the **petty cash**.

中譯

A: 今天我要教你如何做每日銷售摘要。

B: 這會是我身為新助理經理的另一個職責嗎？

A: 如果我人不在這裡自己做，你就要做。看到這個表格了嗎？你需要把它填好。

B: 好，我必須寫下我們今天賺進多少錢。

A: 你也必須記錄手上的現金，包括零用金。

Dialogue 3

A　Fred, can you tell me why I haven't had a daily summary of sales in three days?

B　*That's funny*. I told Martha to do them. She hasn't been giving them to you?

A　No. Now we don't know how much we sold or how much money we have on hand.

B　I'd better talk to Martha. I don't like the sounds of this. I told her to do them.

A　No I'll talk to her. This is one way to hide money that is missing from the cash register.

中譯

A:　佛瑞德，你能告訴我為什麼三天都沒拿到每日銷售摘要嗎？

B:　這就奇怪了。我告訴瑪莎要做。她都沒有拿給你嗎？

A:　沒有。現在我們不知道我們賣了多少，或者手上有多少錢。

B:　我最好跟瑪莎談談，我不喜歡聽到這樣的事。我告訴她要做的。

A:　不，我會跟她談。這是隱藏從收銀機不見的錢的一種方法。

Dialogue 4

A　What have you been doing with the new boy in the sales department?

B　I've been showing him how to do the daily summary of sales.

A　Why does he need to know how to do that? I thought you did it every day.

B　I do it every day that I'm here. All the sales people know how to do it.

A　I suppose they're in and out of the cash drawer all day anyway. It shouldn't matter.

中譯

A:　你跟銷售部門的那個新男孩一起做什麼？

B:　我告訴他怎樣做每日銷售摘要。

A: 他為什麼需要知道那個東西？我以為你每天都會做。

B: 我在這裡的時候，我每天都會做。所有的銷售員都知道怎麼做。

A: 不管如何，我想他們抽屜裡的現金整天進進出出，應該沒什麼關係吧。

Dialogue 5

A Did you do up the daily summary of sales last night?

B No. I didn't get out of here until 6:30 and I had **dinner reservations** for 7:00.

A Is that why you came in early this morning? Are you going to do it now?

B Yes, I'll do it right now. Why are you so **anxious** to get it?

A I have to put it into the **sales and receipts journal**. Do your work so I can do mine.

中譯 ┈┈┈┈┈┈┈┈┈┈┈┈┈┈┈┈┈┈┈┈┈┈┈┈┈┈┈┈┈┈┈┈

A: 你昨晚做了每日銷售摘要嗎？

B: 沒有。我到六點半才離開這裡，我七點有晚餐預約。

A: 這是你今天早來的原因嗎？你現在要做嗎？

B: 對，我馬上就做。你為什麼那麼急著要拿到？

A: 我必須把它放進銷貨與收據簿。你做你的工作，然後我可以做我的。

Dialogue 6

A Boy, what a long day. Lock the door please so no other customers come in.

B I'm tired. I can't believe how late it is. There were so many customers.

A I know. And they all took so long. Let's do the **cash summary** and get out of here.

B　I'll count the money. You get the print out from the **credit card** machine.

A　Okay. Hey, we're out of the sheets we fill out. I'll have to go make a photocopy.

中譯

A:　天啊，真是漫長的一天。請把門鎖上，這樣就沒有其他客人會進來了。

B:　我好累，我不敢相信已經這麼晚了，有這麼多的客人。

A:　我知道，他們都花了很久的時間。讓我們把現金摘要做好，離開這裡。

B:　我來數錢，你去拿從信用卡機器印出來的資料。

A:　好。嘿，我們要填的表格用完了，我必須影印一張。

Dialogue 7

A　Okay. I filled out this sheet like you told me to. Do you want to check it?

B　No. I'm sure you did fine. Now staple it to the read out from the credit card machine.

A　I didn't print that off yet. I don't know how. You haven't shown me yet.

B　Okay. I'll print it off for you today. It's late and I want to get home.

A　I put the money in the **deposit envelope**. Should I drop it off on my way home?

中譯

A:　好，我把表格填好，就像你告訴我的那樣。你要檢查一下嗎？

B:　不用了。我相信你做得很好。現在，把它與信用卡機器的報告釘起來吧。

A:　我還沒把那個印出來，我不知道怎麼做，你還沒有教我。

B:　好，我今天幫你把它印出來。時間已經很晚了，我想回家。

A:　我把錢放在存款信　裡，我回家時應該順道把它存進去嗎？

The daily summary of sales helps us compare sales against cash received.	每日銷售摘要能幫助我們比較銷售量與收到的現金。
It's obvious that one of your duties as assistant manager is to be in charge of petty cash.	身為助理經理的職責之一就是負責零用金,這是很明顯的。
Bill from the sales department is anxious that he'll miss his dinner reservation.	銷售部門的比爾很焦急,擔心會錯過晚餐預約。
The daily summary of sales is how a business can keep track of daily sales.	每日銷售摘要是一家公司追蹤每日銷售的方法。
The daily cash summary is made up of three different parts: the cash receipts, the cash on hand, and the total sales.	每日現金摘要是由三部分所組成:現金收據、手上有的現金與全部的銷售量。
The daily summary of sales is also called the daily summary of cash receipts.	每日銷售摘要也被稱為每日現金收據報告。

Vocabulary 字彙

obvious	*adj.*	當然的
assistant	*n.*	助理
petty cash		零用金
dinner reservations		晚餐預約

anxious	*adj.*	急的
sales and receipts journal		銷貨與收據簿
cash summary		現金摘要
credit card		信用卡
deposit envelope		存款信封

Useful Phrases 實用片語

That's funny. 這就奇怪了

means that something seems strange or unusual

例句 That's funny. I could have sworn I locked this door.
這就奇怪了。我發誓我有鎖門了。

Unit 2 Sales and Receipts Journal
銷貨與收據簿
MP3-15

Each time the daily summary of sales is completed, it goes into the **collection** of daily summary of sales. This collection is called the sales and receipts journal. This journal is used with the journal for **disbursements**, **purchases** and **expenses** to come up with a profit and loss statement. All information that goes into any accounting journal is always recorded in **chronological** order. The journals will be used when it comes time to post entries to the general ledger.

提示　　每一次完成每日銷售摘要，它就進入每日銷售摘要的集合。這個集合被稱為銷貨與收據簿。這個帳簿與付款、進貨與費用簿共同使用，製成損益表。所有進入會計簿的資料總是依照日期先後順序來排列。將帳目寫進總帳的時候，就需要用到這些帳簿。

Dialogue 1

A　You want me to write in a journal? What am I supposed to write about?

B　It's not that kind of a journal. You're going to record accounting information.

A　Okay. I've never taken any accounting so please explain carefully.

B　Each **item** recorded in a journal is called an entry. You are going to make entries.

A　Okay. Is there more than one type of journal? Which journal will I be working in?

中譯

A:　你要我寫日誌？我該寫些什麼？

B:　不是那一種日誌，你要記錄會計資料。

A:　好，我從來沒有學過會計，所以請仔細地解釋。

B:　每一項記錄在帳簿中都叫做帳目，你要記錄帳目。

A:　好，有許多種不同的帳簿嗎？我要做的是哪一種帳簿？

Dialogue 2

A　There's a problem here in the sales and receipt journal, Ted. Something's missing.

B　I thought I had put everything in there. I checked it over. What's wrong?

A Where are your **source documents**? The entries look right but there's nothing else.

B What do you mean? I thought all the receipts and invoices were in there.

A Unless I'm blind, I don't see them. Where did you put them?

中譯 ....

A: 泰德，銷貨與收據簿裡有問題，有東西不見了。

B: 我以為自己把每樣東西都放進去了，我還檢查過一次，什麼有問題？

A: 你的原始文件在哪裡？帳目看起來對，可是沒有其他的東西。

B: 你的話是什麼意思？我以為所有的收據與發票都在那裡。

A: 除非我瞎了，我沒有看到它們。你把它們放在哪裡？

Dialogue 3

A I've had some **complaints** from clients. You're not recording journal entries right.

B I am so. I'm an accountant. I can't believe you would accuse me of *messing up*.

A There are four parts to an entry. The date, debit, the credit, and the source document.

B Oh, my goodness. I've been forgetting to **attach** the source documents. I'm sorry.

A Mistakes are okay here and there but a bad attitude isn't. Don't be rude to me again.

中譯 ....

A: 我聽到有些客戶在抱怨，你帳簿裡的帳目沒有記對。

B: 我記對了。我是一位會計師，我不敢相信你會指責我搞砸了。

A: 一條帳目有四個部分，日期、借方、貸方與原始文件。

B: 喔，我的老天，我一直忘記要把原始文件附上去。抱歉。

A: 偶爾犯錯是沒關係，但是態度不好就不可以。不要再對我無禮了。

Dialogue 4

A   The daily summary of sales gets recorded in the sales and cash receipts journal.

B   The entry is **divided** into five areas. Can you tell me what they are?

A   Cash sales, credit sales, collections, cash from loans, and cash from other sources.

B   Good. How many different types of journals are there?

A   There are different kinds of journals. The type of business **determines** how many.

中譯

A: 每日銷售摘要被記錄在銷貨與收據簿裡。

B: 帳目被分為五個區域,你能告訴我是哪些嗎?

A: 現金銷售、信用卡銷售、收款、來自貸款的現金與其他來源的現金。

B: 很好,有多少種不同的帳簿?

A: 有許多不同種類的帳簿,公司的種類決定帳簿的數目。

Dialogue 5

A   The day-to-day business transactions go into the sales and cash receipts journal.

B   I will also need to know where you keep the cash disbursement journal.

A   I will also show you how we've been keeping the general journal.

B   I won't need that until year end for **adjustments** and closing entries.

A   I'm glad that you're able to come in and help us out on such short notice.

中譯

A: 每天公司的交易會進入銷貨與收據簿裡。

B: 我也需要知道,你將現金付款簿放在哪裡。

A: 我也要告訴你我們怎麼樣記總帳。

B: 在年底需要調整與結算帳目之前，我不需要知道那個。

A: 我很高興臨時通知你，你馬上就能進辦公室，幫助我們。

Dialogue 6

A　Every accounting entry that goes into a journal is based on a business transaction.

B　Does every accounting entry need to be proved with documentation of some kind?

A　Yes. That is called a source document. A receipt or invoice or **pay stub** will work.

B　Are those the transactions that go into the journal?

A　Yes. A journal is where you record transactions as they happen.

中譯

A: 每一個進入帳簿的會計帳目，都是根據一筆公司交易而來。

B: 是不是每一個會計帳目都需要用某種文件來證明？

A: 是的，那叫做原始文件，收據或發票或付款存根都可以。

B: 那些是不是就是記入帳簿的交易？

A: 對。當交易發生時，你需要登入記錄的地方就是帳簿。

Dialogue 7

A　I'm learning how to do accounting entries in the journals. What happens after that?

B　From there you go to the **general ledger**. In there you group entries by their type.

A　Now I'm getting confused. I should stick with what I know for now.

B　You're a good worker. You're also smart. We should get you in an accounting class.

A　That would certainly make my new job duties easier to do, sir.

中譯

A: 我正在學如何在帳簿裡記下會計帳目，在那之後是什麼呢？

B: 從那裡之後，你就會到總帳。在總帳裡，你根據它們的種類
將它們集合在一起。

A: 現在，我被搞混了。我現在應該繼續做我知道的部分就好。

B: 你是一個好員工，你也很聰明，我們應該讓你去上會計課程。

A: 那肯定會使我更容易完成自己的新職責，先生。

Sentence Structure 重點句型

The collection of daily summary of sales is called the sales and receipt journal.	每日銷售摘要的集合被稱為銷貨與收據簿。
Each item that goes into a journal is carefully recorded in chronological order.	記入帳簿的每一項帳目都被仔細地記錄，並依照日期順序排列。
I've had complaints about you not attaching source documents and having a bad attitude.	我聽人抱怨說你不附原始文件，而且態度不好。
Each time the daily summary of sales is completed, it goes into the collection of daily summary of sales.	每次一完成每日銷售摘要，它就進入每日銷售摘要的集合中。
This journal is used with the journal for disbursements, purchases and expenses to come up with a profit and loss statement.	這個帳簿與付款、進貨和費用簿共同使用，製成損益表。
Every accounting entry that goes into a journal is based on a business transaction.	每一筆進入帳簿的會計帳目都是根據一家公司的交易而來。

Vocabulary 字彙

collection	*n.*	集合
disbursements	*n.*	付款
purchases	*n.*	進貨
expenses	*n.*	費用
chronological	*adj.*	按日期先後的
item	*n.*	項目
source documents		原始文件
complaint	*n.*	抱怨
attach	*v.*	附上去
divide	*v.*	分
determine	*v.*	決定
adjustment	*n.*	調整
pay stub		付款存根
general ledger		**總帳**

Useful Phrases 實用片語

Messing up 搞砸

means making a mistake

例句 When I'm tired at work I mess up and make mistakes.
當我工作很疲累時，我就會搞砸犯錯。

Here and there 偶爾

means "once in a while" or "a little bit"

例句 I don't mind you being late for work here and there but every week is too much.
我不介意你偶爾上班遲到，但每個星期就太過份了。

Unit 3 Importance of Financial Documentation
財務文件的重要
MP3-16

Unless a business is an accounting firm or a bookkeeping service, keeping financial records is probably not what that business does best. However, to run a successful business, accurate financial documentation and records are necessary for several reasons. For example, good accounting records can make the difference between getting a loan and not getting a loan. They help a business to do better. They help a business to find other investors or partners. These are just a few of the reasons to keep good books in a business.

提示 除非是一家會計師事務所或簿記服務公司，否則保存財務記錄大概不是該公司的強項。然而，要經營一家成功的公司，擁有準確的財務文件與記錄是必要的，這有幾個原因。例如，好的會計記錄可以造成是否得到貸款的差別，它們能幫助一家公司改善營運狀況，它們幫助一家公司找到其他的投資者或合夥人。這些只是在一家公司中需要保存良好帳簿的少數幾個原因之一。

Dialogue 1

A　Don't you get tired of recording all those different transactions?

B　No. It needs to be done.

A　It looks like a make work project to me. You write all this stuff down and put it away.

B　It doesn't just get put away. The **supervisors** read it to see how the business is doing.

A　I see. They can watch the **success** or **failure** of the business from what you record.

中譯

A：　你記錄所有不同的交易，不會覺得煩嗎？

B：　不會，它是需要做的。

A：　我覺得它看起來像是多此一舉。你把所有的東西寫下來，然後把它放到一邊。

B：　它不是只被放在一邊，管理者讀它以了解公司的營運狀況。

A：　我懂了。他們可以從你的記錄中看出這家公司是成功或失敗。

Dialogue 2

A　You keep good records, Kim. Keep up the good work.

B　Thank you. I'm glad that I'm able to help.

A　More than you know. We need to make some big **decisions.** Your work will help.

B　The books help you see what financial **impact** your decisions will have later on.

A　That's right. Can we afford more sales people? Only the books know for sure.

中譯

A: 金，你的記錄保存得很好。繼續加油。

B: 謝謝，我很高興我能幫得上忙。.

A: 你幫的忙比你知道的多。我們需要做一些重要的決定，你所做的都能幫得上忙。

B: 這些帳簿幫助你看到你的決定之後，會有什麼樣的財務影響。

A: 沒錯。我們可以負擔更多的銷售人員嗎？只有這些帳簿能確定。

Dialogue 3

A We need to apply for a bank loan. We need to **expand** the store.

B Let's take a look at the books to see if a banker will lend us the money.

A Yes. The bank will want to see financial statements before they decide if they'll help.

B We need a balance sheet, income statement, and a cash flow budget.

A Luckily, we keep good records. Everything is documented. We're ready to go.

中譯

A: 我們需要申請一個銀行貸款，我們需要擴展店面。

B: 讓我們來看看帳簿，看看銀行是否會借錢給我們。

A: 好。在銀行決定是否要幫忙之前，他們會要看財務報表。

B: 我們需要有資產負債表、收益表與現金流量表。

A: 幸運的是，我們的記錄保存得很好，每一件事情都被記錄下來了，我們已經準備好了。

Dialogue 4

A Our business has reached a point where we need to take on a partner.

B It has. Anyone who is interested in joining us needs a clear picture of our finances.

A We need **capital** from an outside investor. They'll

want to see all our records.

B　Thank goodness we keep good financial records and good day to day bookkeeping.

A　Our business is in great shape. It'll be easy to see from our documentation.

中譯

A: 我們公司已經發展到了一個階段，我們需要再找一個合夥人。

B: 是。任何有興趣加入我們的人，需要清楚地知道我們的財務清況。

A: 我們需要來自外面投資者的資金，他們會想看我們所有的記錄。

B: 感謝老天，我們保存了很好的財務記錄以及每天的簿記資料。

A: 我們的生意做得很好，從我們的文件裡很容易就看得出來了。

Dialogue 5

A　You mean to tell me you haven't been making a budget each month?

B　That's why we hired you. Please tell us what we're doing wrong and to help us fix it.

A　A budget will help keep your business on track by helping you control expenses.

B　I'm happy to say we have **solid** financial information so we can prepare a budget.

A　That's good news. That'll make my job of preparing a budget for you much easier.

中譯

A: 你要告訴我，你每個月都沒有做預算？

B: 這是我們之所以雇用你的原因。請告訴我我們哪裡做錯了，並幫助我們改正。

A: 預算可以幫助你控制支出以維持公司的營運。

B: 我很高興的說，我們有牢靠的財務資料，所以我們可以準備預算。

A:　這是個好消息，那我要為你們準備預算的工作會更輕鬆些。

Dialogue 6

A　You haven't been filing your **taxes**? How long have you been in business?

B　Only two years. I didn't think I had to pay taxes in my first year of business.

A　It doesn't matter. You need to file taxes. I need to see all your financial records.

B　I keep very good records. I think you'll be pleased.

A　With good records, preparing your taxes will be easy and will not take time at all.

中譯 ....

A:　你一直沒有報稅？你經營有多久了？

B:　只有兩年。我不認為自己在創業的第一年裡必須付稅。

A:　這不重要。你需要報稅，我需要看你所有的財務記錄。

B:　我把記錄保存得很好。我想你會很高興。

A:　有好的記錄，準備你的稅務會很容易，不會花時間。

Dialogue 7

A　Our late payment on the payroll taxes has resulted in a **severe** financial **penalty**.

B　This could have been avoided.

A　If we had kept good bookkeeping practices, we wouldn't have this big fine to pay.

B　Good bookkeeping makes **obeying** these payroll rules easy.

A　Our poor financial records have made it impossible. We need to hire an accountant.

中譯 ....

A:　我們遲交薪資稅導致了嚴重的財務處罰。

B:　這個本來是可以避免的。

A: 如果我們維持良好的簿記習慣，我們就不需要付這麼大的一筆罰款。

B: 好的簿記使得遵循薪資規則變得容易。

A: 我們不良的財務記錄讓它成為不可能，我們需要雇用一個會計師。

Sentence Structure 重點句型

The company's success or failure depends on good supervisors for the finances.	公司的成功或失敗端賴好的財務管理者。
His investment decisions will impact if we have enough capital to expand.	他的投資決定會影響到我們是否有足夠的資金去擴張。
We avoid a severe penalty by paying our taxes on time.	我們準時付稅金，以避免嚴重的罰鍰。
The owners can watch the success or failure of the business from the financial records.	老闆可以從財務記錄中看出公司的成敗。
The books help you see what financial impact your decisions today will have later on.	帳簿可以幫助你看出，你今日的決定將對未來的財務有何影響。
Let's take a look at the books to see if a banker will lend us money to expand our store.	讓我們來看看帳簿，看看銀行是否會借給我們錢擴展店面。

Vocabulary 字彙

supervisors	*n.*	管理者
success	*n.*	成功
failure	*n.*	失敗
decisions	*n.*	決定
impact	*n.*	影響
expand	*v.*	擴展
capital	*n.*	資金
solid	*adj.*	牢靠的
taxes	*n.*	稅
severe	*adj.*	嚴重的
penalty	*n.*	處罰
obey	*v.*	**遵循**

Useful Phrases 實用片語

A make work project 多此一舉

something that doesn't really have to be done

例句 You having to check all the files to make sure they're in order is a make work project.
你檢查所有的檔案確定它們都沒問題，其實是多此一舉的。

Chapter 6

Accounts
帳目

Unit 1　Accounts Receivable
應收帳

MP3-17

Accounts Receivable is also known as AR. This is money that's owed to a business by its customers. Often customers make a purchase but want to pay later. AR is the way to keep track of this money. In order to have good financial records, one of the things that must be **regularly** recorded is any credit that's **extended** to customers.

提示　　應收帳也被稱為 AR，這是客戶欠某家公司的錢。客戶經常買東西，卻想之後再付款，應收帳是記錄這筆錢的方法。為了要有良好的財務記錄，需要定期記錄的許多東西之一就是給予顧客的貸方。

Dialogue 1

A　You must do the books right.　Keep a ledger for each customer that owes us money.

B　That's a lot of work.　Can't I just keep a general ledger for all customers who owe?

A　No.　You need a separate record of each customer's charges and payments.

B　You're **demanding**.　I don't know if I want to do your books.　It's too much work.

A　If a job is worth doing, it's worth doing well.

中譯

A:　你的帳必須做得正確，為每個欠我們錢的客戶建立一本帳。

B:　這樣工作很多。我不能存一本記錄所有欠錢客戶的普通帳本嗎？

A:　不行。你需要每個客戶賒　與付款的分別記錄。

B:　你太苛求了。我不確定我是否要做你的帳，工作量太多了。

A:　如果工作值得做，那就該把它做好。

Dialogue 2

A　Accounts Receivable includes all **unpaid** customer invoices.

B　Does it also include any other money that's owed to our business by customers?

A　Yes. Remember that it's listed as an asset on the balance sheet.

B　Okay. I should keep an accounts receivable ledger for each client, right?

A　Yes. Record a sale in the sales and cash receipts journal. Then add it to the ledger.

中譯

A:　應收帳包括所有未付款的客戶發票。

B:　它是否也包括客戶欠我們公司的其他款項？

A:　是。記住，在資產負債表上，它被列為一項資產。

B:　好。我應該為每個客戶做一本應收帳本，對吧？

A:　對。在銷貨與收據簿記錄銷售，然後再把它加入帳簿裡。

Dialogue 3

A　When a customer makes a purchase, I record it in the sales and cash receipts journal.

B　That's right. Then you enter it in that customer's AR ledger.

A　The AR ledger always tells me what is owed to us by that client.

B　Yes. The journal tells you what is owed to us by all of our clients.

A　Doing the accounts receivable isn't hard. I don't know what all the fuss is about.

A: 當一個客戶要買東西時，我將它記錄在銷貨與收據簿上。
B: 沒錯。然後，你將它記入該客戶的應收帳簿裡。
A: 應收帳簿總是能告訴我該客戶欠我們的帳。
B: 對。帳簿告訴你我們所有客戶欠我們的帳。
A: 做應收帳不困難，我不知道這些抱怨是做什麼的。

Dialogue 4

A   What do I do at the end of the month with the sales and cash receipts journal?

B   All entries in there are **totaled**.

A   And then that total is recorded in the AR account in the general ledger, right?

B   Yes. Do you think you can do that all on your own?

A   Since our bookkeeper quit, I don't think I have any choice, do I?

中譯 ......

A: 到了月底時，我要拿銷貨與收據簿做什麼？
B: 在那裡的所有帳目必須加總。
A: 然後，把加總數額記錄在總帳裡的應收帳，對吧？
B: 對。你認為你可以自己一個人把它完成嗎？
A: 自從我們的簿記員離職後，我認為我沒有選擇，對吧。

Dialogue 5

A   Be careful when extending credit to customers. It could cost us a lot of money.

B   What do you mean? Customers are our friends, aren't they?

A   No, they are customers. Sometimes they don't pay us. Bookkeeping is harder too.

B   If we accept credit cards then we don't have to extend credit as much.

A   That's right. We don't have to invoice as much.
      That's why we take credit cards.

中譯 ┄┄┄┄┄┄┄┄┄┄┄┄┄┄┄┄┄┄┄┄┄┄┄┄┄

A: 讓客戶賒購時要小心,它可能會花我們很多錢。

B: 你的意思是?顧客是我們的朋友,不是嗎?

A: 不,他們是顧客。有時候他們不付我們錢,簿記也比較困難。

B: 如果我們接受信用卡,那我們就不用那樣經常地讓他們賒購。

A: 沒錯,我們也不需要那麼多發票,這是我們為什麼收信用卡
      的原因。

Dialogue 6

A   I hate doing collections. It's embarrassing to phone
      and tell people they owe you money.

B   That's the price we pay for letting people buy
      now and pay later.

A   I think we should stop doing that. It also
      embarrasses the customer.

B   I never thought of that. Embarrassed customers
      might go shop somewhere else.

A   We should have a policy of pay **up front** or you
      can't buy it.

中譯 ┄┄┄┄┄┄┄┄┄┄┄┄┄┄┄┄┄┄┄┄┄┄┄┄┄

A: 我討厭催款,打電話告訴別人他們欠你錢是很尷尬的。

B: 我們讓別人現在買,稍後付款,這就是代價。

A: 我認為我們應該停止那樣做,這也讓客戶覺得尷尬。

B: 我從來不這麼想,覺得尷尬的顧客可能會去別的地方買東西。

A: 我們應該有一個直接付帳、要不然你就不能買的政策。

Dialogue 7

A   Tell me what you've learned in university about
      accounts receivable so far.

B   AR is accounts that owe us money. AR is bills
      that need to be paid by customers.

A　Yes. Do you have any **outstanding** bill?

B　I owe some money for **tuition** to the university. I'm one of their AR accounts.

A　Yes you are. You seem to have a good understanding of accounts receivable.

中譯

A:　告訴我你在大學裡現在學到哪些關於應收帳的事。

B:　應收帳是別人欠我們錢的帳，應收帳是顧客需要付的帳單。

A:　對。你有任何未繳付的帳單嗎？

B:　我欠大學一些學費，我是他們的應收帳之一。

A:　對，你是。你似乎對應收帳了解得很清楚。

Sentence Structure 重點句型

Accounts receivable is money owed to us by customers.	應收帳是客戶欠我們的錢。
Accounts receivable includes credit we've extended to customers.	應收帳包括我們讓客戶賒購的帳。
I'm demanding that all unpaid bills get paid.	我要求所有未償付的帳單都要付清。
The new policy is that all people pay up front.	新政策是所有的人都必須直接付錢買。
Be careful when extending credit to customers. It could cost us a lot of money.	讓客戶賒購時要小心，它可能會花我們很多錢。
If we accept credit cards then we don't have to extend credit as much.	如果我們接受信用卡，那我們就不用那樣經常地讓他們賒。

Vocabulary 字彙

Accounts Receivable		應收帳
regularly	*adv.*	定期地
extend	*v.*	給予
demanding	*adj.*	苛求的
unpaid	*adj.*	未付款的
total	*v.*	加總
up front		直接
outstanding	*adj.*	未繳付的
tuition	*n.*	學費

Useful Phrases 實用片語

Fuss 抱怨、大驚小怪

means "complaining"

例句 So I didn't bring cookies this Friday. Why all the fuss?
我這個星期五的確沒有帶餅乾來，有什麼好大驚小怪的？

Hate 討厭

to dislike or not to like

例句 I hate when she doesn't bring cookies on Friday.
我討厭當她星期五沒有帶餅乾來的時候。

Unit 2 Accounts Payable
應付帳

MP3-18

Accounts Payable is the opposite of AR. It's called AP and it is money that a business owes to its suppliers. Now the business is viewed as the customer of other businesses. AP is the unpaid bills of a business and the money that the business owes to its suppliers and other creditors. Accounts payable information should always be kept separate from accounts receivable information.

提示 　應付帳與應收帳正相反,它被稱為 AP,是一家公司欠自己供應商的錢。現在,這家公司被視為其他公司的客戶。應付帳是一家公司的未付帳款,以及這家公司積欠它的供應商與其他債權人的錢。應付帳資料應該總是與應收帳資料分開放。

Dialogue 1

A　I'm working on accounts payable today. It's a mess. There's lots of work to do.

B　Yes. Our last bookkeeper did a terrible job. That's why he was fired.

A　I'm going to keep a separate AP ledger for each of your suppliers.

B　I don't even know what that is. Please explain it to me.

A　The accounts payable ledger is a record of what you owe to each vendor.

中譯

A: 我今天在處理應付帳，一團亂。有很多事要做。

B: 對。我們上一個簿記員事情做得很糟，這是他被解雇的原因。

A: 我打算為你的每一個供應商保存分別的應付帳簿。

B: 我不知道那是什麼，請解釋給我聽。

A: 應付帳簿是你積欠每個賣方的記錄。

Dialogue 2

A　Will you please tell me how she'll do this from now on?

B　Each of our expenses will be recorded in the cash disbursements journal.

A　After that she'll post the different entries to the different AP ledgers?

B　We'll know how much we owe **in general** and how much we owe to each vendor.

A　Okay. I'm glad you explained this to me. Now I know what to look for.

中譯

A: 請你告訴我現在她要開始怎麼做？

B: 我們每一項支出都會被記錄在現金付款簿裡。

A: 在那之後，她會將不同的帳目登入不同的應收帳簿裡嗎？

B: 我們會知道總體積欠多少，還有我們積欠每個賣方各多少。

A: 好，我很高興你把這個解釋給我聽了。現在，我知道要找什麼了。

Dialogue 3

A　Accounts payable ledgers will help you control your **expenditures**.

B　That's good because this place has been spending way too much money.

A　If you keep accurate ledgers, it will be easy for you to **double check** bills you get.

B　　Great. We've paid a bill twice, a couple of times. *Luckily* our suppliers told us.

A　　It's not just the possible loss of money. Paying a bill twice is embarrassing.

中譯

A: 應付帳簿會幫助你控制自己的支出。

B: 這很好，因為這個地方花了太多錢。

A: 如果你在帳簿上的記錄正確，那你要重複檢查你拿到的帳單就很容易。

B: 太好了。我們曾有好幾次付同一筆帳兩次。幸運地，我們的供應商告訴了我們。

A: 這不僅是可能的金錢損失。一筆帳付兩次是很令人尷尬的。

Dialogue 4

A　　I'm working on AP today. I have lots of cheques to send out.

B　　Do you photocopy the invoice and send the copy back with the cheque?

A　　Yes, I like to do that. Some people think it's a waste of paper.

B　　It's better to be safe than sorry.

A　　I'm the same way. Besides if they don't want to keep it, they will shred it.

中譯

A: 我今天在處理應付帳，我有很多支票要送出去。

B: 你有影印發票，並把發票與支票一起寄回去嗎？

A: 有，我喜歡這樣做，一些人認為這麼做浪費紙。

B: 安全總比出錯好。

A: 我也是這麼認為。除此之外，如果他們不想要保留它，他們會把它用碎紙機裁掉。

Dialogue 5

A　　The one thing about AP is that it always goes up

as a business does better.

B Yes. The more you make, the more you spend.

A It's not just that. If you're making more, you're busier. You need to expand.

B Yes. Then you spend more because your operation is bigger.

A But it works the other way too. If there are fewer sales, there's less AP to do.

中譯

A: 關於應付款的一件事是，當公司狀況愈好，它的金額總是向上升。

B: 對。你賺愈多錢，你花得就愈多。

A: 不只是這樣，如果你賺更多錢，你也更忙。你需要擴張。

B: 對。因為你的營運更大，你就會花更多錢。

A: 但是，反之亦然。如果銷售比較少，應付帳就少。

Dialogue 6

A The key to good accounts payables is to **delay** payment as long as possible.

B I don't agree. You don't want to get into trouble with late **fees** to the vendors.

A No, but you do want to put off paying as long as you don't hurt your credit.

B I think that's rude. When you get a bill, pay it. Why make them wait?

A The longer you take to pay, the longer that money collects interest for you.

中譯

A: 好的應付帳關鍵在盡可能的延遲付款時限。

B: 我不同意。你不想與賣方陷入遲繳款項的麻煩中。

A: 不，但只要你在不傷害自己信用的情況下，你是希望要將付款時間向後延的。

B: 我認為這樣很無禮。當你拿到帳單時，就付清。為什麼要讓他們等？

A: 你等愈久付款，錢就有更長的時間為你生利息。

Dialogue 7

A   I'm glad account receivable collected from those two major clients who owed us.

B   Me too. Now we can get those filing cabinets we need for the office.

A   Not only that. Now I can get to work on accounts payable and cut some cheques.

B   Do we owe lots of money? Are we in financial trouble?

A   No. I've been holding off on paying some bills so I don't empty the bank account.

中譯

A: 我很高興那兩個主要客戶欠我們的應收帳都收回來了。

B: 我也是。現在我們可以將那些我們辦公室需要的檔案櫃買回來。

A: 不只那些。現在我們處理一些應付帳，簽出一些支票。

B: 我們欠了很多錢嗎？我們的財務有問題嗎？

A: 不是。我延遲一些帳單的付款，這樣銀行帳戶才不會空掉。

Sentence Structure 重點句型

Accounts payable is the money that you owe to your suppliers, creditors, and vendors.	應付帳是你積欠你的供應商、債權人與賣方的錢。
In general, it's a good idea to double check expenditures.	總體來説，重複檢查支出是個好主意。

AP is the unpaid bills of a business and the money owed to its suppliers and creditors.	應付帳是一家公司的未付帳款，以及這家公司積欠它的供應商與債權人的錢。
I'm going to keep a separate AP ledger for each of your suppliers.	我打算為你每一個供應商分別保存應付帳簿。
The accounts payable ledger is a record of what you owe to each vendor.	應付帳簿是你積欠每個賣方的記錄。
The one thing about AP is the more you make, the more you spend.	關於應付款的一件事是，當你錢賺得越多，你花得也越多。

Vocabulary 字彙

Accounts Payable		應付帳
creditors	n.	債權人
in general		總體
expenditures	n.	支出
double check		重複檢查
delay	v.	延遲
fees	n.	款項

Useful Phrases 實用片語

Luckily 幸運地

means "it's good that"

例句 Luckily, we were able to find the accounting error before it was too late.
幸運地，我們能在太遲之前，找到會計錯誤。

Unit 3　Petty Cash
零用金

MP3-19

All businesses should have a **petty cash fund** for small **miscellaneous** purchases. **Retail** businesses can go without a petty cash fund. Money can be taken out of the cash register as long as a note is placed in the cash drawer. The note should say who took out money, how much was taken, and what it was for. There should not be a lot of money kept in the petty cash and it should always be locked up. Only one or two people should be allowed access to the petty cash. It's when too many people have their hands in it that things can get recorded wrong or money can go missing.

提示 所有的公司應該都有零用金基金，以花在各種各樣的小型採 。零售業可以不用零用金基金，錢可以從收銀機拿出來，只要把字條放在現金抽屜裡就可以。這張字條應該有寫誰拿了這筆錢，拿了多少，以及拿錢的原因。在零用金裡不應該放太多錢，而且它應該一直被鎖起來，只有一或兩個人被允許取得零用金。當太多人管理那種東西，記錄可能就會有錯誤，或者錢會不見。

Dialogue 1

A   I need some money. We're out of **paper clips** and pens.

B   Just take it out of the cash register. Leave a note saying how much you took.

A   Okay. Should I write on there why I'm taking out money?

B   You don't have to. Get a receipt and put it in the cash drawer along with your note.

A   Okay. When I get back, I'll staple the receipt to my note so neither gets lost.

中譯

A: 我需要一些錢，我們的迴紋針與筆用完了。

B: 從收銀機拿錢出來，留一張字條，註明你拿了多少。

A: 好。我應該在上面寫我為什麼拿錢嗎？

B: 你不需要這麼寫。拿一張收據，將它跟你的字條一起放在現金抽屜裡。

A: 好。當我回來時，我會把收據釘在我的字條上，否則它會不見。

Dialogue 2

A   How do we set up a petty cash fund for our new business?

B   Write a cheque from your business. Make it out to petty cash. Cash that cheque.

A   I see. Then I put that money in a drawer in my desk?

B   I'd put it in a petty cash box. That way if you want to, you can lock it.

A   Then whenever I take money out of there, I put a receipt or a note in it, right?

中譯

A: 我們要怎樣為我們的新公司設立零用金基金？

B: 你從公司開出一張支票，把它標為零用金，將支票兌現。

A: 我懂了。然後我把錢放在我桌子的抽屜裡？

B: 我會把它放在零用金箱子裡，這樣你如果要的話，你可以把它鎖起來。

A: 然後，每當我從裡面拿錢出來，我就將收據或字條放進去，對吧？

Dialogue 3

A   I need to go buy pens but we're out of petty cash.

B   No problem. Add up the receipts in petty cash. Write a new cheque to petty cash.

A   Do you want me to go cash it or will you do it on your lunch break?

B   You can do it. Put the money in petty cash and take out what you need to buy pens.

A   Okay. I'll put the receipt in when I get back. I'll put my **initials** on the receipt.

中譯

A: 我需要去買筆，可是我們的零用金用完了。

B: 沒問題，把零用金裡的收據加總起來，開一張新支票做零用金。

A: 你要我去兌現，或是你要在午休的時候去做？

B: 你可以去做。將錢放在零用金裡，拿出你需要買筆的錢。

A: 好，當我回來時我會將收據放進去，我會將我名字的起首字母寫在收據上。

Dialogue 4

A   The petty cash fund will be for expenses that are too small to write a cheque for.

B   Okay. Who will have **access** to the petty cash box?

A Only me and the manager. If you need money for something, ask one of us.

B How much will we keep in the petty cash fund?

A I think a hundred dollars is too much. We'll keep sixty dollars.

中譯

A: 零用金基金是花在金額太小，不能付支票的支出上。

B: 好。誰能取用零用金箱子？

A: 只有我跟經理。如果你需要錢買東西，問我們其中一位。

B: 我們在零用金基金中有多少錢？

A: 我想一百元就太多了，我們會放六十元。

Dialogue 5

A All businesses should have a petty cash fund for small day to day expenses.

B That's right. You don't want to have to ask the store to invoice you for some pens.

A They want payment when you buy small things.

B At times like this it's best just to take some money out of petty cash.

A Do you want to go to the store or should I go instead?

中譯

A: 所有公司都應該有零用金基金，用來應付每天的支出。

B: 沒錯。你不想要店家為一些原子筆開發票給你。

A: 當你買小東西時，他們會要你付錢。

B: 像這樣的時候，最好就是從零用金裡拿出一些錢來。

A: 你想去商店嗎？或者應該由我去？

Dialogue 6

A Where is this petty cash box kept? Will I have access to it?

B　　We have a petty cash box we keep locked in a drawer. You're too new.

A　　What happens if I have to pay for something?

B　　You won't. You're too new yet. In a few months *we'll see*.

A　　What happens when petty cash is empty? When all that's in there is receipts?

中譯

A:　零用金箱子放在哪裡？我可以去拿嗎？

B:　我們有一個零用金箱子，鎖起來放在一個抽屜裡。你還太資淺。

A:　如果我必須為某東西付款時，怎麼辦？

B:　你不會遇到。你還太資淺。幾個月過後，我們會再看情況。

A:　當零用錢沒有時怎麼辦？裡面都是收據時怎麼辦？

Dialogue 6

A　　It's time to **replenish** petty cash. The only thing left in there is receipts.

B　　Okay. I'll get Bill to write a cheque to petty cash. You can go cash it.

A　　It's cold out. I don't want to go all the way to the bank.

B　　I know. We'll send the new guy. He's excited to do anything.

A　　While he's out there tell him to bring back a coffee with cream for me.

中譯

A:　該是增補零用金的時候了，裡面只剩下收據了。

B:　好。我會要比爾開一張支票給零用金，你可以去把它兌現。

A:　外面很冷，我不想走這麼長的一段路到銀行。

B:　我知道。我們要那個新來的人去，他做任何事都很興奮。

A:　當他出去時，叫他為我帶一杯加奶的咖啡。

Sentence Structure 重點句型

A petty cash fund is used to pay for small miscellaneous expenses.	零用金基金用來支付各式各樣的小額支出。
You can buy a petty cash box that will lock and some paper clips in a retail store.	你可以在一家零售商店裡買到一個可以鎖的零用金箱子與一些迴紋針。
He will need to initial this form before he's given access to the bank accounts.	在他可以使用銀行帳戶前，他會需要簽上起首字母。
Please replenish petty cash because it's almost empty.	請增補零用金，因為它已經幾乎用完了。
All businesses should have a petty cash fund for little day to day purchases.	所有公司都應該有零用金基金，用來應付每天的支出。
Money can be taken from the cash drawer in a store as long as a receipt gets put in.	在一家商店裡，可以從現金抽屜拿出錢來，只要有把收據放進去就好。

Vocabulary 字彙

petty cash fund		零用金基金
miscellaneous	*adj.*	各種各樣的
retail	*n.*	零售

paper clips		迴紋針
initials	*n.*	起首字母
access	*n.*	取用
replenish	*v.*	**增補**

Useful Phrases 實用片語

Day to day 每天的

every day

例句 We use the petty cash fund for the little day to day expenses.
我們用零用金做每天的小額支出。

We'll see 我們再看情況

means we'll talk about this some other time

例句 Can I take one afternoon off this month?
我這個月可以找一天下午休假嗎？

I don't know yet. We'll see.
我還不知道。我們再看情況。

Chapter 7

Adjustments
調整

Unit 1 Depreciation
折舊

MP3-20

Depreciation is an expense. It's **listed** in the income statement. Depreciation is the loss of value as an asset gets older and experiences wear and tear. A good example is a car. The longer you own a car, the less it's worth. The worth of the car goes down due to age, wear and tear. Another example would be office equipment like computers and printers. The opposite of depreciate is appreciate. When things appreciate, they go up in value, not down.

提示　折舊是一種支出，它被列在收益表裡。折舊是當資產變舊，並經歷一些磨損時所產生的價值損失。一輛車就是一個好例子，你擁有一輛車的時間愈長，它的價值就愈低。這輛車的價值因為年齡、磨損而下降。另一個例子是辦公室設備，例如電腦與印表機。折舊的相反就是增值，當東西增值時，他們的價值會往上升，而非下降。

Dialogue 1

A　All of the **fixed assets** of a business will decrease in value over time.

B　Still, it's not fair. It's not my fault but it hurts me because my assets **dwindle**.

A　It's just a cost of doing business. Everyone else in business faces that too.

B　I guess. It's just that we're not doing so good right now. Every cost hurts.

A   Depreciation is a fact of life. There's nothing you can do about it.

中譯 ....

A: 一家公司所有的固定資產都會隨著時間而貶值。

B: 這不公平。這不是我的錯，不過它讓我遭受損害，因為我的資產逐漸變少。

A: 它只是做生意的一個成本，每個做生意的人也都面臨到。

B: 我猜也是，只是我們現在狀況沒有那麼好，每個成本都有損害。

A: 折舊是生存的一部份，你無法做任何事改變它。

Dialogue 2

A   Depreciation like all other expenses is **deducted** from income.

B   Okay. I understand that part. How do you **calculate** depreciation on something?

A   There are several ways. The easiest is the **declining** balance method.

B   What's that?

A   A percent of the declining value you deducted each year over the life of the asset.

中譯 ....

A: 折舊就像其他的支出是從收入中扣除。

B: 好，我了解那個部分。你怎麼計算某樣東西的折舊？

A: 有好幾種方法，最容易的是餘額遞減法。

B: 那是什麼？

A: 你每年由資產中扣除遞減值的百分比。

Dialogue 3

A   The value of your long-term assets will change from year to year.

B   Is that change **represented** by **accumulated**

depreciation?

A   Yes. Depreciation is an expense even though no cash goes out of the bank account.

B   I'm good at being a business owner but not at doing accounting stuff.

A   That's what I'm here for. I'm good at the accounting stuff. Just leave it to me.

中譯

A: 你長期資產的價值會一年年改變。

B: 那個改變是由累積折舊所代表的嗎？

A: 對，折舊是支出，即使沒有現金由銀行帳戶流出去。

B: 我做公司老闆很在行，但對會計就不行。

A: 這就是我在這裡的原因，我對會計事務很在行，交給我就好了。

Dialogue 4

A   We just bought a new **cash register**. Do you know what the depreciation is on that?

B   The rate of depreciation on cash registers is thirty percent a year.

A   It cost us three thousand dollars. What's the depreciation in the first year?

B   What's thirty percent of three thousand dollars? Is it nine hundred dollars?

A   I can't believe I'm going to lose nine hundred dollars in the first year.

中譯

A: 我們剛買了一台收銀機。你知道它的折舊是如何嗎？

B: 收銀機的折舊率是一年百分之三十。

A: 它花了我們三千元，第一年的折舊是多少？

B: 三千元的百分之三十是多少？是九百元嗎？

A: 我不敢相信第一年內，我將損失九百元。

Dialogue 5

A   Does the government set the rate of depreciation?

B   No. The government sets **capital cost allowances**. That's **slightly** different.

A   Who sets the rate of depreciation?

B   The business sets that for itself. It's based on how much the asset gets used.

A   We rarely use the photocopier. I don't think it depreciates much.

中譯 ....

A: 折舊率是政府設定的嗎?

B: 不是,政府設定資產成本減免額,這有些許不同。

A: 誰設定折舊率?

B: 公司自己設定。這是基於這個資產被使用的程度而定。

A: 我們很少使用影印機,我不認為它會折舊得這麼多。

Dialogue 6

A   We need a new company car. Do you know what we should buy?

B   As your accountant I'd advise you not to buy. You should **lease**.

A   If we buy it becomes as asset. You told me company assets are good.

B   They're not so good if they depreciate. They need to increase in value to be good.

A   I see. Are you suggesting that we lease our next company car?

中譯 ....

A: 我們需要一輛新的公司車,你知道我們應該買哪一輛嗎?

B: 身為你的會計師,我建議你不要買,你應該去租。

A: 如果我們買了,它就變成資產,你告訴我有公司資產是好的。

B: 如果他們會折舊,那它們就沒有這麼好。它們需要會增值,這樣才好。

A:　我懂了。你建議我們下一輛公司車用租的嗎？

Dialogue 7

A　The photocopier just died. What are we going to do?

B　We need to think about not replacing it. It's a big expense.

A　It was bought and paid for. It wasn't an expense.

B　It depreciated in value. That's an expense. We do very little copying.

A　Well, there is a copy store right beside us. Maybe we should just make copies there.

中譯

A:　影印機剛剛停機了。我們要怎麼辦？

B:　我們需要想想要不要換掉它，它是一項很大的支出。

A:　我們已經把它買下來，款也付清了，它不是一項支出。

B:　它會折舊貶值，這是一項支出，我們很少影印。

A:　嗯，我們隔壁就是一家影印店，或許我們應該到那裡去影印。

Sentence Structure　重點句型

Depreciation is listed as an expense on the income statements.	折舊在收益表上被列為支出。
The value of a fixed asset dwindles as it experiences age and use.	固定資產的價值隨著它的年齡與使用而逐漸降低。
Depreciation is deducted from the value after it is calculated.	在計算之後，折舊從它的價值裡扣除。
Capital cost allowance helps you decide how much depreciation has accumulated.	資產成本減免額幫助你決定折舊已累積多少。

| Depreciation is the loss of value as an asset gets older and experiences use. | 當資產變舊並有使用時，折舊就是價值的損失。 |
| All of the fixed assets of a business, like cars and computers, will decrease in value. | 一家公司的所有固定資產，例如汽車與電腦，都會貶值。 |

Vocabulary 字彙

depreciation	*n.*	折舊
list	*v.*	列
fixed assets		固定資產
dwindle	*v.*	變少
deduct	*v.*	扣除
calculate	*v.*	計算
declining	*adj.*	遞減
represent	*v.*	代表
accumulate	*v.*	累積
cash register		收銀機
capital cost allowances		資產成本減免額
slightly	*adv.*	些許
lease	*v.*	租

Useful Phrases 實用片語

Face 面臨、面對

to face something means to have to deal with something

例句 Everyday I have to face my boss and tell him I can't do my job.
每天我都必須面對我的老闆，告訴他我無法做自己的工作。

Died 停機、當機

when a thing has died it has stopped working

例句 My computer just died so can I use yours?
我的電腦剛剛當機，我可以用你的嗎？

Unit 2 Trial Balance 試算表

MP3-21

The trial balance is a worksheet. All general ledger accounts and their debit or credit balances are listed on it. It's used as a tool to alert a business to errors that have been made in the books. The total debits must equal the total credits. If they don't, there's a mistake. It must be traced down and fixed. Good accounting staff will always do a trial balance more than once.

提示　試算表是工作底稿，所有的總帳帳戶與它們的借方或貸方平衡都會列在上面。它被當作一個工具使用，用來警告公司在帳簿裡產生的錯誤。借方的總額與貸方的總額必須相等，它必須被追蹤並糾正，好的會計人員試算表總是做兩次以上。

Dialogue 1

A　When you close the books at year end you must do three trial balances.

B　But what if I balance on the first try? Do I still have to do two more?

A　Yes. What if you're only balancing because you keyed in a number wrong?

B　I see what you're thinking. If I balance I might have made a mistake.

A　Exactly. That mistake could be correcting a mistake we'd never find.

中譯

A:　當你在年底結算時,你必須做三張試算表。

B:　但是,如果我第一次做就平衡了呢?我還需要再做兩次嗎?

A:　對。如果你只是因為鍵入一個錯誤的數字才得到平衡的,怎麼辦?

B:　我懂你在想什麼了,如果平衡,我還是有可能犯錯。

A:　沒錯。那個錯誤可能是改正了一個我們永遠不會發現的錯誤。

Dialogue 2

A　What happens if she's made mistakes? She's new and it's so close to year end.

B　That's why we're having the accountant do the trial balance for this year. He'd find the mistakes if she made any.

A　Would he make the adjustments as well?

B　Yes. He'll make any adjustments that are needed and post them to the general ledger.

A　That will make sure the books are in balance before she prepares financial statements.

中譯

A:　如果她犯錯的話,怎麼辦?她是新手,而且很靠近年底了。

B:　這是為什麼我們今年要會計師來做試算表。如果她有犯錯,他會找出來。

A:　他也會做調整嗎？

B:　對。他會做任何需要的調整，然後再把它們登入總帳中。

A:　這樣在她準備財務報表之前，能確保帳簿都平衡。

Dialogue 3

A　When doing a trial balance total debits must equal the total credits, right?

B　Yes. Don't be **discouraged** if they don't. Bookkeeping errors happen.

A　But I want to be a good assistant to you. I like working in accounting.

B　Errors happen all the time. They're usually made by the person who made the entry.

A　Yes. I guess it'd be hard for me to get it right if it wasn't done right in the first place.

中譯

A:　做試算表時，借方的總額與貸方的總額必須相等，對吧？

B:　對。如果它們不相等，不要沮喪。簿記錯誤是會發生的。

A:　但是，我要做好你的助理工作，我喜歡做會計工作。

B:　錯誤時時發生，它們通常是由登入帳目的人所犯下的。

A:　沒錯。我猜，對我來說，如果首先沒有做對，就很難做對了吧。

Dialogue 4

A　I need to think of the trial balance as a way to find errors.

B　Yes. Be sure the numbers on your trial balance are the same as in the general ledger.

A　I also need to make sure I wrote debits as debits and credits as credits.

B　Yes. Sometimes people will copy one down as the other.

A　It's not hard work but it takes time and patience.

A: 我需要把試算表想成尋找錯誤的一種方法。

B: 對。要確定在你試算表上的數字與總帳中的一樣。

A: 我也需要確定自己把借方寫在借方欄，貸方寫在貸方欄。

B: 對。有時候人們會把一個抄到另一個去。

A: 它不是很困難的工作，但需要時間與耐心。

Dialogue 5

A If you can't seem to find where the mistake was made, go back to the journals.

B Right. I should check that the journal totals were posted correctly in the general ledger.

A Yes. You need to check that the amounts were **copied** correctly.

B I should also check if the total debits equal total credits in each journal.

A That's what lots of errors are. Things get copied down wrong somewhere else.

A: 如果你似乎不能找出錯誤在哪裡，那就回日記帳裡找。

B: 好。我應該去查查帳簿的總額是否正確地登入總帳裡。

A: 對。你需要檢查數額是否正確地抄寫下來。

B: 我應該也檢查每一本帳簿中借方的總額是否與貸方的總額相等。

A: 很多的錯誤都是那樣，一樣東西被抄錯成另外的東西。

Dialogue 6

A I need some fresh eyes. Can you help me? I've been going over this for hours.

B What's the problem? Can't get the books to balance? Here, let me try.

A You get to a point where you can't see anything anymore. I need a rest.

B   Look at this. Someone wrote down a 62 in the ledger but it's 26 in the journal.

A   Let me see for a minute. You're right. The books balance. Thank you so much.

中譯

A: 我需要另一個人來看。你能幫我嗎？我已經花了好幾個小時檢查這個了。

B: 是什麼問題？沒有辦法使帳簿平衡嗎？拿來，讓我試試看。

A: 當你到一個程度時，就看不出任何東西了。我需要休息。

B: 看看這個，有人在帳簿裡寫 62，但在日記帳裡是 26。

A: 讓我看一下。你說的沒錯，帳簿平衡了，非常謝謝你。

Dialogue 7

A   I hate trying to balance the books. Isn't there someone else who can do it?

B   Seeing as you're an accountant I think you'd better do it yourself.

A   Isn't there some accounting technician on staff who can do it for me?

B   Everybody has their own work to do. Just sit down and get at it.

A   Okay. I'll start by comparing the totals in the ledger to the totals on the trial balance.

中譯

A: 我討厭試著使帳簿平衡，有沒有其他人可以做這件事？

B: 因為你是會計師，我想你最好還是自己做。

A: 公司裡沒有會計技術員可以幫我做嗎？

B: 每一個人都有他們的工作要做，你最好坐下來開始做。

A: 好。我會開始比較帳簿裡的總額與試算表的總額。

The trial balance is a worksheet that is used as a tool to alert you to errors in the books.	試算表是工作底稿，被當作一個工具使用，用來警告公司在帳簿裡產生的錯誤。
Don't be discouraged if a mistake happens. Just have patience and make it right.	如果錯誤發生，不要感到沮喪，只要有耐心，並把錯誤改正。
Find errors by comparing numbers and making sure they were copied or keyed in right.	利用比較數字來找錯誤，並確定他們被正確地抄寫或鍵入。
All general ledger accounts and their debit or credit balances are listed on it.	所有的總帳帳戶與他們的借貸平衡都列在上面。
Start by comparing the totals in each of the ledgers to the totals on the trial balance.	從比較帳簿裡的總額與試算表的總額開始。
If you can't seem to find where the mistake was made, go back to the journals.	如果你似乎找不到錯誤在哪裡，就回日記帳去找。

Vocabulary 字彙

trial balance		試算表
worksheet	*n.*	工作底稿
alert	*v.*	警告
trace down		追蹤

| discouraged | *adj.* | 沮喪的 |
| copy | *v.* | 抄寫 |

Useful Phrases 實用片語

Fresh eyes 另一個人來看

said when a person needs help finding something that should be easy to find

例句 I've looked for my car keys everywhere. I need a fresh set of eyes.
我到處找過我的車鑰匙了。我需要另一個人來看。

Unit 3　Closing the Books
結算

MP3-22

When a business reaches the end of an **accounting period** they need to **close the books**. Closing the books is what takes place at year end so it happens at least once a year. In order to prepare financial statements a business will close the books. Some businesses close the books monthly even if they aren't preparing financial statements.

提示　當一個公司遇到會計期即將結束時,他們需要做結算。結算是在年底發生的事,所以它至少一年發生一次。為了要準備財務報表,

一家公司要結算，一些公司即使並不是要準備財務報表，他們每個月
也做結算。

A   I'm going to teach you the basics on how to close
    the books.

B   Okay. If I'm going to be an accountant one day,
    I'd better know how to do that.

A   After you finish entering the day to day
    transactions in the journals you're ready.

B   Okay. So first I make all my entries in the
    journals and then I can close the books.

A   Right. Now the business can do some of the work
    and the accountant can do some.

中譯 ······

A: 我打算教你結算的基本手續。

B: 好。如果我打算有一天成為會計師，我最好知道要怎麼做。

A: 在你把每日交易記入日記帳之後，你就準備好了。

B: 好。所以，我首先將我所有的帳目登入日記帳裡，然後我就
    可以結算了。

A: 對。現在公司可以做一些工作，會計師也可以做一些。

A   What are you doing? I thought today was
    supposed to be your day off.

B   I'm posting entries to the general ledger accounts
    so I can close the books.

A   Weren't you supposed to do that last week? Boy
    you're **behind**.

B   That's why I'm not taking the day off. I need to
    do a trial balance.

A   Make sure you do the income statement and
    balance sheet also.

A: 你在做什麼？我以為你今天該休假一天。

B: 我在將帳目登入總帳的帳戶中，這樣我就可以結算。

A: 你不是上個星期就該做這件事嗎？老天，你的進度落後了。

B: 這就是為什麼我今天沒有休假，我需要做一張試算表。

A: 要確定你把收益表與資產負債表也要做好。

Dialogue 3

A　Okay. We need to close the books and Janet is off sick. Who can help me?

B　That's a big job. Can't we just leave it until she gets back?

A　She's really sick. They say she might be out for three weeks.

B　That's too bad. Okay, I'll help you. I'm a little *rusty* though.

A　Let's check to see that all of the journal entries have been done.

中譯

A: 好。我們需要結算，而珍納生病請假了，誰能幫我忙？

B: 那是一份很重大的工作，我們不能把它放著等到她回來上班嗎？

A: 她病得很重。他們說，她可能會有三個星期不在。

B: 這很糟糕。好，我會幫你。不過，我有點生疏。

A: 讓我們檢查一下所有的日記帳的帳目是否都做好了。

Dialogue 4

A　Doing our own books takes too much time. I'd like to get an accountant.

B　We can't afford an accountant for these day to day things.

A　What about closing the books? Could we at least get someone to do that for us?

B   I'll think about it. **In the meantime,** let's get started on that.

A   Okay. I'll transfer the journal totals to the general ledger.

中譯 ....

A: 做我們自己的帳花太多時間了，我想要請一位會計師。

B: 我們負擔不起請一個會計師來做每天事務的費用。

A: 那結算呢？我們至少可以找人來幫我們做那件事吧？

B: 我還在考慮。現在這段時間，讓我們先開始做那件事吧。

A: 好。我會將日記帳的總額轉到總帳裡。

Dialogue 5

A   Closing the books is something that takes place at the end of an accounting period.

B   Is that when you make adjusting entries? When the books are being closed?

A   Yes. First you do that and then the income and expense accounts are closed.

B   After that do you transfer the **net profit** to an equity account?

A   Yes. You can transfer it to the retained earnings equity account.

中譯 ....

A: 結算是在會計期結束時所發生的事。

B: 你是在那時候做帳目調整的嗎？在結算的時候？

A: 對。首先，你做那件事，然後收入與支出的帳戶就結算好了。

B: 在那之後，你會將淨利轉到一個權益帳戶？

A: 對。你可以將它放入保留盈餘帳戶。

Dialogue 6

A   We were talking about the accounting system the other day in class.

B   Yes. Do you want to review where closing the

books **fit** in?

A   Yes. I know it all starts with a business transaction. That gets entered in a journal.

B   Correct. Those journal entries get posted to the general ledger.

A   From which you can do a trial balance. Then closing the books comes from that.

中譯

A: 之前有一天，我們在課堂上談到會計系統。

B: 對。你想要複習，結算是過程中的哪個位置？

A: 是。我知道它是從一個商務交易開始，它被記入一個日記帳裡。

B: 對。這些日記帳的帳目被登入總帳中。

A: 你可以從那裡做出一張試算表，然後結算就是從那裡來的。

Dialogue 7

A   It's year end. We need to close the books. We need to file an income tax return.

B   Okay. Can we do it ourselves this year or should we give it to the accountant?

A   I think we've learned a lot. We could probably muddle through it.

B   Muddling through isn't good enough. If it's worth doing, it's worth doing well.

A   Okay. You're right. Let's get the accountant to do it for us for one more year.

中譯

A: 年底了。我們需要做結算，我們需要申報所得稅。

B: 好。今年我們可以自己做，還是我們應該將它交給一位會計師？

A: 我想，我們學了很多。我們大概可以應付得來。

B: 應付是不夠好，如果它值得做，那就值得做好。

A: 好。你是對的。我們今年再找會計師幫我們做一年。

Sentence Structure 重點句型

At the end of the accounting period all businesses close the books.	在會計期結束時，所有的公司都做結算。
An accountant can teach a business how to transfer the net profit into an equity account.	會計師可以教公司如何將淨利轉到一個業主權益帳戶中。
Closing the books is what takes place at year end so it happens at least once a year.	結算是在年底發生的事，所以它至少一年發生一次。
In order to prepare any financial statements a business will have to close the books.	為了要準備財務報表，一家公司要結算。
Some businesses close the books every month whether or not they're preparing financial statements.	一些公司即使並不是要準備財務報表，他們每個月也做結算。
We need to close the books at year end because we need to file an income tax return.	我們在年底需要結算，因為我們需要申報所得稅。

Vocabulary 字彙

accounting period		會計期
close the books		結算
behind	*adv.*	進度落後
In the meantime		現在這段時間
net profit		淨利

fit	v.	適合

Useful Phrases 實用片語

Boy 老天

an exclamation expressing surprise

例句 Boy, am I glad to see you. I locked my keys in my car.
老天，我真高興見到你，我將自己的鑰匙鎖在車上。

Rusty 生疏的

Out of practice. Said when something hasn't been done in a long time.

例句 I'll help you close the books but I haven't done that in years so I'm a little rusty.
我會幫你做結算，不過我已經很多年沒做了，所以我有點生疏。

Muddle through 應付

said when you know you're going to make a lot of mistakes

例句 I think the books are too important for us to just try and muddle through them.
我想這些帳簿對我們來說太重要了，不能試著自己虛應了事。

Chapter 8

Alternatives
替代方案

Unit 1　**Bookkeepers**
簿記員

MP3-23

A **bookkeeper** is a person who does the books for a business. Bookkeepers are often **self-employed** and work for a business on a contract basis. It's more cost effective for a business to have them work on a contract basis than it is to have them as an employee. Bookkeepers are not accountants. Accountants have a university degree.

提示　簿記員就是為一家公司作帳的人。簿記員經常是自由業，以定契約方式為一家公司工作。對一家公司來說，讓他們以契約方式工作，比雇他們為員工更有成本效益，簿記員不是會計師，會計師有大學學位。

Dialogue 1

A　Now that we are open for business, we have to discuss our financial **situation**.

B　We don't have a financial situation yet. We haven't started bringing in money.

A　I'm talking about taking care of the books. Who's going to do that for us?

B　I think we should get a bookkeeper. We're a small company that's just starting out.

A　I agree. We can't afford an accountant and we won't need one for quite a while.

中譯

A:　現在，我們要開公司，我們必須討論一下我們的財務狀況。

B:　我們還沒有財務狀況，我們還沒開始賺錢。

A:　我講的是處理帳簿的事，誰要為我們作帳？

B:　我想，我們應該請一位簿記員，我們是一家剛開始的小公司。

A:　我同意。我們負擔不起一位會計師，而且我們會有一段時間
　　都不需要會計師。

Dialogue 2

A　I know you're an accountant and I know we're at
　　a party. Can I ask you one thing?

B　Sure. Go ahead. What do you want to know? My
　　age? Am I married?

A　Actually, I want your **professional** opinion on
　　whether or not I need a bookkeeper.

B　I'm an accountant. You realize that don't you? I
　　might not be the right person to ask.

A　You're right. I'm sorry. I shouldn't ask you that.

中譯 ....

A:　我知道你是一位會計師，而且我知道我們正在一個派對上。
　　我可以問你一件事嗎？

B:　沒問題，請說。你想要知道什麼？我的年齡？我結婚了嗎？

A:　實際上，我要你的專業意見，看看我需不需要一位簿記員。

B:　我是一位會計師。你知道，對吧？你可能不該問我。

A:　你說得對，我很抱歉，我不應該問你那件事的。

Dialogue 3

A　What are your **credentials** as a bookkeeper?

B　I took a course called bookkeeping for small
　　business at the local community college.

A　That's it? Those don't sound like very good
　　credentials to me.

B　If you want someone with a degree, you're
　　looking at hiring an accountant.

A But I can't afford an accountant. How long have you been doing books?

A: 你做簿記員有什麼憑證嗎？

B: 我在地方社區大學修了一門叫做簿記的課。

A: 就這樣？我聽起來似乎沒有很好的憑證。

B: 如果你要一個有學位的人，你要雇用的是會計師。

A: 但是，我負擔不起一位會計師。你作帳作多久了？

Dialogue 4

A As our new bookkeeper you'll need to know where we keep our records.

B Yes. I also want to know if I can do some work right here without getting in the way.

A Yes. Since you will be coming in after hours you can work at the secretary's desk.

B That will be just fine. It'll allow me to be close to the files and records I need.

A Yes. All of that is kept in this filing cabinet right beside his desk.

A: 身為我們新的簿記員，你需要知道我們將記錄保存在哪裡。

B: 對。我也需要知道，我是否可以在這裡工作，而不會干擾到你們。

A: 對。既然你在下班後來，你可以在秘書的位子上工作。

B: 那沒有問題，我會與需要的檔案與記錄很靠近。

A: 對。所有的東西都被保存在他桌子旁邊的這個檔案櫃。

Dialogue 5

A I brought you the income statement and balance sheet for the last month.

B That's great. Thank you. You work very hard. I'm **grateful**.

A I like helping out small businesses. I like finances. I'm happy to do it.

B You're much more affordable than an accountant. Why can they charge so much?

A They have to pay for their university educations I suppose.

中譯

A: 我幫你帶來了上個月的收益表與資產負債表。

B: 太好了,謝謝你。你很努力地工作,我很感激。

A: 我喜歡幫助小公司,我喜歡財務,很高興可以做這件事。

B: 我們比較能負擔你的費用,而無法負擔會計師。為什麼他們收費這麼高?

A: 我想,他們必須支付自己的大學教育。

Dialogue 6

A As a bookkeeper, what do you have to offer for me? What can you do here?

B As a bookkeeper, I can teach you how to do your own books to start.

A That'd be nice. Since this is a new business, I can't afford to pay out for that.

B Once you get busy enough, I would manage your finances for you.

A Will you show me how to record all transactions and how to post to ledgers?

中譯

A: 身為一個簿記員,你可以提供我什麼?你在這裡能做什麼?

B: 身為一個簿記員,我可以從教你如何做自己的帳開始。

A: 那會不錯。因為這是新公司,我無法負擔讓外面的人來做這件事。

B: 你一旦變得很忙,我就可以為你管理財務。

A: 你能告訴我如何記錄所有的交易,以及如何登入帳簿嗎?

Dialogue 7

A　Okay. I've decided that I'll do your bookkeeping for you. When do I start?

B　You can start today. I have a lot of receipts in this **shoe box**. *Good luck.*

A　This is bad. To have a bookkeeping system that works, you need to be organized.

B　That will be your first job. Organize our finances and then you'll maintain them.

A　All right. From now on promise me you will at least record every transaction.

中譯

A:　好。我決定為你做簿記工作,我什麼時候開始?

B:　你今天就可以開始,我在這個鞋盒裡有很多收據,祝你好運。

A:　這很糟糕,要有一個能運作的簿記系統,你需要有組織。

B:　那將是你的第一個工作,將我們的財務組織起來,然後你可以維持它們。

A:　好吧。從現在開始,你至少會將每筆交易記錄下來。

Sentence Structure 重點句型

Bookkeepers are usually self-employed and work for a company on a contract basis.	簿記員通常是自由業,以定契約的方式為一家公司工作。
If someone says they are a professional accountant, ask what credentials they have.	如果某人說他們是專業的會計師,問問他們有哪些憑證。
A bookkeeper is a person who does the books for a business.	簿記員就是為一家公司作帳的人。

It's more cost effective for a business to have them work on a contract basis than it is to have them as an employee.	對一家公司來說，讓他們以契約方式工作，比雇他們做員工更有成本效益。
Bookkeepers are not accountants. Accountants have a university degree.	簿記員不是會計師，會計師有大學學位。
To have a bookkeeping system that works you need to be organized.	要有一個能運作的簿記系統，你需要有組織。

Vocabulary 字彙

bookkeeper	n.	簿記員
self-employed		自由業
situation	n.	狀況
professional	adj.	專業的
credentials	n.	憑證
grateful	adj.	感激的
shoe box		鞋盒

Useful Phrases 實用片語

Good luck 祝你好運

this means the person wishes you well with a difficult job

例句 Okay the new filing cabinet is ready to have all the old files moved into it. Good luck.
好，新的檔案櫃已經準備好，可以把所有的舊檔案移進去了。祝你好運。

Unit 2 Computerized Accounting
電腦化會計
MP3-24

It used to be that all bookkeeping was done by hand on paper. Now all accounting can be done by computer. This means that more and more businesses are getting someone on staff to do some of the accounting. Bookkeepers work more with the self-employed than with small businesses. Accountants do less of the day-to-day things and more of the big jobs like year end.

提示　以前所有的簿記工作都是書面手寫而成。現在，所有的會計都可以用電腦完成，這表示有愈來愈多的公司，要公司裡的人做一些會計工作。簿記員與自營商合作比與小公司要來得多。會計師比較少做每天的例行工作，而較常做像年底（結算）那樣的重大工作。

Dialogue 1

A　Good news Phil. We're going to be getting some computers.

B　I'd **rather** not get one if that's okay with you. I'm happy to do the books **manually**.

A　Oh come on. It'll save you a lot of time to do them on the computer.

B　It won't. Doing books by hand is what I know. That's how I've always done them.

A　I'll talk to the boss and see what she says. I'll think she'll be surprised though.

中譯 ....

A:　好消息，菲爾。我們打算買一些電腦。

B:　如果你不介意的話，我寧可不要，我對人工做帳很滿意。

A:　喔，拜託，用電腦做可以節省你很多時間。

B:　並不會，手寫作帳是我懂的，這是我一直使用的方式。

A:　我會和老闆談談，看看她怎麼說。不過，我想她會被嚇一跳。

Dialogue 2

A　We're getting a new computer **operating system** put on all of our machines.

B　Oh great. Now I'm going to have to **switch** brands of accounting software.

A　Hmm. That sounds like more money going out. Is that what it means?

B　Of course. You switch the operating system and I have to switch the software.

A　We'll have to compare the cost of staying the same to the cost of switching over.

中譯 ....

A:　我們正準備在我們所有的機器上裝一個新的電腦作業系統。

B:　喔，這下可好，我得更換會計軟體了。

A:　嗯。聽起來要花更多錢，是不是這個意思？

B:　當然。你更換作業系統，我就必須更換軟體。

A:　我們必須比較維持原樣的成本以及更換的成本。

Dialogue 3

A　Excuse me. I need to buy some accounting software for my computer.

B　Okay. We have several different accounting

software **packages**.

A   I have the Windows operating system.

B   Then you can choose from Simply Accounting or Quickbooks.

A   Quickbooks is for a very small business. I think I better stick with Simply.

中譯 ....

A: 打擾一下,我需要為自己的電腦買會計軟體。

B: 好。我們有好幾種不同的會計套裝軟體。

A: 我有 Windows 作業系統。

B: 那你可以選 Simply Accounting 或者是 Quickbooks。

A: Quickbooks 是給非常小型的公司用的,我想我最好用 Simply。

Dialogue 4

A   If I'm going to be doing the books here I need access to a computer.

B   No problem. You can use this one here. I'll give you the **password**.

A   Before you do that what version of Simply do you run on it?

B   Our version is a few years old now. I don't know exactly which one it is.

A   I'll be doing work on my machine at home too. We need the same **version**.

中譯 ....

A: 如果我打算在這裡做帳,我需要用到一部電腦。

B: 沒問題,你可以用這裡的這一部,我會給你密碼。

A: 在你這麼做之前,你(電腦)裡面跑的是 Simply 的哪個版本?

B: 我們的版本是好幾年前的,我不知道它究竟是哪一個版本。

A: 我也會在家裡用我的機器工作,我們需要用同一個版本。

Dialogue 5

A   Okay. Now you have the right operating system to run the software I like to use.

B   So, are you ready to go then? Are you able to get started now?

A   I'll need to use spreadsheets as well. Do you have spreadsheet software?

B   No but I have a feeling I'm about to purchase it. Just write down what you need.

A   Okay. While you're at it will you get me a **flat screen monitor**?

中譯 ....

A: 好。現在你有正確的作業系統來跑我喜歡用的軟體了。

B: 那，你準備好要做了嗎？你可以現在開始嗎？

A: 我也需要使用試算表，你有試算表的軟體嗎？

B: 沒有，不過我會去買，只要把你需要的寫下來。

A: 好。既然你要辦這件事，你可以幫我買一個平面螢幕嗎？

Dialogue 6

A   Where are you going to keep all the journals and ledgers?

B   Everything will either be in the computer or in one of these two drawers.

A   You can fit everything into two drawers of one filing cabinet? That's great.

B   It wasn't always like that. Thanks to computers you don't need as much space.

A   I would like you to print off a copy of the financial statements for me each month.

中譯 ....

A: 你打算把所有帳冊與帳簿放在哪裡？

B: 每樣東西不是在電腦裡，就會在這兩個抽屜裡。

A: 你能將所有的東西放進一個檔案櫃的兩個抽屜裡？那真是太

好了。

B: 以前並不是這樣的，幸虧有電腦，你不需要那麼多空間。

A: 我會要你每個月為我印出這些財務報表。

Dialogue 7

A Do you use **database** much when you're doing the computerized accounting?

B No. I don't seem to need it. I do use electronic spreadsheets though.

A I can see how that'd be very useful. Did you have to take a course to learn?

B I took a course in computerized accounting because you need good computer skills.

A I thought I saw a course like that being offered at the community college.

中譯

A: 當你在做電腦化會計時，你有常使用資料庫嗎？

B: 沒有。我似乎不需要它。不過，我有用試算表。

A: 我可以看出它是很有用的，你必須去上課學習如何用嗎？

B: 我上了一堂電腦化會計的課，因為你需要善於使用電腦。

A: 我想，我在社區大學看到有提供像那樣的課程。

Sentence Structure 重點句型

The bookkeeping and accounting used to be done manually.	以前所有的簿記工作與會計都是書面手寫而成。
Accounting can now be done by computer.	會計現在都是利用電腦完成。
Make sure the version of software you buy works with your computer operating system.	確定你買的軟體版本能在你電腦的作業系統上運作。

Computers used for accounting should have a password to protect them.	用來做會計的電腦應該有密碼來保護它們。
More businesses are getting someone on staff to do at least some of the accounting.	愈多公司找公司裡的人多少做一些會計工作。
Today, bookkeepers work more with self-employed people than with companies.	現在，簿記員大多為自營商工作，而比較沒有為公司工作。
Accountants do fewer of the little jobs and more of the big jobs, like year end.	會計師較少做小事情，而是較常做像年底結算那樣的重大工作。

Vocabulary 字彙

rather	adv.	寧可
manually	adv.	人工
operating system		作業系統
switch	v.	更換
packages	n.	套裝
password	n.	密碼
version	n.	版本
flat screen monitor		平面螢幕
database	n.	資料庫

Useful Phrases 實用片語

By hand 手寫

means manually or without a computer

例句 Many years ago, before there were computers, she used to do the books by hand.
許多年以前,在電腦出現之前,她都用手寫作帳。

Unit 3 Do it Yourself
自己動手做

`MP3-25`

More people with small businesses are doing some of the **computerized accounting** themselves. Courses are **inexpensive** and can be **claimed** as a **business expense**. The more people are able to do themselves, the less money they have to spend on getting help. It can be cost effective to do it yourself. Some people even use accounting software to help manage their household finances.

提示 愈來愈多擁有小公司的人,自己做一些電腦化的會計。課程不貴,而且可以報商務支出。愈多人可以自己做,他們就可以花愈少的錢來找人幫助,自己做符合成本效率,一些人甚至使用會計軟體來管理家庭財務。

Dialogue 1

A　I'll tell you the basic things you need to do to keep your own finances.

B   Thank you. We will come to you for the more difficult **tasks**.

A   Okay. Keep all receipts and **issue** receipts for all payments.

B   We'll also issue invoices for all purchases made without payment.

A   Good. You will need to record all of these transactions. I'll show you how.

中譯 ....

A: 我會告訴你管理自己的財務所需要做的基本東西。

B: 謝謝你。我們遇到更困難的工作會來找你。

A: 好。把所有收據收好，所有的收款都必須開收據。

B: 我們也有對所有未付款的購買開發票。

A: 很好。你需要記錄所有的交易，我會告訴你如何做

Dialogue 2

A   It will help you to understand the basics of accounting if you know this **formula**.

B   What formula? Tell me.

A   Remember this. All assets are equal to the liabilities plus the equity.

B   Is that the **accounting equation**?

A   You've heard of it. Yes. Does that help? Or is that too advanced to start with?

中譯 ....

A: 如果你知道這個公式，它會幫助你了解會計的基本原則。

B: 什麼公式？告訴我。

A: 記得這一個，負債加上業主權益等於所有的資產。

B: 這是會計等式嗎？

A: 你聽過它，是的。這樣有幫助嗎？或者，這樣的開始太進階了？

Dialogue 3

A Those people want to open a business. They don't have a lot of money.

B We can help them. They should do their own books to start.

A Once they get too busy to do them, we can do them.

B Yes. They need us to tell them how to do their own books. You will teach them.

A I'll tell them to record all transactions, enter them in the journals and I'll do the rest.

中譯

A： 那些人想要開一間公司,他們沒有很多錢。

B： 我們能幫助他們,他們應該從自己作帳開始。

A： 他們一旦忙得做不來時,我們可以做。

B： 是。他們需要我們告訴他們如何自己作帳,你要教他們。

A： 我會告訴他們要記錄所有的交易,將它們記入日記帳裡,然後我會把剩下的完成。

Dialogue 4

A We don't need you anymore. We'll save money by doing the books ourselves.

B That's a bad idea. I do more than bookkeeping. I help you plan for the future.

A That's a good point. But we still need to save money.

B I help you save money by finding **loopholes** with your taxes.

A Okay. You're hired back. How could I ever get rid of you? You save us money.

中譯

A： 我們不再需要你了,我們要自己作帳來省錢。

B： 那是一個不好的主意,我做的事比記帳多,我幫助你們計畫未來。

A: 這是一個不錯的論點，但我們仍需要省錢。

B: 我可以利用找尋報稅的漏洞幫你省錢。

A: 好，你被重新雇用了。我哪能擺脫你呢？你讓我們省錢。

Dialogue 5

A I talked to the accountant. There are things we can do ourselves.

B Like what? If you're talking about recording the daily transactions, we do that.

A We do? Oh. Well, there are other things we can do ourselves.

B I already make the entries in the journals and maintain the ledgers.

A You do? Oh. I'm beginning to think I don't pay you enough money.

中譯

A: 我跟這個會計師聊過天。有些事情我們可以自己做。

B: 類似什麼？如果你是在說記錄每天的交易，我們有做。

A: 我們有？喔，我們還有其他事情可以做。

B: 我已經在日記帳中做記錄，並處理帳冊的事宜。

A: 你有做？喔。我開始覺得自己付給你的薪水不夠。

Dialogue 7

A I just completed a course in accounts payable and accounts receivable.

B That's great. We use a **payroll service** but it's expensive. Could you do it?

A I could do payroll yes. I can also do the invoicing and collecting.

B It'd be great if you knew how to do balance sheets and income statements.

A I do. I can even close your books each month for

you.

中譯

A: 我剛完成一個關於應付帳款與應收帳款的課程。

B: 真好，我們使用一個薪資服務，但它很昂貴。你可以做嗎？

A: 我可以處理薪資，沒問題，我也可以做開發票與收款。

B: 如果你知道如何做資產負債表與收益表就太好了。

A: 我知道，我甚至可以每個月為你結算帳冊。

Dialogue 8

A　I'm glad we do our own accounting. Why doesn't everybody do it themselves?

B　Some people don't have time. Others don't know how.

A　All it takes is a course in computerized accounting.

B　Some people don't have any computer skills. That course would be too advanced.

A　I'm going to do a cash flow statement. Will you give me the balance sheet please?

中譯

A: 我很高興我們自己做會計，為什麼每個人不都自己做？

B: 有些人沒有時間，其他的人不知道怎麼做。

A: 他們所需要的是一門電腦會計課。

B: 有些人沒有任何電腦技能，那個課程會太過進階。

A: 我要做一張現金流量表，請你把資產負債表拿給我好嗎？

Sentence Structure 重點句型

People in small businesses can do some of the computerized accounting themselves.	在小公司的人可以自己做一些電腦化的會計工作。

Course and classes in computerized accounting are inexpensive.	教電腦化會計的課程與班級很便宜。
These courses from a school can be claimed as a business expense.	這些學校裡的課程可以申報為一項商務支出。
People need basic computer skills before they can do computerized accounting.	他們做電腦化會計之前，需要基本的電腦技能。
The more people are able to do accounting on the computer by themselves, the less money they will have to spend on help from a bookkeeper or accountant.	愈多人可以在電腦上自己做會計工作，他們求助於簿記員與會計師所花的錢就愈少。
Some people use accounting software to help manage their household finances.	一些人使用會計軟體來幫助他們管理自己家庭的財務。

Vocabulary 字彙

computerized accounting		電腦化的會計
inexpensive	*adj.*	不貴的
claim	*v.*	架
business expense		商務支出
tasks	*n.*	工作
issue	*v.*	開
formula	*n.*	公式

accounting equation		會計等式
loopholes	*n.*	漏洞
payroll service		薪資服務

Useful Phrases 實用片語

Get rid of 擺脫

is used when talking about an employee; it means to fire

例句 If you don't start getting your work done on time they might try to get rid of you.
如果你不開始準時完成你的工作，他們或許會試著擺脫你

Chapter 1

Overworked
工作過度

Unit 1 Come Have Coffee
來喝咖啡

MP3-26

Jane is just leaving the staff room. She sees Dick on his way to his office.

珍正要離開員工休息室。她看到迪克正要去他的辦公室。

Jane Hello, Dick. I haven't seen you all day. How are you doing?

哈囉，迪克。我一整天都沒看到你。你好嗎？

Dick Hey, Jane. Not good. I have so much work to do.

嗨，珍。我不太好。我有好多工作要做。

Jane Do you have that much?

真有那麼多工作嗎？

Dick I haven't been able to get out of my office. There's a mountain of **paperwork** in there. It's **blocking** the door.

我根本離不開我的辦公室。那裡有堆積如山的文書檔案，把門都擋住了。

Jane You're so funny.

你講話真有趣。

Dick I'm serious. I can't seem to get caught up. I have too much work to do.

我是說真的。我似乎沒辦法趕上進度，有太多工作要做了。

Jane
I have **noticed** that you have been working very hard.
我注意到你近來工作很努力。

Dick
Yes.
是的。

Jane
You don't seem to take many breaks.
看起來你不常休息。

Dick
I feel like I can't get caught up in my work no matter how hard I try.
我感覺無論我多努力，都無法趕上進度。

Jane
Dick, why don't you sit down? Come to take a break for a minute.
迪克，為什麼你不坐下呢？過來休息一下。

Dick
I can't.
我不能。

Jane
Come on. Have a coffee. I just made a fresh pot.
來吧！喝杯咖啡。我才剛煮好一壺。

Dick
I can't. I don't have time.
我不能。我沒有時間。

Jane
Of course, you down here. Just take fifteen minutes to sit down here and visit.
你當然有時間。只要花十五分鐘，來這裏坐一下看看。

Dick
All right.
好吧！

> *Dick and Jane go into the staff room and sit down. She pours coffee for him.*
>
> 迪克和珍去員工休息室坐了下來。她幫他倒了咖啡。

Dick Is there any cream?
有奶精嗎？

Jane There's only milk. The cream went bad. I threw it out.
只有牛奶。奶精壞了。我把它扔了。

Dick Milk is fine. Is there any sugar?
牛奶也好。有糖嗎？

Jane No. All of the sugar is gone. There is some honey. Do you want that?
沒有。糖用完了。有一些蜂蜜，你要嗎？

Dick No. Honey tastes funny in coffee. I will just have some milk in my coffee.
不要。蜂蜜加在咖啡裏味道很怪。我的咖啡裡只要加一些牛奶。

Jane Here it is.
咖啡來了。

Dick Thanks.
謝謝。

Jane So tell me more about your work.
多告訴我一點有關你工作的事。

Dick I feel like I never see anybody here any more.
我覺得好像我在這裡都見不到任何人。

Jane You don't take many breaks.

你不太常休息。

Dick I never take breaks. I leave late and come early. I eat lunch at my desk.

我從不休息。我早早到，晚晚離開。還在辦公桌吃午餐。

Jane Why?

為什麼呢？

Dick I told you already. I'm so busy. I feel like I'm doing the work of two people.

我告訴過你了。我太忙了。我覺得我好像在做兩人份的工作。

Jane Maybe you are. Have you talked to your boss?

也許這是實情。你有和上司談過嗎？

Dick No.

沒有。

Jane Why not?

為什麼不呢？

Dick I don't want to. It's not a problem. I am just busy. Everyone is busy.

我不想要這樣做。這不是什麼問題。我只是忙。每個人都忙啊！

Jane No one else here is as busy as you. Talk to him. Maybe your boss is nice.

在這裏，沒有人像你一樣忙。和他談談，也許你上司人很好。

Dick You mean talk to her. My boss is a lady.

你該說「和她談談」。我上司是女的。

Jane Maybe she's nice. Maybe she is someone who is easy to talk to.

也許她人很好。也許她是那種很容易溝通的人。

Dick She does seem nice. Everybody says that she is a good boss.

她看起來人似乎真的很好。每個人都說她是個好上司。

Jane You have to do something. You are very stressed out. You don't look good.

你必須採取一些行動。你壓力太大了,看起來不太好。

Dick Well, that's not a nice thing to say.

嗯,對別人那樣說不太好吧?

Jane It is just an observation. I did not say it to be mean. I am concerned.

這只是我的觀察。我不是出於惡意才那麼說。我是關心你。

Dick That's nice of you.

妳人真好。

Jane You need to take care of yourself. Talk to your boss.

你要照顧好自已,和你的上司談談吧!

Dick No. I don't need to talk to my boss. I can handle it.

不,我不需要和上司談。我可以處理。

Jane If you say so.

如果你這麼說,那就算了。

Dick I should get back to work now. Thanks for the coffee.

我現在應該回去工作了。謝謝妳的咖啡。

Jane Okay. Try to relax.

嗯,試著放輕鬆些。

Dick I'm fine. I'm just very busy. There's no problem. Thanks anyway.

我沒事。我只是很忙。沒問題的。無論如何，謝謝妳了。

Comprehension Questions 理解測驗

___ (1) Who threw away the cream?

A) Jane threw away the cream.

B) Dick threw away the cream.

C) Dick's boss threw away the cream.

D) It was milk that was thrown away.

___ (2) What is wrong with Dick?

A) He is stressed out about his boss.

B) He is stressed out about Jane.

C) He is stressed out about his job.

D) All of the above

___ (3) When is Dick going to talk to his boss?

A) He will talk to her after coffee break.

B) He is talking to her right now during coffee break.

C) He will talk to her tomorrow.

D) He will think about it.

___ (4) Where is Dick?

A) He is in his apartment.

B) He is at work.

C) He is in Jane's apartment.

D) None of the above

Vocabulary 字彙

overworked	adj.	工作過度的
staff	n.	工作人員
paperwork	n.	文書工作
block	v.	堵塞；阻礙
notice	v.	注意
pour	v.	倒
stressed out		緊張的；感到有壓力的
observation	n.	觀察
concern	v.	關心
mean	adj.	惡劣的

Answers 解答   (1) A   (2)C   (3) D   (4) B

Unit 2 There's a Problem
有問題

MP3-27

Dick almost walks right past Jane in the hallway at work.

迪克差點與珍在辦公室的走廊擦身而過。

Jane Hi, Dick.What's going on?

嗨，迪克。最近怎樣？

Dick Hey, Jane. Sorry. I wasn't ignoring you. I just didn't see you.

嗨，珍。抱歉，我不是故意對妳視而不見。我只是沒看到妳。

Jane	I know. You were staring at the ground.You almost walked right past me.
	我知道。你剛才瞪著地板看，幾乎與我擦身而過。

Dick	I have a lot on my mind. What can I do for you?
	我腦子裏有一大堆事。有什麼我可以為你效勞的嗎？

Jane	What can you do for me? Dick, this is your friend Jane speaking. I'm not a client.
	有什麼你可以為我效勞的呢？迪克，你講話的對像是你的朋友珍，我不是你的客戶。

Dick	Sorry, Jane. I'm so busy. I didn't mean to be rude.
	抱歉，珍。我太忙了。我不是故意無禮的。

Jane	You really do have a problem.
	你真的有問題。

Dick	Sorry.
	抱歉。

Jane	You need to relax. Come in my office for a minute and sit down.
	你需要放鬆。到我的辦公室坐一下。

Dick	I don't have time.
	我沒時間。

Jane	Make time, Dick. It's for your own good.
	找時間，迪克。這是為了你好。

Dick gives up and they go into Jane's office.

迪克放棄與珍爭辯，就去了珍的辦公室。

Jane   Sit down, please.
請坐。

Dick   Thanks. You have a nice office.
謝謝。妳的辦公室不錯。

Jane   It's been a long time since you visited me in my office.
從你上次來我的辦公室，已經有好一陣子了。

Dick   Yes. It seems like I never see you.
是的。好像我從來沒有看到妳。

Jane   Have you thought about talking to your boss?
你想過要和上司談談了嗎？

Dick   I don't know. I don't want to sound like I am **complaining**.
我不知道。我不想讓人覺得我在抱怨。

Jane   I know.
我明白。

Dick   This is a very good job. I'm thankful for it.
這是份很好的工作。我對此很感恩。

Jane   You don't look good. You look stressed.
你看起來臉色不太好，壓力很大。

Dick   I feel stressed.
我也這麼覺得。

Jane   You're not taking breaks. You're working way too hard.
你都沒有休息，實在工作太賣力了。

Dick   I don't want to complain.
我不想抱怨。

Jane	If you don't say anything, your boss might not know.
	如果你什麼都不說，你的上司也許不會知道。

Dick	Maybe you're right. Maybe I should say something.
	也許妳說得對。也許我應該表達一些意見。

Jane	Good.
	很好。

Dick	But I'm worried. I don't want to get into trouble.
	但我很擔心。我不想惹麻煩。

Jane	You won't. You said yourself that your boss is nice.
	不會的啦！你自己說過你上司人很好的。

Dick	That is what I hear. Jane, I've been thinking about what you said the other day.
	那是我聽說的。珍，我一直在想妳前幾天講的話。

Jane	It wasn't the other day. That was three weeks ago.
	不是前幾天。那是三星期前了。

Dick	Oh. I do have a problem.
	喔，我真的有問題。

Jane	That's the first step to getting your problem fixed.
	那是解決你問題的第一步。

Dick	What's that?
	這話怎講？

Jane	**Admitting** that you have a problem is the first

step to solving it.

「承認你有問題」是解決問題的第一步。

Dick Really?
真的嗎？

Jane Talk to your boss. Tell her that you're behind. Just tell her what you told me.

和你的上司談談。告訴她你進度落後，只要告訴她，你和我說的事就可以了。

Dick If she asks me what needs to be done to fix it, I don't know what to tell her.

如果她問我要怎麼解決這問題，我不知道該如何回答她。

Jane You don't need to know how to fix it. That's the manager's job. She'll know what to do.

你不需要知道如何解決問題。那是主管的工作。她會知道該怎麼做的。

Dick Are you sure?
妳確定？

Jane It's your duty as a good employee to communicate with your manager.

與主管溝通是身為一個好員工的職責。

Dick I suppose.
我想是吧！

Jane It is the manager's job to solve the problem.
解決問題則是主管的工作。

Dick Okay. I will talk to her.
好。我會和她談的。

___ (1) What is Jane telling Dick to do?

    A) She is telling him to talk to her.

    B) She is telling him not to talk to her.

    C) She is telling him not to talk to his manager.

    D) She is telling him to talk to his manager.

___ (2) When did Jane last speak with Dick?

    A) It has been three weeks.

    B) It has been three days.

    C) It has been three hours.

    D) It has been three months.

___ (3) Where are Dick and Jane taking a break?

    A) They are taking a break in his office.

    B) They are taking a break in her office.

    C) They are in his manger's office.

    D) They are not taking a break.

___ (4) How is Dick feeling?

    A) He is upset at Jane for bothering him.

    B) He is feeling really good.

    C) He is feeling stressed about his work.

    D) He is upset that Jane has a nice office.

Vocabulary 字彙

hallway	*n.*	走廊

ignore	v.	忽視；不理會
ground	n.	地面
client	n.	客戶
rude	adj.	無禮的
complain	v.	抱怨
admit	v.	承認
solve	v.	解決
communicate	v.	溝通
suppose	v.	猜想

Answers 解答 (1) D (2) A (3) B (4) C

Unit 3 Ask for Help
尋求幫助
MP3-28

Ann's office door is open. Dick stands in the doorway and clears his throat.
安辦公室的門是開的。迪克站在門口清清喉嚨。

Ann　Hello, Dick. How are you today?
嗨，迪克。你今天好嗎？

Dick　Good morning, Ann. I'm fine. Can I talk to you for a moment?
早安，安。我很好。我可以和妳談一下嗎？

Ann　Yes. Come into my office. Have a seat.
安：可以。進來辦公室。坐下吧！

Dick   Okay.
好的。

Ann   Would you like a cookie? My son baked them yesterday. They are very good.
你要不要一塊餅乾？這些是我兒子昨天烤的，吃起來很不錯。

Dick   Thank you. I like cookies. This cookie looks delicious.
謝謝妳。我喜歡餅乾。這餅乾看起來很好吃。

Ann   I am glad that you have come to see me, Dick.
我很高興你來見我，迪克.

Dick   You are?
為什麼呢？

Ann   Yes. I never see you. You are always in your office working.
我從來見不到你。你總是在辦公室裡工作。

Dick   Yes.
是的。

Ann   You always work hard. That's nice to see.
你總是努力工作。那是人樂見的。

Dick   Thank you.
謝謝。

Ann   There are one or two people here who are lazy. They should follow your example.
這辦公室裡有一兩個人很懶。他們應該以你作榜樣。

Dick   Yes.
嗯。

Ann What did you want to talk to me about?
你想和我談些什麼？

Dick Nothing. I just was walking by and I saw that your door was open.
沒什麼。我只是走過來，看到妳門是開的，所以打聲招呼。

Ann That's all?
就只是這樣嗎？

Dick Yes. I just wanted to say hi. I'm going to get back to work now.
是的。我只想打個招呼。我現在要回去工作了。

Ann I know that you came here for a reason. Don't worry. You can talk to me.
迪克，我知道你來這裏，一定有原因。不要擔心。你可以和我説的。

Dick Are you sure?
妳確定？

Ann Yes. I'm an understanding manager.
是的，我是一個通情達理的主管。

Dick Everybody says that you are a nice boss.
每個人都説妳是一個好上司。

Ann Tell me what's bothering you.
告訴我什麼事在困擾你？

Dick stands up and looks out the window.
迪克站起來看著窗外。

Dick I'm worried. I don't want to get into trouble.

我很擔心。我不想惹麻煩。

| Ann | Please, Dick. I cannot help you if you do not tell me what's wrong.
拜託，迪克。如果你不告訴我是怎麼回事，我無法幫你的。 |

| Dick | Okay. I am so busy. I can't seem to get caught up. I am always behind.
好吧！我忙得要命，但好像趕不上進度，進度一直落後。 |

| Ann | I see.
這樣子啊 |

| Dick | I come here early and I leave late. I take work home with me. I'm really stressed.
我早來、晚走，還把工作帶回家。我真的壓力好大。 |

| Ann | That's not good. Do you really have that much work to do?
那樣不太好吧？你真的有那麼多工作要做嗎？ |

| Dick | I'm a good employee. I don't want to get in trouble. I'm telling the truth.
我是一個好員工。我不想惹麻煩，但我說的是事實。 |

| Ann | We need to look closer at this problem. Can we go to your office?
我們需要對這問題深入瞭解，可以去一下你的辦公室嗎？ |

| Dick | Why?
為什麼呢？ |

| Ann | I want to see what you're working on. I want to see why you have so much work.
我想看看你在做哪一樣工作，想瞭解為什麼你有這麼多工作。 |

Dick Maybe this was a bad idea. I don't want to cause trouble.
也許這是個壞主意。我不想找麻煩。

Ann No. Don't worry. I don't think that you're just not working hard enough.
不，別擔心。我不認為你工作不夠努力。

Dick You don't?
真的嗎？

Ann No. I'm wondering why you have to work so hard.
是的，我只是好奇為什麼你為什麼必須如此辛苦工作。

Dick Okay.
嗯。

Ann Maybe you're doing work that's supposed to be done by someone else.
也許你在做的，是別人應該做的工作。

Dick Okay.
嗯。

Ann Let's go to your office.
我們去一趟你的辦公室吧！

Dick My desk is messy.
我的桌上很亂。

Ann I am sure that it is not that bad.
我很確定不會那麼糟的。

Dick My office is messy, too.
我的辦公室也很亂。

Ann Don't worry. I'm here to help. I'm not concerned with a messy office.

別擔心。我是來幫忙的。我不在乎一間亂糟糟的辦公室。

Comprehension Questions 理解測驗

____ (1) When is Ann going to see Dick's office?

    A) They are going to his office later today.

    B) They are going to his office this afternoon.

    C) They are going to his office tomorrow.

    D) They are going to his office right now.

____ (2) Where are Ann and Dick talking?

    A) They are talking in Dick's office.

    B) They are talking in Ann's office.

    C) They are talking in Jane's office.

    D) None of the above

____ (3) How does Dick's office look?

    A) It is messy.

    B) It is clean.

    C) It is dark.

    D) None of the above

____ (4) Why is Dick worried?

    A) He doesn't want Ann's help.

    B) He doesn't want Jane to be upset.

    C) He doesn't want to get into trouble.

    D) He isn't worried about anything.

Vocabulary 字彙

delicious	*adj.* 美味的
follow	*v.* 跟隨
understanding	*adj.* 善解人意的
manager	*n.* 經理
bother	*v.* 使困擾
employee	*n.* 員工
messy	*adj.* 混亂的
concern	*v.* 關心

Answers 解答

(1) D (2) B (3) A (4) C

Chapter 2

Solving the Problem
解決問題

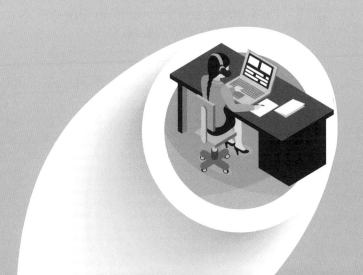

Unit 1　A Solution
一個解決之道

Dick is in his office hard at work. Ann enters his office.
迪克在他辦公室努力工作。安進來他的辦公室。

Ann　Hello, Dick. How are you feeling today?
哈囉，迪克。你今天覺得如何？

Dick　Very good, thank you.
很好，謝謝妳。

Ann　Please be honest with me, Dick.
請你要對我坦誠，迪克。

Dick　Okay. I'm stressed out. I'm worried about my work. I can't seem to catch up.
好的。我壓力很大。我擔心我的工作，好像趕不上進度。

Ann　Okay.
嗯。

Dick　I'm worried about not having time to do a good enough job for my clients.
我擔心沒有充份的時間為客戶提供好的服務。

Ann　I'm glad that you told me about all of this last week.
我很高興你上星期把這一切告訴我。

Dick　You are?
真的嗎？

Ann   Yes. I've been meeting with my superiors to come up with a solution.

是的。我已經與我的上司們開會，找到了一個解決辦法。

Dick   What do they think?

他們認為如何？

Ann   You're being overworked. There is no doubt.

你工作過度，那是毫無疑問的。

Dick   Really? What a relief. I feel better already. Someone understands me.

真的嗎？這樣我就放心了。我已經覺得好多了，因為有人瞭解我。

Ann   I do. My superiors had a suggestion. I would like to see what you think.

我真的瞭解。我的上司提了個建議。我想聽聽你的看法。

Dick   Yes? What is it?

是嗎？什麼建議？

Ann   Let's step into the coffee room. Everyone is working and it's not break time yet.

讓我們去咖啡間。每個人都在上班，現在還不是休息時間。

Dick   Okay. I could use the break.

好的。我真的需要休息一下。

Ann   I know. And since everyone else is working, we can talk and not be bothered.

我知道。因為每個人都在上班，我們的談話可以不被打擾。

Dick and Ann go to the coffee room.
Dick picks up the coffee pot.

迪克和安去咖啡間。迪克拿起咖啡壺。

Dick　There is some coffee in the pot. It smells fresh. Do you want some?

壺裏還有一些咖啡，聞起來像是剛煮好沒多久的。妳要喝一點嗎？

Ann　No, thanks. Go ahead if you do.

我不要，謝謝。如果你要的話，請便。

Dick　I will have some.

我要喝一點。

Ann　As I was saying before, I talked to my superiors about how overworked you are.

正如我剛剛所說的。我與上司們提到你工作過度的情形。

Dick　Okay.

是。

Ann　There's no money in our budget right now to get you some help.

在我們的預算中，現在沒有錢可以雇人來幫你。

Dick　All right.

好的。

Ann　There's no one else we can give your work to.

我們也沒有辦法把你的工作給其他人。

Dick　Oh.

喔。

Ann	Cheer up. They did have two good ideas.
	高興點。但他們後來提出了兩個好點子。

Dick	They did?
	真的？

Ann	They will be doing the budget for the next year in two or three months.
	在兩三個月內，他們會編下年度的預算。

Dick	What does that mean for me?
	對我來說有什麼意義呢？

Ann	They have decided to budget some money to get you some help.
	他們已經決定編預算，為你找個幫手。

Dick	That's great. I am sure that I can hang in there for a couple months.
	太好了。我確定我可以再撐幾個月。

Ann	Wait. There's more. They will budget money for a part time assistant for you.
	等等，還沒了呢。他們會編列經費，給你一個兼職助理。

Dick	That's great. What a relief!
	太好了。我可以放心了。

Ann	They want some help for you right now. They want to find a volunteer.
	他們現在就要幫你。他們要人自願幫你。

Dick	They want us to find someone who will help me right now, but not get paid for it?
	他們要我們現在找幫手，但不付薪水給那個人？

Ann	There are lots of people who would like to learn more about accounting. 有很多人想多學一些會計方面的知識。
Dick	They can go to school. 他們可以去學校學啊！
Ann	Some people can't **afford** school. 但有些人付不起學費。
Dick	So they volunteer. 所以他們會自願來幫忙。
Ann	They learn on the job. We get some help for you and they get free education. 他們在工作中學習。我們找到人幫你，而他們則可以獲得免費教育。
Dick	I don't know. 我不知道這樣做好不好。
Ann	For now, just think about it. Come to see me in my office tomorrow. You can tell me what you think then. 目前你先考慮看看。明天到我辦公室來，到時再告訴我你的想法。

Comprehension Questions 理解測驗

____ (1) Where is Dick to meet with Ann tomorrow morning?

A) He is to meet with her in her office.

B) He is to meet with her in the coffee room.

C) He is to meet with her in his office.

D) He is to meet with Ann, not with Jane.

___ (2) How does Dick like the manager's suggestion?

A) He likes it a lot.

B) He thinks it is a good idea.

C) He is happy with it.

D) None of the above

___ (3) Why would someone want to work for free?

A) They can learn on the job.

B) They want the knowledge.

C) They cannot afford school.

D) All of the above

___ (4) Who has a coffee in the break room?

A) Dick has a coffee.

B) Jane has a coffee.

C) Ann has a coffee.

D) No one has a coffee.

Vocabulary 字彙

superior	*n.*	上司；管理者
solution	*n.*	解決之道
doubt	*n.*	懷疑
suggestion	*n.*	建議
budget	*n.*	預算
relief	*n.*	放心

afford	v.	有足夠金錢 (財力)
volunteer	n.	志願者;義工

Answers 解答 (1) A (2) D (3) D (4) A

Unit 2 Try it Out
試試看

MP3-30

Jane is working in her office. Dick comes in.
珍在她辦公室工作。迪克走了進來。

Dick Hi, Jane. What are you doing?
嗨,珍。妳在做什麼?

Jane Hi, Dick. I'm working. What are you doing?
嗨,迪克。我在工作。你呢?

Dick I was wondering if you had a minute. I need to ask you something.
我想知道妳有沒有時間,有事想問妳。

Jane Sure. Come on in. Have a seat.
沒問題。進來吧!請坐。

Dick Thanks.
謝謝。

Jane Do you want a candy?
你要不要顆糖果?

Dick No, thanks. I don't eat candy. It's bad for your

teeth.

謝謝，不用。我不吃糖。它對牙齒不好。

Jane　I love candy. Why are you laughing?

我愛糖果。你為什麼要笑？

Dick　It just seems that people around here eat and drink a lot.

似乎這裏的人常常吃吃喝喝。

Jane　That's the way it is when you work in an office. What did you want to ask me?

那是辦公室的工作方式。你想問我什麼？

Dick　I talked to Ann last week.

上星期我和安談過。

Jane　That's good. How did it go?

那很好。談得怎麼樣？

Dick　Good. She was very nice.

很愉快。她人很好。

Dick　I told you she would be. Did she have any suggestions on how to help you?

我告訴過你她是這樣的人。對於如何幫你，她有任何建議嗎？

Dick　Today she did. I saw her again this morning.

今天她提了建議。我今天早上又和她見了一次面。

Jane　What did she say?

她説了些什麼呢？

Dick　She told me that I should get a volunteer for now.

她告訴我目前應該找個義工。

Jane A volunteer?
義工？

Dick And in two or three months, I might be able to get a part time assistant.
而且兩三個月內，我也許可以有一個兼職助理

Jane In two or three months?
在兩三個月之內？

Dick Right now, she wants me to have help but it would have to be a volunteer.
目前，她希望有人幫我，但必須是義工。

Jane Why is that?
為什麼呢？

Dick The company can't afford to pay for a part time assistant right now.
公司目前無法支付一個兼職助理。

Jane I think that having a volunteer is a great idea.
我想有個義工是個好主意。

Jane helps herself to another candy.
珍又吃了另一顆糖。

Dick You do?
妳真的這麼想嗎？

Jane Yes. I think you should try it out. You don't pay a volunteer.
是的。我想你該試試看。義工是不支薪的。

Dick	Maybe they don't work hard. 也許他們工作就會不認真。
Jane	A volunteer works hard. They want to learn as much as they can. Try it out. 義工工作認真。他們想要盡量多學一點。試試看嘛！
Dick	But I have to teach them everything. They won't know anything. 但我必須教他們每件事。他們什麼都不懂。
Jane	They will learn everything exactly as you want it. 他們會學會一切，如你想要的。
Dick	So? 然後呢？
Jane	They won't bring in ideas from a different job. You won't have to correct them. 他們不會把其他工作的想法、點子帶進來，所以你不需要改正他們。
Dick	True. But it will take so much time to teach them. 那倒是真的。但是我要花很多時間去教他們。
Jane	But you will have help right away. They can help you with little things right away. 但你馬上就有人幫你。他們馬上可以從小事上幫你。
Dick	Yes. That will make a difference. 是的。那對我就會有差別。
Jane	Give it a try. If you don't like it, Ann will understand. 試一試。如果你不喜歡的話，安會瞭解的。

Dick It wasn't Ann's idea. The idea to get a volunteer came from her superiors.

這不是安的主意。讓義工來是她上司們出的主意。

Jane Dick, those are the **partners**. Those are the people who own this accounting firm.

迪克，那些人是合夥人。他們就是擁有這間會計師事務所的人。

Dick Oh.

喔。

Jane I would try it out. The partners may not like it if you **refuse** their idea.

我會試試看。如果你拒絕了他們的主意，這些合夥人也許會不高興。

Dick Right.

這倒是真的。

Jane They are good people and they are very smart. If they think this is a good idea, you should **at least** try it.

他們人很好，而且很聰明。如果他們認為這是個好主意，你至少該試試看。

Dick You are right. Tomorrow morning I'll tell Ann that I want to try having a volunteer to help me.

妳說得對。明天早上我會告訴安，我想試試看請義工來幫我忙。

Jane Good for you.

這是為了你好。

_____ (1) How does Jane like Ann's suggestion?

　　A) She thinks it is a bad idea.

　　B) She thinks it is a good idea.

　　C) She thinks Ann is silly.

　　D) She thinks Ann doesn't know what she is talking about.

_____ (2) Why does Dick go talk to Jane?

　　A) He wants to know what she thinks about Ann's suggestion.

　　B) He wants some candy.

　　C) He wants to give Jane some candy.

　　D) He wants her to talk to Ann.

_____ (3) Who likes candy?

　　A) Ann likes candy.

　　B) Dick likes candy.

　　C) Jane likes candy.

　　D) Dentists like candy.

_____ (4) In what kind of office does Dick work?

　　A) He works in a law firm.

　　B) He works in an accounting office.

　　C) He works in a dentist's office.

　　D) Dick does not work.

Vocabulary 字彙

wonder	*v.*	想知道
volunteer	*n.*	志願者；義工
assistant	*n.*	助理
exactly	*adv.*	完全的
correct	*v.*	改正
partner	*n.*	合夥人
refuse	*v.*	拒絕
at least		至少
dentist	*n.*	牙醫

Answers 解答

(1) B (2) A (3) C (4) B

Unit 3 Getting Ready
作準備

MP3-31

Dick is working in his office. Ann knocks on the open door and comes in.
迪克在辦公室工作。安敲敲已敞開的門，然後進來。

Ann   Dick, can I talk to you for a minute?
迪克，我可以和你講一下話嗎？

Dick   Of course, Ann. Come on in. Let me clear that pile of papers off of that chair for you.
當然可以，安。進來吧。讓我把椅子上的一堆文件清出來，這樣妳才可以坐。

Ann	Okay. 好的。

Dick	I will just put them on top of this other pile on the floor. Have a seat. 我先將它們放在地上另一堆文件上面。請坐。

Ann	Thank you. When you get some help, your office will be very tidy again. 謝謝你。當你有助手時，辦公室將會再度有條不紊。

Dick	I'm not a messy person. I just don't have enough places to put all of my work. 我不是個邋遢的人。我只是沒有足夠的空間，來放置所有的工作文件。

Ann	I am glad that you agreed to have a volunteer. What do you think? 我很高興你同意找個義工。你認為怎麼樣？

Dick	I'm willing to give it a try. 我願意試一試。

Ann	That's good. That is all we can do right now. We can't afford to hire someone. 那很好。我們目前只能那樣做。我們沒辦法負擔另外再雇人。

Dick	I understand. 我瞭解的。

Ann	You need help. You're our best accounting technician. We want you to be happy. 你需要幫忙。你是我們最好的會計專員。我們想要你快樂。

Dick　I'm glad to know I work for a company who cares about their *employees.*

我很高興瞭解到我所工作的公司很關心員工。

Ann　Of course, we do. Your volunteer is named Bob. I have met him. He is very nice.

我們當然是如此。你的義工叫鮑伯。我已經見過他了。他人很好。

Dick　That's good.

那很好。

Ann　He is also very smart. He wants to be an accounting technician just like you.

他也很聰明。他想要成為會計專員，就像你一樣。

Dick smiles. He is happy.
迪克笑了，他很快樂。

Ann　Great.

太好了。

Ann　Bob wanted to learn more before he spends any money on university.

鮑伯想在付更多大學學費之前，學習更多的東西。

Dick　That's a good idea.

那是個好主意。

Ann　All of his *former employers* had good things to say about him.

他以前所有的雇主對他都有好評。

Dick	That's good. 那很好。
Ann	He will be your assistant until we can hire someone for you. 直到我們可以幫你雇人之前，他將會是你的助理。
Dick	Okay. 好的。
Ann	Teach him everything that he needs to know. He is here to help you get caught up. 教導他所需要知道的一切。他來這裏是要幫你趕上進度。
Dick	Thank you, Ann. I hope this goes well. 謝謝妳，安。我希望這件事進行順利。
Ann	Me too. Bob will start tomorrow morning. 我也希望如此。鮑伯會從明天早上開始上班。
Dick	Okay. I should get some things ready for tomorrow for Bob. 好的。我應該為鮑伯明天要來做一些準備。
Ann	What do you think needs getting ready? 你認為應該準備好些什麼？
Dick	He will need a place to put his personal belongings. 他會需要一個地方，放置他的私人物品。
Ann	Right. 沒錯。
Dick	I will clear out a drawer in my desk. He can keep his things in there.

我會把辦公桌的一個抽屜清出來。他可以把東西放在裏面。

Ann	That's nice of you. I'll let you get back to work. 你人真好。我讓你回去工作了。
Dick	Thanks again, Ann. 再次感謝妳，安。

Comprehension Questions 理解測驗

_____ (1) Why does Dick clear a pile of papers off of a chair?

A) He does not want Ann to see them.

B) He is making room so Ann can sit down.

C) He does not want Bob to see them.

D) He is making room so Bob can sit down.

_____ (2) Who is going to start helping Dick tomorrow?

A) The volunteer

B) Ann

C) Bob

D) Jane

_____ (3) What is Dick going to get ready for tomorrow?

A) He is going to empty a desk drawer and put a coat hook on the office door.

B) He is going to put all of the piles of paper on the floor.

C) He is going to make a batch of cookies.

D) He is going to bake some cookies.

_____(4) When is the volunteer starting?

A) Tomorrow

B) In the morning

C) At eight o'clock

D) All of the above

Vocabulary 字彙

knock	v.	敲
tidy	adj.	整齊的
accounting technician		會計專員
employee	n.	員工
former	adj.	以前的
employer	n.	雇主
hire	v.	雇用
belongings	n.	所有物
drawer	n.	抽屜
hook	n.	掛鉤

Answers 解答 (1)B (2)C (3)A (4) D

Chapter 3

First Day
第一天

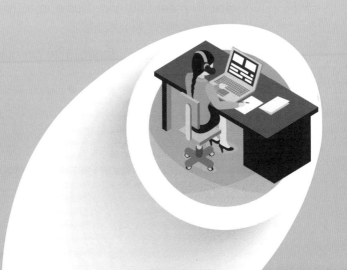

Unit 1 The Basics
基本概念

Dick is walking to his office. He sees Bob waiting by his office in the hall way.

迪克正走向他的辦公室。他看見鮑伯在他辦公室外的走廊等候。

Dick Good morning. You must be Bob.
早安。你一定是鮑伯。

Bob Good morning. Yes, my name is Bob. Are you Dick?
早安。是的，我的名字是鮑伯。你是迪克嗎？

Dick Yes. You're here early.
是的。你早到了。

Bob I find that I'm at my best in the morning. It is nice to meet you.
我發現我在早上時狀況最佳。很高興見到你。

Dick It is nice to meet you, too. Come in to my office.
我也很高興見到你。進來我辦公室吧。

Bob Thanks. I am looking forward to working with you.
謝謝。我很期待與你一起工作。

Dick That's good.
那很好。

Bob I think that I want to be an accounting technician.
我想要成為一個會計專員。

Dick
That's good.
那很好。

Bob
But I want to learn more before I decide for sure.
但我想在確定決定前，學更多的東西。

Dick
This will be a good learning experience.
這將會是好的學習經驗。

Dick unlocks his office door and the two men enter.
迪克打開他辦公室的門鎖，然後兩人進去。

Dick
Hang up your coat behind the door. You can put your car keys in this drawer.
把你的外套掛在門後。你可以把汽車鑰匙放在這抽屜裏。

Bob
Thanks.
謝謝。

Dick
Do you need a coffee before we get started?
在我們開始之前，你需要咖啡嗎？

Bob
No, thanks. I had a coffee at home before I came. I'm ready to get to work.
謝謝，不用。我在出門前已經在家裏喝過了。我準備好要工作了。

Dick
That's great. There are some basics we should cover.
那太好了。有些基本概念我們應該先講一下。

Bob
Okay.
好的。

Dick To do good accounting, you need good records.
要做好會計，你需要好的記帳。

Bob Okay.
好的。

Dick You need records that are well organized.
你的記帳需要有條有理。

Bob Do most clients keep good records that are well organized?
大多數的客戶都有保存良好的記帳嗎？

Dick No. It is up to you to make what they give you into good records.
不。是你要把他們所給你的資料變成好的記錄。

Bob Okay.
好的。

Dick That's why you need to be an organized person.
那也就是為什麼你需要是一個有條有理的人。

Bob Right.
是的。

Dick You need to work hard. Are you ready to work hard?
你需要努力工作。你準備好要努力工作了嗎？

Bob Yes. I'm ready to learn.
是的。我準備好要學習了。

Dick Okay. Remember that our clients do not understand accounting. They don't like it. They think it's difficult. It's our job to make it easy.
好的。你要記住，我們的客戶不瞭解會計。他們不喜歡會計，他們認為它很難，而我們的工作是要讓它變得容易。

Bob Okay.

好的。

Dick The information that we give them helps them to run their businesses well.

我們給他們的資訊將可幫助他們經營好他們的事業。

Bob Why don't people just use computers to do their accounting?

為什麼他們不用電腦去做會計呢？

Dick You still need the time to sit at the computer.

你仍需要花時間坐在電腦前面。

Bob Right.

是的。

Dick You still need to know how to use a computer and the accounting program.

你仍需知道如何使用電腦和會計電腦程式。

Bob Right.

是的。

Dick And some people just want other people to do their accounting.

有些人只想要別人幫他們做會計報告。

Bob I understand. Tell me more.

我明白了。再多告訴我一些吧！

Dick I think that I had better show you around first.

我想我最好先帶你四處看看。

Bob Okay.

好的。

Dick You'll want to know where the washrooms are and where the break room is.

你需要知道洗手間和休息室的位置。

Bob Is your staff room nice?

你們的員工休息室很不錯嗎？

Dick Yes, it is. Come with me and I will show you.

是的。跟我來，我帶你去看。

Comprehension Questions 理解測驗

____ (1) Who is Dick talking about to Bob?

    A) Ann

    B) Jane

    C) Clients

    D) Bob

____ (2) Who is going to teach Bob ?

    A) Ann is going to teach him about accounting.

    B) Jane is going to teach him about life.

    C) Ann is going to teach him about being an adult.

    D) It is Dick who will teach Bob.

____ (3) When did Bob get to the office?

    A) He got to the office before Dick.

    C) He got to the office at the same time as Dick.

    D) He never showed up.

____ (4) Where is Dick taking Bob?

A) To the lunch room

B) To the washrooms

C) He is showing him around.

D) All of the above

Vocabulary 字彙

experience	*n.*	經歷
unlock	*v.*	打開
hang up		掛；懸
cover	*v.*	包括
organize	*v.*	使有條理
program	*n.*	程式
show (sb) around		帶領 (某人) 參觀
washroom	*n.*	洗手間
adult	*n.*	成年人

Answers 解答　(1)C (2)D (3)A (4) D

Unit 2　Debits and Credits
借和貸
MP3-33

As Dick walks to his office, he sees that Bob is already waiting for him.
當迪克走到辦公室時，他看到鮑伯已經在等他了。

Bob　Good morning, Dick. How are you this morning?
早安，迪克。你今天早晨好嗎？

Dick   I am good, Bob. How are you?
　　　　　我很好，鮑伯。你好嗎？

Bob   Good.
　　　　　我很好。

Dick   You're here bright and early again. I hope that you weren't waiting long.
　　　　　你又一清早到。我希望你沒有等太久。

Bob   No.
　　　　　沒有。

Dick   Are you ready for your second day?
　　　　　你準備好要上第二天的班了嗎？

Bob   I sure am.
　　　　　我完全準備好了。

Dick   Okay. Great. Today I am going to tell you about **debits** and **credits**.
　　　　　好的，那很好。今天我要告訴你關於借方和貸方。

Bob   What are those?
　　　　　那些是什麼？

Dick   They are the most important part of accounting.
　　　　　它們是會計最重要的部份。

Bob   Yes?
　　　　　是嗎？

Dick   There's a thing that is called the **general ledger**.
　　　　　有一樣東西叫做總分類帳。

Bob   Should I be writing this down?
　　　　　我應該把這個記下來嗎？

Dick I don't think so. We will start to do work with debits and credits. We will work with the general ledger. Once we are working, all of this will be clear.

我想不用。我們將會開始做借與貸方面的帳,就會做到總分類帳。一旦我們開始工作,所有這些東西就會變得很清楚。

Bob Okay. Go on.

好的。請繼續。

Dick Every entry that you make in the general ledger must have a debit and a credit.

你在總分類帳所登錄的每一個項目都會有借貸雙方。

Bob So when you do one, you always do the other. The books must always balance.

所以當你做到借方,就會做到貸方。帳目一定要平衡。

Dick That's right. But let's stop talking in the hallway. Come inside.

沒錯。但不要在走廊上講話。進去裏面吧!

Dick unlocks the door to his office. The two men go in and sit down.

迪克打開門鎖。兩人進去,並且坐了下來。

Dick Now. Where were we?

我們剛剛說到哪裏了?

Bob The books must always balance. All debits must equal all credits.

帳目應該要保持平衡。所有的借方金額應等於貸方金額。

Dick Right. If they don't, it means the books are not balancing.

是的。如果它們不相等的話，就代表帳目不平衡。

Bob And that isn't good.

那樣是不好的情況。

Dick Out of balance *entries* mean that the whole *record* system is out of balance.

失去平衡的帳目登錄代表著這整個記錄系統都失去平衡。

Bob That's a good way of *explain*ing accounting. It's a record of the finances of a business.

那是個解釋會計的好方式。它是企業的財務記錄。

Dick Yes. Now, tell me. What have you learned so far?

是的，告訴我，到目前為止你學了些什麼？

Bob You help clients to have good records of the *finances* of their businesses.

你幫助客戶，讓他們的企業有好的財務記錄。

Dick Yes.

是的。

Bob We will make entries in a general ledger for each client.

我們會為每個客戶在總分類帳系統做登錄。

Dick Yes.

是的。

Bob Our entries will be debits and credits. Whenever we do one, we do the other.

我們的登錄將會有借貸雙方。只要我們做了一個，就會做另一個。

Dick This is so the books balance. Our goal is to always have the books balance.

這就是帳目平衡的道理。我們的目標就是讓帳目永遠保持平衡。

Bob Right.

是的。

Dick You're good at this. I'm glad you are here. You learn fast. You'll be a great help to me.

你對這個很在行。我很高興你在這裏。你學得很快,對我將是很大的幫助。

Bob Thank you. I'm excited to learn more.

謝謝。對於要學更多東西,我感到很興奮。

Dick I'll show you how it's done. Pull up a chair. Come sit beside me so you can learn.

我將會做給你看。拉把椅子過來,坐在我旁邊,那樣你可以學。

Comprehension Questions 理解測驗

___ (1) What is another name for entries made to the general ledger?

A) Debts and credits

B) Debits and creditors

C) Debits and credits

D) Depths and credit cards

___ (2) When did Dick arrive at work?

A) He got to work after Bob.

B) He got to work before Bob.

C) He got to work at the same time as Bob.

D) He did not go to work.

_____ (3) Where are Dick and Bob working?

A) In the coffee room

B) In Bob's office

C) In the washroom

D) None of the above

_____ (4) How does Dick think that Bob is doing so far?

A) He thinks Bob is terrible.

B) He thinks Bob is a fast learner and that he is good at it.

C) He thinks that Bob smells funny.

D) He thinks that Bob tells bad jokes.

Vocabulary 字彙

debit	*n.*	借方
credit	*n.*	貸方
general ledger	*n.*	總分類帳
balance	*n.*	平衡
entry	*n.*	項目
record	*n.*	記錄
explain	*v.*	解釋
equal	*v.*	等於
finance	*n.*	財務狀況

Answers 解答

(1)C (2)A (3)D (4)B

Unit 3 **Working Out**
問題解決了

MP3-34

Dick is walking to his office. Jane is on the way to her office.

迪克正走向他的辦公室。珍也在去她辦公室的路上。

Dick Good morning, Jane. How are you today?
早安,珍。妳今天好嗎?

Jane Good morning, Dick. I am good. How are you?
早安,迪克。我很好。你呢?

Dick Good. I'm feeling pretty good. It's the first time in a long time.
好。我覺得還不錯,已經很久沒這種感覺了。

Jane That is great. Why do you think you are feeling so good?
那太好了。你想為什麼你感覺會這樣好呢?

Dick Because of Bob. He is a big help.
是因為鮑伯。他是很大的幫助。

Jane Excellent. I am glad to hear that he is working out.
太棒了。我很高興聽到他幫你解決了問題。

Dick Yes. Everything is going to work out fine now that Bob is here.
是的。現在有鮑伯在,每件事都會很順利的。

Jane What have you been teaching him?
你教了他些什麼?

Dick I've been showing him some basics. We're looking at different kinds of accounts.
我已經教了他一些基本概念。我們正在查看不同的帳戶。

Jane Oh?
哦？

Dick Yes. We're talking about assets and liabilities.
是的。我們在討論資產和負債。

Jane What did you tell him about assets?
關於資產，你告訴他些什麼？

Dick I told him that a debit increases the account balance in assets.
我告訴他借方會增加資產帳戶結餘。

Jane Come in my office for a second.
進來我辦公室一下。

Jane and Dick go sit in Jane's office.
珍和迪克走進去，坐在珍的辦公室裏面。

Jane Finish what you were saying.
把你說的繼續說完。

Dick And a credit decreases the account balance in assets.
而貸方減低在資產帳戶上的結餘。

Jane What did you tell him about liabilities?
關於負債，你告訴他些什麼？

Dick I told him that a debit to that account decreases the account balance.

我告訴他借方對負債帳戶而言，會減少結餘。

Jane Good.
很好。

Dick And a credit increases the account balance.
而貸方則會增加負債帳戶的結餘。

Jane Are you going to tell him about income accounts?
你打算告訴他關於收入帳戶嗎？

Dick Yes. I will tell him about expense accounts also.
是的，我也會告訴他關於支出帳戶。

Jane What are you going to tell him about those?
關於這些，你打算告訴他什麼呢？

Dick I will tell him that a debit to an income account decreases the account balance.
我將告訴他借方對收入帳戶而言，會減少結餘。

Jane Yes.
是。

Dick And a credit to Income accounts increases the account balance.
而貸方會增加收入帳戶的結餘。

Jane That's right. Does he understand accounting?
沒錯，他懂會計嗎？

Dick Yes, he does.
是的，他懂。

Jane What a great volunteer. What are you doing for lunch?
多麼好的義工啊！你午餐時要做什麼？

Dick I don't know. What did you have in mind?
我不知道。妳有什麼打算嗎？

Jane Why don't you and Bob come to have lunch with me in the break room?
你與鮑伯和我一起在休息室吃午餐，好嗎？

Dick Sure. We've just been eating in my office. I would like that.
當然好。我們一直都在我辦公室吃。這主意不錯。

Jane That will give me a chance to get to know Bob.
那給我一個機會認識鮑伯。

Dick Good. See you at lunch.
那午餐見了。

Comprehension Questions 理解測驗

____ (1) When will Jane get to know Bob?

    A) She will meet him after work in the coffee room.

    B) He will have supper with her in the staff room.

    C) He will see her at the coffee break in the lunch room.

    D) He will have lunch with her in the break room.

____ (2) Where will Dick have lunch today?

    A) He will eat at his desk.

    B) He will eat in the lunch room.

C) He will eat in his office.

D) He will eat in Jane's office.

___ (3) How is Dick feeling today?

A) He is feeling pretty good.

B) He is tired.

C) He is grumpy.

D) He is sad.

___ (4) Why does Dick like Bob?

A) Bob is a big help.

B) Bob smells good.

C) Bob eats lunch with Dick.

D) Dick is happy to have a new friend.

Vocabulary 字彙

work out		解決問題
excellent	adj.	太棒了
asset	n.	資產
liability	n.	負債
increase	v.	增加
decrease	v.	減少
income account		收入帳戶
expense account		支出帳戶

Answers 解答 (1)D (2)B (3)A (4)A

Chapter 4

Settling In
進入狀況

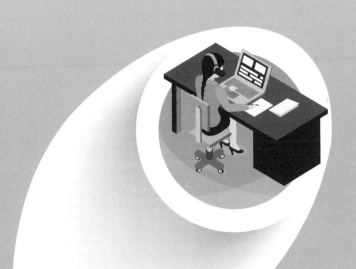

Unit 1 Happy to be Here
在這裡很開心

MP3-35

Ann goes in to Dick's office.
Dick is not there but Bob is.
安去迪克的辦公室。迪克不在那裏，但鮑伯在。

Ann Hello. Is Dick here?
哈囉。迪克在嗎？

Bob Hi. No. Dick is in the lunchroom. He's getting a coffee.
嗨，不，迪克在午餐室。他去拿咖啡了。

Ann Oh. Okay.
喔，好的。

Bob You're Ann, right?
妳是安，對嗎？

Ann Yes. How did you know my name?
是的。你怎麼知道我的名字呢？

Bob I am Bob. We met before.
我是鮑伯。我們以前見過。

Ann Hello, Bob. I didn't recognize you.
嗨，鮑伯。我剛剛沒認出你來。

Bob It's been a while since I saw you.
從我上次見到妳，已經有一段時間了。

Ann Are you enjoying working with Dick?
你喜歡與迪克一起工作嗎？

Bob Yes. I'm happy to be here. I'm learning so much. He's very smart.

是的。我很高興在這裏。我現在在學很多東西。他很聰明。

Ann Yes, he is. We're happy to have him.

是的，他很聰明。我們很高興有他一起工作。

Ann sits down.
安坐了下來。

Ann So. What are you working on?

那麼，你現在在做什麼工作呢？

Bob I've been helping him get organized. He hasn't had time to keep organized.

我一直在幫他整理東西。他以前一直沒時間整理。

Ann I know.

我知道。

Bob I've been filing. Things are going faster now. He's getting more done in less time.

我一直在歸檔文件。現在事情進行地比較快。他現在用比較少的時間完成更多的事。

Ann Great. What has he been teaching you?

太好了。他教了你些什麼呢？

Bob He's been teaching me about assets. I also know what an asset is.

他在教我關於資產的事。我也知道什麼叫做資產。

Ann What is it?

那資產是什麼呢？

Bob　Anything of value that a company owns. A company car would be an asset.
一家公司所擁有的任何有價物。例如,一輛公司車就是一項資產。

Ann　I think that you are an asset to Dick.
我想你對迪克而言是一項資產。

Bob　Thank you. I enjoy learning about accounting. I'm happy to be here.
謝謝你。我喜歡學會計。我很高興來這裏。

Ann　What else are you learning?
你還學其他東西嗎?

Bob　I am learning about liabilities. They are another balance sheet account.
我學了有關負債,它們是另外一個資產負債表帳戶。

Ann　Yes, they are.
是,它們是的。

Bob　They are the opposite of an asset. Your accounts payable is a liability.
它們是資產的反面。你的應付帳款就是負債。

Ann　Why?
為什麼呢?

Bob　Because that is money that you owe to someone else. A loan is a liability.
因為那是你欠別人的錢,貸款是負債。

Ann　Unless you are the person who loaned the money.
除非你是出借錢的人。

Bob　Right. Then to you, the loan is an asset.
對。如果是這樣的話,對你而言,借款是資產。

Ann　You know a lot. You're doing well. Thank you again for all of your help.

你知道很多。你做得很好。再次謝謝你的幫忙。

Bob　Thank you, Ann.

謝謝妳，安。

Ann　Tell Dick I came by to see how things are. Things look like they're going well.

告訴迪克我來過這裡，看看情況。情況看起來很好。

Bob　I will tell him.

我會告訴他的。

Comprehension Questions 理解測驗

____ (1) Where is Dick?

A) He is in his office.

B) He is talking to Anne.

C) He is getting a coffee.

D) He is talking to Bob.

____ (2) How does Ann think things are for Bob and Dick?

A) She thinks that things are going well.

B) She thinks that Bob should work for her.

C) She thinks that Bob is not very smart.

D) She thinks that Dick needs a coffee.

____ (3) Why didn't Ann recognize Bob?

A) She has not seen him before.

B) It's been a long time since she saw him.

C) She has new glasses.

D) He has a new haircut.

___ (4) Who sees a loan as an asset?

A) The person who owes the money.

B) The company that owes the money.

C) The person or company who lends the money.

D) No one sees a loan as an asset.

Vocabulary 字彙

settle in		(工作) 安定下來
recognize	v.	認出
file	v.	歸檔
value	n.	價值
balance sheet		資產負債表
opposite	n.	相反的
payable	adj.	應支付的
owe	v.	欠(債)
loan	n.	貸款

Answers 解答 (1)C (2)A (3)B (4)C

Unit 2 Financial Statements
財務報表

MP3-36

Dick comes into the staff room to talk to Jane. Jane is having a coffee.

迪克到員工休息室和珍談話。珍正在喝咖啡。

Bob	Hi, Jane. How are you this morning? 嗨，珍。妳今天早上好嗎？
Jane	I am good, Bob. How are you? 我很好，鮑伯。你呢？
Bob	I need your help. Dick is sick today. He is not coming to work. 我需要妳的幫忙。迪克今天生病了，不會來上班。
Jane	I'll be happy to help you, Bob. I just poured myself a coffee. Do you want some? 我很高興能幫你，鮑伯。我正幫倒咖啡給自己。你要喝咖啡嗎？
Bob	Yes, thank you. I did not have time to make any at home this morning. 要，謝謝妳。我今天早晨在家沒時間煮咖啡。
Jane	So, tell me, Bob. What do you need help with? 告訴我，鮑伯。你需要什麼忙？
Bob	I've been learning about financial statements. 我最近一直在學有關財務報表的事。
Jane	Yes? 是嗎？
Bob	All businesses must produce financial statements at the end of each fiscal year. 所有企業在每一會計年度結束時，一定要提出財務報表。
Jane	That's right. 沒錯。
Bob	All the financial statements produced at year-end are called the annual report.

在年終時所提出的所有財務報表，稱為年報。

Jane Right.

對。

Bob What are all of the financial statements that go into the annual report?

年報所包含的財務報表內容是什麼呢？

Jane You need a balance sheet.

你需要作一份資產負債表。

Bob Yes.

是。

Jane You also need an *income statement*. Let's go to talk in my office.

你同時也需要一份收益表。我們去我的辦公室談吧。

Bob Okay. Your office is so *neat* and tidy.

好，妳的辦公室很整齊，井然有序！

Jane I work better when everything is in its place.

當一切都井然有序時，我工作會較有效率。

They leave the coffee room and go into Jane's office.

他們離開咖啡間，然後去珍的辦公室。

Jane Have a seat. Do you want a candy?

請坐。你要糖果嗎？

Bob No, thanks. Candy is bad for your teeth.

我不要，謝謝。糖果對牙齒不好。

Jane That is what Dick says.
迪克也這樣説。

Bob So. Income statements. Some people call that a profit and loss statement.
剛剛談到收益表吧？有些人稱它為損益表。

Jane Yes, some people do. You also need a statement of owner's equity.
是的，有些人這麼稱呼它。你也需要業主的權益表。

Bob Is that one sometimes called a statement of retained earnings?
它是不是有時會被稱為保留盈餘表？

Jane Yes.
是的。

Bob I wonder why there is more than one name for some of these things.
我很好奇為什麼這些事都有一個以上的名稱。

Jane I don't know.
我不知道原因。

Bob Are there any other financial statements that make up the annual report?
年報裏還有任何其他財務報表嗎？

Jane There's the statement of changes in financial position.
還有財務狀況變動表。

Bob Okay.
好的。

Jane　It depends on the type of business. Some companies need forms that others don't.

要視企業型態而定。有些公司所需要的表格，別家並不需要。

Bob　Like what?

像是什麼？

Jane　Some businesses need an auditor's report. Some need a management report.

有些企業需要審計報告，另一些則需要經營狀況報告。

Bob　How do you know?

妳怎麼知道這些？

Jane　I can't explain it all just by telling you. It's best Dick shows you.

我無法只靠言語來跟你解釋。最好讓迪克做給你看。

Bob　Okay.

好的。

Jane　What have you been working on?

你目前在做什麼？

Bob　He wants me to learn financial statements so I know what goes in the annual report.

他要我學財務報表，這樣我才知道該把什麼列入年報。

Jane　You will probably learn about the income statement soon.

你很可能很快就會學到收益表。

Bob　Yes.

是的。

Jane　Do you like it here?

你喜歡這裏嗎？

Bob	Yes I do.
	是的，我喜歡。

Jane	Dick sure likes having you here and so do I. So, does Ann.
	迪克很喜歡有你在這裏，我也是，安也是。

Bob	Everyone is so nice. I should get to work.
	大家人都很好。我應該回去工作了。

Jane	Let me know if there's anything else I can help you with.
	如果還有其他我可以幫上忙的事，讓我知道。

Bob	Thanks, Jane.
	謝謝，珍。

Jane	Bye, Bob.
	再見，鮑伯。

Comprehension Questions 理解測驗

___ (1) How is Dick feeling today?

A) Dick is very busy.

B) Dick is lonely.

C) Dick is sick at home.

D) Dick is grumpy.

___ (2) Why is Bob getting help from Jane?

A) Dick is very busy.

B) Bob is lonely.

C) Dick is sick at home.

D) Dick is grumpy.

_____ (3) Who had a coffee?

A) Dick

B) Jane

C) Bob

D) Both Jane and Bob

_____ (4) What goes into an annual report?

A) Financial statements

B) Income statement

C) Balance Sheet

D) All of the above

Vocabulary 字彙

financial statement		財務報表
fiscal year		會計年度
produce	_v._	提出
annual report		年報
neat	_adj._	整潔的
profit and loss statement		損益表
equity	_n._	權益；股份
auditor	_n._	審計員
management	_n._	經營；管理
income statement		收益表

Answers 解答
(1)C (2)C(3)D (4)D

Unit 3 Income Statement
收益表

MP3-37

Bob is waiting outside Dick's office as Dick walks down the hall way.

當迪克走在走廊上時，鮑伯正在迪克的辦公室外頭等候。

Bob　How are you feeling today, Dick?
你今天感覺如何，迪克？

Dick　I am feeling much better. How about you, Bob? How are you today?
我覺得好多了。你呢？鮑伯。你今天好嗎？

Bob　Good. Welcome back.
很好。歡迎你回來。

Dick　I hope you were okay without me. Sorry to leave you here by yourself.
我希望我不在的期間，你一切都還好。抱歉讓你自已獨自一人。

Bob　Don't worry. The three days that you were away went by quickly.
別擔心。你不在的這三天，時間過得很快。

Dick　Good.
還好。

Bob　Besides, sick people don't get much work done. And they can make others sick.
何況生病的人做不了很多工作。他們還會讓別人生病。

Dick That wouldn't be good.
那就不好了。

Bob I bet it feels like you were never gone.
我敢打賭，一切感覺就好像你從來沒有離開過一樣。

Dick No. It didn't go by quickly for me. I was bored. I hate being sick.
不，對我來說，時間並沒有過得很快。我好無聊。我討厭生病。

Bob I know what you mean.
我知道你的意思。

Dick I don't like to be away from work. Did anything happen while I was away?
我不喜歡離開工作。當我不在時，有什麼事嗎？

Bob Some clients called. I took messages. I said that you would be back next week.
有些客戶打電話來。我記下他們的留言。我告訴他們你下週會回來。

Dick Great. Thank you. We'll call them back today.
很好。謝謝。我們今天會回他們電話。

Bob Yes. The only one that was urgent was Mr. Smith. He wants an income statement.
是。唯一一個緊急事件是史密斯先生。他需要收益表。

Dick We'll take care of him first.
我們會先處理他的事。

Dick and Bob go into the office and sit down.
迪克和鮑伯進去辦公室，坐了下來。

Dick What have you learned about income statements?

關於收益表，你學到了些什麼？

Bob They're also called profit and loss statements.

它們也被稱為損益表。

Dick Yes, they are.

是的，沒錯。

Bob Revenue is money that a business makes. Expenses are what a business spends.

營收是商家所賺的錢。費用是商家所花的錢。

Dick Yes.

是的。

Bob Income statements show revenue and expenses.

收益表中顯示了營收和費用。

Dick Yes.

是的。

Bob Profit and loss statements show what money came in and went out of the business.

損益表顯示商家金錢的進出。

Dick During what time?

在什麼時間之內？

Bob Income statements are usually done once a month.

收益表通常一個月做一次。

Dick So an income statement shows what money came in and went out for the month?

所以收益表顯示某個月金錢的進出項目。

Bob　I think so.
　　　　我想是這樣。

Dick　Good work. You seem to understand that.
　　　　做得好。你似乎都弄懂了。

Bob　Yes.
　　　　是的。

Dick　So tell me what else happened while I was gone.
　　　　那麼告訴我，我不在時還發生了什麼事。

Bob　Not much.
　　　　沒什麼事。

Dick　I thought there'd be a big pile of things to do on my desk, there isn't. How nice.
　　　　我本以為在我桌上將會有堆積如山的事情要做。結果沒有，真好。

Bob　I did some of the basic accounting procedures you showed me.
　　　　我做了一些你教過我的基本會計程式。

Dick　That's great. Thank you.
　　　　那太好了。謝謝你。

Bob　I only did the things that I know how to do. I didn't try anything that I don't know.
　　　　我只做了那些我知道怎麼處理的事，沒有去試我不懂的東西。

Dick　Bob, I would like to buy you lunch today.
　　　　鮑伯，今天我想請你吃午飯。

Bob What for?

為什麼？

Dick I want to thank you for doing so much work for me while I was sick.

我要謝謝你在我生病時，為我做了那麼多的事。

Bob No problem.

小意思。

Dick Do you want to go to that fast food burger place down the street?

你想去這條街底的那間速食漢堡店嗎？

Bob No. I would like to eat something that won't make me fat.

不。我想要吃一些不會讓我發胖的東西。

Dick What a good idea! Let's go to get a healthy lunch instead.

多好的主意啊！我們改吃健康午餐吧！

Comprehension Questions 理解測驗

____ (1) Why doesn't Bob want a fast food burger?

A) He doesn't eat meat.

B) He used to work there.

C) He doesn't want to get fat.

D) He wants ice cream for lunch.

___ (2) Who wants an income statement?

A) Ann

B) Mr. Smith

C) Dick

D) Bob

___ (3) What does an income statement show?

A) Money that came in and went out of a business

B) Balance sheet

C) Mathematical formula

D) Auditor's report

___ (4) When does Dick want to take Bob out?

A) At breakfast

B) At lunch

C) At supper

D) At coffee break

Vocabulary 字彙

message	n.	留言
urgent	adj.	緊急的
revenue	n.	收益；營收
expenses	n.	支出；費用
pile	n.	堆
procedure	n.	程序
instead	adv.	作為替代

Answers 解答

(1)C (2)B (3)A (4)B

Chapter 5

My Right Hand
得力助手

Unit 1 What Would We Do?
我們將做什麼？

MP3-38

Bob is walking by Ann's office. She gets up and calls after him.

鮑伯經過安的辦公室。她起身叫住他。

Ann　Bob, can I have a word with you, please?
鮑伯，我可以和你講幾句話嗎？

Bob　Of course, Ann.
當然可以，安。

Ann　Come into my office for a second. Here. Sit down.
進來我的辦公室一下。來，坐下。

Bob　Thank you.
謝謝。

Ann　Would you like a muffin? My son made them.
你要不要吃個鬆餅？我兒子做的。

Bob　I would love a muffin. I hear that your son is an excellent cook.
我喜歡吃個鬆餅。我聽說你兒子是個很棒的廚師。

Ann　He likes to bake. You should try his cheesecake.
他喜歡烘焙。你應該嚐嚐他的起士蛋糕。

Bob　You always have some kind of baking.
妳這裡總有些糕點。

Ann	Yes.
	是的。
Bob	If I had all this delicious baking all the time, I'd weigh four hundred pounds.
	如果我總是吃這些可口糕點,我會重達四百磅的。
Ann	I like to share it. Everybody likes muffins.
	我喜歡與別人分享。每個人都喜歡鬆餅。
Bob	So. What's on your mind, Ann?
	你有什麼想法嗎,安?
Ann	I thought you should know that it is Dick's birthday tomorrow.
	我想應該讓你知道明天是迪克的生日。
Bob	I know.
	我知道。
Ann	Good. I would like you to organize a short little party in the lunchroom.
	那好。我想請你在午餐室安排一個小型聚會。
Bob	Okay.
	好的。
Ann	Everyone can have a piece of birthday cake on their coffee break.
	每個人可以在咖啡休息時間時,吃塊生日蛋糕。
Bob	Sounds good.
	聽起來不錯。
Ann	Would you be willing to do something like that?
	你願意負責那事嗎?

Bob Actually, it is already done.
事實上，我已經安排好了。

Ann What would we do without you? You're terrific. You're so well organized.
我們如果沒有你，怎麼辦呢？你真是太棒了。你是這麼地有條理。

Bob Thank you.
謝謝。

Ann No. Thank you, Bob. Thank you for doing this.
不，謝謝你，鮑伯。謝謝你做了這件事。

Bob Dick has been good to me. I'm happy to do this for him.
迪克一直對我很好。我很高興可以為他做這件事。

Ann offers Bob another muffin but he declines.
安想給鮑伯另一個鬆餅，但他婉拒了。

Ann What have you been working on lately?
你最近都在做些什麼？

Bob We have been talking about the accounting equation.
我們最近在討論有關會計計算式的事。

Ann What do you know about the accounting equation?
關於會計計算式，你學到了些什麼？

Bob　Well, anything that the business owns is called an asset.

嗯，企業擁有的任何東西，都稱為資產。

Ann　Yes.

是的。

Bob　Equity is when you have financial rights to the asset.

權益（股份）是你對資產的財務權。

Ann　Good.

很好。

Bob　If I have equity in a business that means that I put money into it.

如果我對某企業有權益（股份），那表示我對它投資了金錢。

Ann　Yes.

是的。

Bob　I'll expect to get that money back.

我會想要回收那筆錢。

Ann　Right.

對。

Bob　Equity and capital are pretty much the same.

權益（股份）和資本幾乎是一樣的東西。

Ann　Almost, yes.

幾乎是。

Bob　The accounting equation is assets are equal to the liabilities plus the equity.

會計計算式是資產等於負債加上權益（股份）。

Ann You got it.

你答對了。

Bob The accounting system is explained in that equation.

那計算式解釋了會計系統。

Ann Yes. Accounting people like to explain ideas as though they are formulas.

是的。做會計的人喜歡用公式來解釋一些觀念。

Bob Yes. The accounting equation sounds like a mathematical formula, doesn't it?

是的。會計計算式聽起來像數學公式，不是嗎？

Ann Yes. Now, tell me. What kind of cake did you get?

是的。現在，再告訴我，你訂了什麼蛋糕？

Bob I got a white cake with vanilla icing. I know that Dick does not like chocolate.

我訂了一個有香草口味的蛋糕。我知道迪克不喜歡巧克力。

Ann You did your homework. I don't know what we would do without you.

你做了一些功課。我不知道沒有你，我們該怎麼辦。

Bob Thank you. I really like it here.

謝謝妳。我真的很喜歡這裏。

Ann And I really like cake. I will see you in the lunchroom tomorrow afternoon.

而我真的喜歡蛋糕。明天下午午餐室再見了。

Bob　　Make sure you bring your singing voice.
　　　　確定妳把唱歌的嗓子帶來。

____ (1) Where will the birthday party take place?

　　　A) In the office lunchroom

　　　B) In Ann's office

　　　C) In Bob's office

　　　D) In Dick's office

____ (2) How does Bob know that it is Dick's birthday tomorrow?

　　　A) Ann told him.

　　　B) Jane told him.

　　　C) Dick told him.

　　　D) He already knew.

____ (3) Why did Bob get a white cake?

　　　A) Bob doesn't like chocolate.

　　　B) Ann wanted white cake.

　　　C) Dick doesn't like chocolate.

　　　D) All of the above

____ (4) Who will sing Happy Birthday to Dick?

　　　A) Ann

　　　B) Bob

　　　C) The whole staff

　　　D) All of the above

Vocabulary 字彙

muffin	*n.*	鬆餅
weigh	*v.*	重量
decline	*v.*	拒絕
terrific	*adj.*	極好的
lately	*adv.*	最近地
equation	*n.*	計算式
equity	*n.*	（股東）權益；股份
capital	*n.*	資本
plus	*prep.*	加上
mathematical	*adj.*	數學的
formula	*n.*	公式
vanilla	*n.*	香草
icing	*n.*	（糕餅的）糖霜

Answers 解答   (1)A (2)D (3)C (4)D

Unit 2 Wonderful
太棒了

MP3-39

Jane has just made coffee in the staff room. Dick comes in and pours some for himself.

珍剛在員工休息室煮好咖啡。迪克進來幫自己倒了一些咖啡。

Jane	Dick, did you have a happy birthday yesterday?
	迪克，你昨天生日快樂嗎？

Dick	Yes, I did, Jane.
	是的，珍，我過得很快樂。

Jane	That's good. That birthday cake was wonderful. I wonder where Bob got it.
	那很好。那個生日蛋糕真是太棒了。我好奇鮑伯是在哪裏買的。

Dick	He got it from the bakery down the street. That bakery is called Harry's Bakery.
	他從這條街底的糕餅店買的。那糕餅店名叫哈瑞西點麵包。

Jane	I've bought bread there before. Harry's Bakery is a good bakery.
	我以前在那裏買過麵包。哈瑞西點麵包是一間很好的西點麵包店。

Dick	Yes.
	是的。

Jane	Lots of people buy there. I wonder why Bob didn't get a chocolate cake.
	很多人光顧那裡。我好奇為什麼鮑伯沒有買個巧克力蛋糕。

Dick	I don't like chocolate.
	我不喜歡巧克力。

Jane	Oh.
	喔。

Dick	Bob is great, isn't he?
	鮑伯很棒，對不對？

Jane	He is.
	他是的。

Dick	I call him my right hand.
	我稱他為我的右手。

Jane	Really?
	真的？

Dick	Yes. He is like my right hand. I would be lost without him.
	是的。他是像我的右手。沒有了他，我會迷失。

Jane	Too bad that he doesn't get paid.
	可惜的是他沒法領薪水。

Dick	Maybe when they hire someone to help me, they can hire Bob.
	也許當他們要雇人來幫我時，他們可以雇用鮑伯。

Jane	That would be smart.
	那樣做是明智之舉。

Dick	I'd like him to be my assistant. He is already. I'd like to see him get paid for it.
	我想要他當我的助理。他現在已經是了。我希望看到他領薪水。

Jane	Don't forget. He's getting something out of it. He is getting a free education.
	別忘了。他也從中得到了一些東西。他獲得了免費的教育。

Dick	I guess so.
	我想是的。

Jane	Lots of people have to pay lots of money to

learn what he is learning.
很多人必須付一大筆錢去學他現在所學的東西。

Dick I guess.
我猜也是。

Jane What are you teaching him right now?
你目前在教他什麼？

Dick I'm teaching him about the daily summary of sales. I need to get to work.
我在教他關於每日的銷售摘要。我得回去工作了。

Jane I'll walk with you.
我和你一塊走。

They leave the coffee room and walk together down the hallway.
他們離開咖啡間，一起在走廊上走著。

Jane What have you told him about daily summary of sales?
關於每日銷售摘要，你教了他什麼？

Dick That this is how a business can compare receipts against cash received.
商家利用銷售摘要來比較收據與現金收款。

Jane Yes.
是的。

Dick It's also how they can keep track of daily sales.
它也是商家瞭解每日銷售額的方法。

Jane The daily summary of sales is made up of three parts.

每日銷售摘有三個組成部份。

Dick Cash receipts, cash on hand, and total sales. Yes. We have talked about that.

現金收據、手頭現金及銷售總額。是的，我們已經談過那個了。

Jane When will you tell him about journal entries?

你何時要教他記日記帳？

Dick I told him that information from the daily summary goes into a journal everyday.

我告訴他每日摘要的資訊需每天登入日記帳。

Jane Good.

很好。

Dick That journal is called the sales and receipts journal.

日記帳被稱為是銷售和收據日記帳。

Jane Sounds good.

聽起來不錯。

Dick He's been working with sales and receipts journals already.

他最近已經在做銷售和收據日記帳了。

Jane Good. What about journals for disbursements, purchases and expenses?

那好。關於支付款、購買和費用的日記帳呢？

Dick We haven't got to that yet.

我們還沒講到哪裏。

Jane Because it's through those journals that he can create profit and loss statements.

因為他必須要完成那些日記帳，才能做損益表。

Dick Yes. I'm doing the profit and loss statements. I don't let him do those yet.

是的。損益表是我在做。我還沒讓他做那些。

Jane Do you think there is any of that cake left?

你想有剩下任何蛋糕嗎？

Dick Yes. It is in the fridge in the coffee room.

有的。在咖啡間的冰箱裡。

Jane I want some. I'm going back to the break room to get a piece. Do you want some?

我要吃一點。我要回去休息室去拿一塊。你要嗎？

Dick No. Cake is not a very good breakfast.

不。蛋糕不是很好的早點。

Jane Oh, no? What if I put some candy on top of it? Will it be a good breakfast then?

哦，是這樣嗎？如果我放些糖果在上面呢？這樣它會是好早點嗎？

Dick Your dentist must think that you are wonderful.

妳的牙醫一定很喜歡妳。

Comprehension Questions 理解測驗

____ (1) What does Jane buy at the bakery?

　　A) She buys cake there.

　　B) She buys candy there.

　　C) She buys bread there.

D) None of the above

_____ (2) When was Dick's birthday?

A) Yesterday

B) Today

C) The day before yesterday

D) The day after tomorrow

_____ (3) Where is the birthday cake?

A) In Dick's fridge.

B) In Bob's fridge.

C) In Dick's office

D) None of the above

_____ (4) How does Jane want to eat her cake?

A) She wants to eat it for breakfast.

B) She wants to eat it now.

C) She wants to put candy on it.

D) All of the above

Vocabulary 字彙

pour	v.	倒
bakery	n.	麵包店
lost	adj.	迷失的
summary	n.	摘要
sales	n.	銷售
compare	v.	比較
receipt	n.	收據
keep track of		追蹤瞭解；記住

journal	n.	日記帳；流水帳
disbursement	n.	支付（款）
purchase	n.	買
fridge (=refrigerator)	n.	電冰箱
dentist	n.	牙醫

Answers 解答 (1)C (2)A (3)D (4)D

Unit 3 Like Family
像家人一樣
MP3-40

Dick goes to Ann's office and knocks.
She yells for him to come in.
迪克去安的辦公室敲門。她大聲要他進來。

Dick Ann, I have to talk to you for a minute. Can I come in?

安，我要和妳談一下。我可以進來嗎？

Ann Of course, Dick. What is going on? Are you all right?

當然，迪克。怎麼了？你沒事吧？

Dick Yes. I'm fine. I just wanted to tell you something about Bob.

是的，我很好。我只是要告訴你關於鮑伯的事。

Ann Is there something wrong?

有什麼事不對嗎？

Dick   Not at all. My car didn't start this morning. The taxis were all busy.
沒事。我車子今早無法發動。計程車都載了客人。

Ann   Wow.
哇。

Dick   I know. I was worried that I would be late for work.
我知道。我那時還擔心我上班會遲到。

Ann   You're never late for work. You're always early.
你上班從未遲到。你總是早到。

Dick   Exactly. Bob was already here. He always comes to work as early as I do.
沒錯。那時鮑伯已經到了辦公室。他總是跟我一樣，很早來上班。

Ann   Does he? I can't believe it.
是嗎？我不敢相信。

Dick   I know. He doesn't have to but he does.
我知道。他不需要如此，但他都這樣做。

Ann   Impressive.
真教人印象深刻。

Dick   Yes. When I didn't show up at my usual time, he was worried.
是的，當我在一般上班時間沒出現時，他很擔心。

Ann   Oh?
哦？

Dick He looked up my number in the phone book. He phoned my house.

他在電話簿裏查到我的電話。他打電話到我家。

Ann Really?

真的？

Dick When I told him that I was waiting for a taxi, he said he would come to get me.

當我告訴他我在等計程車時，他說他要來接我。

Ann Really?

真的？

Dick He came to my house and drove me to work today. Isn't that nice?

他今天來我家載我來上班。他人是不是很好？

Ann He is wonderful.

他是非常好。

Dick He's like family to me. If I had a brother, I would want him to be like Bob.

對我來説，他像家人一樣。如果我有兄弟，我會希望他像鮑伯一樣。

Ann He's a good worker. He's a good part of our team.

他是個好員工。他是我們團隊中很好的一份子。

Dick Yes, he is, Ann. And he is going to be a great accounting technician.

是的，他是，安。而且他將會是個很好的會計專員。

Ann I'm sure he will one day.

我很確定有一天他會是。

Dick He's so good. He could be an accountant.

他真的很好，他有可能成為一位會計師。

Ann Maybe.

也許。

Dick He could even be a partner in an accounting firm. He is that smart.

他甚至可能成為某家會計師事務所的合夥人。他是那麼聰明。

Ann Any accounting firm would be lucky to have him.

任何一家會計師事務所有他，都會很幸運。

Dick Yes. I agree. We would be lucky to have him. Maybe we should pay him.

是的，我同意。有他的話，我們會很幸運。也許我們應該付他薪水。

Ann Dick, I would like to. We don't have the money in the company budget.

迪克。我很想要那麼做。但在公司的預算中，我們沒有這筆錢。

Dick I know. But when you hire someone to help me, you could hire him.

我知道。但當你們要雇別人來幫我時，可以雇用他。

Ann I never thought of that. Give me time to think about it. It might be a good idea.

我從未想到這個。給我點時間考慮。這可能是個好主意。

Dick Okay.

好的。

Ann	Okay.
	好的。

Dick gets up to leave.
迪克正站起來要離開。

Ann	How much has he learned?
	他已經學了多少？

Dick	We are talking more about ledgers now.
	我們現在在深入地談分類帳。

Ann	What has he learned about ledgers?
	關於分類帳，他學了多少？

Dick	He knows that a ledger is a group of accounts.
	他知道分類帳是帳戶的集合。

Ann	Okay. What else does he know?
	好。他還知道別的嗎？

Dick	That if it has all the financial statement accounts, it is called the general ledger.
	那個，如果一個帳戶有所有的財務報表，那就稱為總分類帳。

Ann	Have you talked about the chart of accounts?
	你們談到帳戶的圖表嗎？

Dick	Yes. I told him that each account in a ledger has a name and number.
	是的。我告訴他在分類帳的每一帳戶，都有名字和代號。

Ann	Okay.
	是的。

Dick Each of those names is called an account title.
每一個名字叫做帳戶名稱。

Ann Yes.
是的。

Dick Each of those numbers is called an account number.
每個號碼稱作帳號。

Ann Go on.
繼續講。

Dick An account number shows where an account is in the ledger.
每一帳號顯示帳戶在分類帳的位置。

Ann And?
然後呢？

Dick The list of account titles and numbers is what we call a chart of accounts.
帳戶名稱的清單就是我們所謂的帳戶圖表。

Ann Good. You explain things very well. He is moving very quickly.
很好。你將事情解釋得很好。他學的很快。

Dick Yes. There's a lot to learn in accounting.
是的。在會計裏還有很多要學的。

Ann Keep going with Bob. I will think about hiring him.
繼續教導鮑伯。我會考慮雇用他。

Dick Thank you, Ann.
謝謝妳，安。

Comprehension Questions 理解測驗

____ (1) When did Bob give Dick a ride to work?

A) When Dick's car wouldn't start

B) When Dick couldn't get a taxi

C) This morning

D) All of the above

____ (2) Where is Dick meeting with Ann?

A) In his office

B) In her office

C) In the coffee room

D) In a taxi

____ (3) How does Dick feel about Bob?

A) Dick doesn't like him.

B) He is like family to Dick.

C) Dick thinks he smells funny.

D) None of the above

____ (4) Why did Dick talk to Ann?

A) He wants her to hire Bob.

B) He wants her to give him a ride.

C) He wants her to phone for a taxi.

D) He wants to tell her that he will be late.

Vocabulary 字彙

yell	v.	大叫
start	v.	發動
impressive	adj.	予人深刻印象的
taxi	n.	計程車
team	n.	團隊
firm	n.	公司
ledger	n.	分類帳
chart	n.	圖表
title	n.	名稱
explain	v.	解釋

Answers 解答

(1)D (2)B (3)B (4)A

Chapter 6

Something New
新鮮事

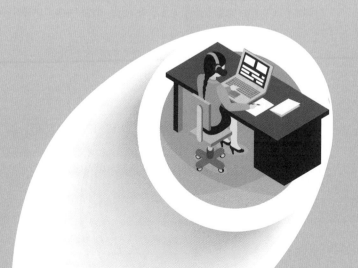

Unit 1 **Talking to Clients**
與客戶談話

Dick comes into the office where Bob is working. He sits down.

迪克進入鮑伯正在工作的辦公室，坐了下來。

Dick Today, we are going to try something new, Bob.
今天我們要做點新鮮的事，鮑伯。

Bob What are we going to try, Dick?
我們要做什麼呢，迪克？

Dick You are going to try meeting with clients.
你要試試與客戶會面。

Bob Do you think I am ready for that?
你認為我已經做好準備了嗎？

Dick I will be right here beside you. I'll be here to help if you need it.
我會在你旁邊。如果你需要幫忙，我會幫你。

Bob Okay. As long as I know that you are here to help me.
好的。只要我知道你會在這裏幫我，那就好。

Dick Of course.
當然。

Bob I don't want to do a bad job. I want to do it right.
我不想把事情搞砸。我想要把事情做好。

Dick You will do well. I know it.
你會做得很好。我知道。

Bob What will I be meeting with clients for?
我與客戶碰面的目的何在？

Dick There are some people coming in today. They are thinking of opening a business. They don't have a lot of money.
今天有一些人要來。他們想開始做生意。他們並沒有很多錢。

Bob Okay.
好的。

Dick They'll do their own books to start. Once they have more money, we'll do them.
一開始時，他們打算自己記帳。一旦他們有較多的錢，就由我們來做。

Bob All right.
好的。

Dick They need us to tell them how to do their own books. You will teach them.
他們需要我們告訴他們如何自己做帳。而你將教他們。

Bob Okay. I think I know what to tell them. Can I tell you what I will tell them?
好的。我想我知道該告訴他們什麼。我可以告訴你我計畫要告訴他們什麼嗎？

Dick If you want.
如果你想要的話。

Bob Can we do that before they get here? You can tell me if I am right.

我們可以在他們來這裏，做這件事嗎？你可以告訴我我說得對不對。

Dick Go ahead.

好啊！

Bob This is what I will tell them. Keep all of your receipts. Keep all of your papers.

我想這樣告訴他們。留下所有收據和所有文件。

Dick Yes?

然後呢？

Bob Throw them in a box. Bring it to us. A box of papers and receipts is all we need.

把它們丟在一個箱子裏。把箱子帶來給我們，一箱的文件和收據是我們需要的一切。

Dick What?

你說什麼？

Dick is shocked.
迪克很震驚。

Dick That's not right, Bob. That's terrible. That is exactly what we don't want.

那樣不對，鮑伯。那很糟糕。那正是我們不想要的。

Bob Really?

真的嗎？

Dick I can't believe you would say that to a client.

我不敢相信你會和客戶那樣說。

Bob No! I'm joking!

不，我是開玩笑的。

Dick   Oh! Thank goodness. I thought you were serious. Oh, Bob. That's funny!

喔！謝天謝地。我以為你是認真的。喔，鮑伯。那真的很好笑。

Bob   I was trying not to laugh when I said that. I didn't want to mess up my joke.

當我講那些話時，我強忍著不笑出來。我不想搞砸我的玩笑。

Dick   Okay. Tell me what you will tell them. What you will really tell them.

好的。告訴我你想告訴他們什麼，這次來真的。

Bob   To have a bookkeeping system that works, you must be organized.

要有一個有用的簿記系統，你一定要很有條理。

Dick   Yes.

是的。

Bob   Record all transactions. Record all bills you pay and all money you get.

記錄所有的交易。記錄所有你支付的帳單和收到的錢。

Dick   Yes.

是的。

Bob   You must record every time money comes in and every time money goes out.

每一筆金錢進帳和出帳，都要記錄下來。

Dick   That's right. Keep going.

對的。繼續說。

Bob   They will need to identify what they are doing.

Are they paying a *bill*? Show that.

他們需要確認自己在做什麼。是在支付帳單嗎？記錄要顯示那些。

Dick That's right.

沒錯。

Bob Show what bill you paid and when you paid it.

顯示你付了什麼帳單、何時付的。

Dick Good.

很好。

Bob Show how you paid and how much the bill was.

顯示你如何付款、帳單的金額是多少。

Dick Very good.

非常好。

Bob If you paid by cheque, write down the cheque number.

如果你用支票付款，記下支票號碼。

Dick And what else?

還有呢？

Bob *Post* to the accounts.

把它記入帳戶。

Dick Yes.

是的。

Bob Get a *total* from the account.

從帳戶得到總額。

Dick Yes.

是的。

Bob　Write that total in the financial statements.
把總額記到財務報表上。

Dick　Good.
好。

Bob　You think so? You think that I know what to tell them?
你這麼認為嗎？你覺得我知道該告訴他們什麼嗎？

Dick　Yes. I think you do. And I will be right here in case you forget.
是的，我想你知道。而且萬一你忘掉的話，我就在這裏。

Bob　I'm **pleased** that you think I am good enough to talk to clients. Thank you, Dick.
我很高興你認為我好到可以和客戶會面。謝謝你，迪克。

Comprehension Questions　理解測驗

____ (1) Where did Bob say that clients should keep their records?

A) In a drawer

B) In a bag

C) In a shoe

D) In a box

____ (2) How did Dick know that Bob was joking?

A) Bob told him.

B) Bob couldn't stop laughing.

C) Bob was smiling.

D) Dick had already heard the joke.

_____ (3) Why is Dick going to stay with Bob?

A) In case the phone rings

B) In case Bob needs help

C) Ann told him to.

D) In case there is a fire

_____ (4) Who is coming to talk to Bob?

A) Some people who have receipts in a box

B) Some people who have some papers in a box

C) Some people who want to open a business

D) Some people who have a business

Vocabulary 字彙

shock	*v.*	震驚
bookkeeping	*n.*	簿記
transaction	*n.*	交易
identify	*v.*	確認
bill	*n.*	帳單
cheque	*n.*	支票
post	*v.*	過（帳）
total	*n.*	總額
pleased	*adj.*	高興的

Answers 解答

(1)D (2)A (3)B (4)C

Unit 2 **Ways We Help**
我們可以幫忙的地方

MP3-42

Ann comes into the coffee room. Jane is drinking coffee and reading a magazine.
安進來咖啡間。珍正在喝咖啡、看雜誌。

Ann　Jane, is there any coffee made?
珍，有煮好的咖啡嗎？

Jane　Yes, there is, Anne. I just made a fresh pot. Help yourself.
有的，安。我剛煮了一壺，請自便。

Ann　Great. How are you doing today?
太好了。妳今天好嗎？

Jane　I'm tired. That's why I came in here. I'm moving slow today. I needed a break.
我很累。這就是為什麼我人在這裏。我今天工作進展緩慢，需要休息一下。

Ann　I know what you mean. I didn't sleep well last night.
我知道妳的意思。我昨晚沒睡好。

Jane　Join the club.
我也一樣。

Ann　I hope a cup of coffee and a short visit with you will help me to wake up.
我希望一杯咖啡和與妳的短暫談話可以幫我清醒。

Jane	Ann, I have always wanted to know. What education do you have? 安，我一直想知道。妳有什麼樣的教育背景？
Ann	I have a Bachelor of Commerce. 我有一個商業學士學位。
Jane	So you do have a university degree in accounting? 所以妳真的有大學會計學位？
Ann	Yes. I also have an MBA. 是的。我也有企管碩士學位。
Jane	You have a Masters in Business Administration? 你有企業管理的碩士學位？
Ann	Yes. 是的。
Jane	Good for you. 妳真的很棒。
Ann	Why do you want to know, Jane? 妳為什麼想要知道這個，珍？
Jane	I think that I would like to do what you do. I think it would be fun. 我想要做妳在做的事，我想那會很有趣。
Ann	Are you not happy with your job? 妳不喜歡妳的工作嗎？
Jane	I'm very happy with my job. But I'm young. I have a lot of years ahead of me. 我很喜歡我的工作。但我還年輕，未來還有很長的歲月。

Ann	That's right. 沒錯。
Jane	I might want some more education. I might want to try something new later on. 我也許想再多念個學位，也許以後想要嘗試一些新的事情。
Ann	Something new? 新的事？
Jane	I might want to get into management down the road. Like you. 將來我也許想要走管理這條路，像妳一樣。
Ann	I love being a manager. I love working in finance with people and with numbers. 我很喜歡當主管。我喜歡在財務領域裏，與人和數字一起工作。
Jane	Me, too. 我也是。
Ann	Accounting has a lot of math in it. I've always liked math. 會計用到很多數學。我一直很喜歡數學。

Jane fills up her coffee cup and pours some more in Ann's cup.
珍在她的咖啡杯再倒了一些咖啡，並且倒了一些在安的杯子裏。

Jane	There are so many ways we help people. We

do their accounting.

我們幫助別人的方式有很多種。我們幫他們做會計的工作。

| Ann | That's right. |
| | 對。 |

| Jane | We can do their bookkeeping. We can show them how to do it themselves. |
| | 我們可以做他們的帳，可以教他們如何自己做帳。 |

| Ann | Yes. |
| | 是的。 |

| Jane | When you are in accounting, you help people organize their finances. |
| | 當你在會計這行業裡，你幫助人們使他們的財務狀況有條理。 |

| Ann | You can help them plan their finances for the future. |
| | 你可以幫他們規劃未來的財務。 |

| Jane | That's right. You can help them with their income tax. |
| | 沒錯。你可以幫他們算所得稅。 |

| Ann | You can help them with the taxes for their business or their firm. |
| | 你可以在他們的企業或公司稅務上提供他們協助。 |

| Jane | You can help them with their personal taxes. |
| | 你可以在個人稅務上幫助他們。 |

| Ann | There are so many ways that we help people. Have you ever done estate planning? |

我們幫助人們的方式有很多種。你做過遺產規劃嗎。

Jane Do you mean helping people decide their will? Who gets what when they pass on?

你是說幫助別人決定遺囑？當他們過世時，其他人可以得到什麼？

Ann Yes.

是的。

Jane I thought only lawyers did that.

我以為那只有律師會做。

Ann Whenever money and numbers are involved, accountants are involved.

任何時候只要牽涉到金錢和數字，就有會計師的介入。

Jane That's true. No, I haven't worked in estate planning yet.

那倒是真的。不，我還沒有做過遺產規劃。

Ann It's very rewarding. So is planning trusts.

這經驗很有益處。信託規劃也是如此。

Jane What's a trust?

什麼是信託？

Ann That's money left to young people after a loved one passes on.

那是親人過世後，留給年幼小孩的錢。

Jane Oh.

哦。

Ann They don't get the money until a certain age. It grows while they grow up.

他們直到某一個年紀，才能拿到這筆錢。當他們長大時，錢也因利息而增加了。

Jane What a good idea.

這是多好的一個主意啊！

Ann Yes.

是的。

Jane Sometimes the people we leave behind are too young to be given a lot of money.

有時候我們過世留下的人，他們年紀太小了，以致不能繼承一大筆錢。

Ann That's right.

沒錯。

Jane They would not use it well. They are too young to know what to do with it.

他們不會好好利用這筆錢。他們太年輕，不知要怎麼運用這筆錢。

Ann Exactly.

正是如此。

Jane I would like to help people in that way.

我想要用這種方式來幫助別人。

Ann I will call you when I am working in estate or trust planning again.

當我在作遺產或信託規劃時，我會打電話給你。

Jane Thank you. It is time for me to get back to work. Bye, Ann.

謝謝妳。是我該回去工作的時候了。再見，安。

Ann Bye.

再見。

Comprehension Questions 理解測驗

___ (1) How is Ann feeling this morning?

A) She is happy.

B) She is bored.

C) She is tired.

D) She is lonely.

___ (2) Why is Ann tired?

A) Because Jane is tired too.

B) Ann did not sleep well.

C) She does not drink coffee.

D) She drinks too much coffee.

___ (3) Who else is tired this morning?

A) Dick

B) Jane

C) Bob

D) Ann

___ (4) What other job would Jane like to try?

A) Garbage man

B) Truck driver

C) Management

D) Door to door salesman

Vocabulary 字彙

Bachelor	n.	學士
Commerce	n.	商業

university	*n.*	大學
degree	*n.*	學位
masters	*n.*	碩士
administration	*n.*	管理
income tax		所得稅
estate	*n.*	財產
lawyer	*n.*	律師
involve	*v.*	牽涉
rewarding	*adj.*	有益的
trust	*n.*	信託
certain	*adj.*	某種（或一定）程度的

Answers 解答 **(1)C (2)B (3)B (4)C**

Unit 3 Wear and Tear
磨損

MP3-43

Dick and Jane are sitting in the staff room. Dick pours himself a coffee.
迪克和珍坐在員工休息室裏。迪克幫自己倒了杯咖啡。

Dick Jane, pass the cream, please.
珍，請遞奶精給我。

Jane There is no cream, Dick.
奶精沒了，迪克。

Dick Why is there no cream? It seems like there is never any cream here.

為什麼沒有奶精？看起來好像這裏從來沒有奶精。

Jane Sorry.

抱歉。

Dick Pass the milk, please.

請遞給我牛奶。

Jane Here you are.

來，給你。

Dick Thank you. Can I get you to pass the sugar, please?

謝謝妳。可以再請妳遞一下糖嗎？

Jane I hate to tell you this, Dick.

我討厭告訴你這件事，迪克。

Dick What?

什麼事？

Jane There is no sugar. It is all gone.

糖也沒了，都用完了。

Dick I can't believe it. Why does it seem like there is never any sugar?

我不敢相信這個。為什麼好像從來都沒糖呢？

Jane There's honey. Do you want to use honey instead?

有蜂蜜，要不要用蜂蜜代替？

Dick No. I've told you before. Honey goes in tea. It doesn't go good in coffee.

不，我以前告訴過妳。蜂蜜用在茶裏，和咖啡配在一起不適合。

Jane I know. I am just trying to help.
我知道。我只是想幫你。

Dick Thanks anyway.
無論如何,謝了。

Dick drinks his coffee silently.
Jane stares at him.
迪克沉默地喝著咖啡。珍看著他。

Jane You seem a little **grumpy** today. What is going on?
你今天看起來有點耍脾氣。怎麼了?

Dick My computer has worn out. It has died. It was getting old. I need a new one.
我的電腦報廢,它太舊了,我需要一台新的。

Jane That's too bad.
那真是太糟了。

Dick Bob and I can't do any work until I get a new one. That's why I am grumpy.
直到有新的電腦,鮑伯和我什麼事都不能做。那正是為什麼我想發脾氣的原因。

Jane There has to be something you can work on while your computer is on order.
當你在訂購電腦的同時,一定有什麼工作是你可以做的。

Dick I don't know.
我不知道。

Jane	Have you taught Bob about depreciation? 你教鮑伯關於折舊了嗎？
Dick	No, I haven't. 不，還沒。
Jane	That might be a good thing for him to know about. 讓他知道這個也許是件好事。
Dick	Of course. He must know about depreciation. What a good time to talk about it. 當然。他應該要知道關於折舊，現在正是談這個的好時機。
Jane	It is. All of the fixed assets of a business will lose their value over time. 的確如此。所有企業的固定資產都會隨時間而有所折舊。
Dick	A good example of a fixed asset is a computer. 固定資產的最佳例子之一就是電腦。
Jane	Right. They will lose their value through age and wear. 對。它們會因年限和損耗而失去價值。
Dick	Yes. They just wear out. Like mine did. 是的，它們會有損耗，像我的一樣。
Jane	Depreciation allows for that. It allows for loss of value due to wear, tear and age. 折舊允許那樣的情形。它允許東西由於磨損和年限而失去價值。
Dick	Exactly like my computer. 正像我的電腦一樣。

Jane It's a cost of doing business. It's deducted from income like any other expense.

它是作生意的成本之一，要從收入扣除，就像其它費用一樣。

Dick What a great lesson for Bob. The timing is perfect. Thank you, Jane.

對鮑伯來說，這是很好的一課。這時機再恰當不過了。謝謝妳，珍。

Jane You're welcome.

不客氣。

Dick Hey. What do you know? I'm not grumpy anymore.

嘿，妳知道嗎？我不再想耍脾氣了。

Comprehension Questions 理解測驗

____ (1) Why did Dick's computer wear out?

    A) It was getting old.

    B) It was not a good computer.

    C) He did not treat it well.

    D) It was broken to begin with.

____ (2) Who needs to learn about depreciation?

    A) Jane

    B) Bob

    C) Dick

    D) Ann

___ (3) What can depreciate in value?

A) Friends

B) Cookies

C) Teeth

D) Fixed assets

___ (4) When will Dick get his new computer?

A) Tomorrow

B) Tuesday

C) Two days from now

D) It does not say.

Vocabulary 字彙

grumpy	*adj.*	氣暴躁的
wear out		磨損
depreciation	*n.*	折舊
fixed assets		固定資產
allow	*v.*	允許
deduct	*v.*	扣除
depreciate	*v.*	折舊

Answers 解答

(1)A   (2)B   (3)D   (4)D

Chapter 7

Give and Take
互相讓步

Unit 1　Better to Give
施比受更好

MP3-44

Bob is trying to carry several boxes at the same time. Jane walks up to him.
鮑伯正試著要同時拿好幾箱東西。珍走向他。

Jane What are you doing, Bob?
你在做什麼，鮑伯？

Bob This is Dick's new computer, Jane. I am going to set it up for him.
這是迪克的新電腦，珍。我要幫他組裝。

Jane That's nice of you. Where is Dick?
你人真好。迪克人在哪裏？

Bob He just met with some clients. He's just walking them out.
他剛與一些客戶見面，正要送他們出去。

Jane Do you need a hand with that?
你需要幫忙嗎？

Bob Yes, please. I can't carry all of these boxes at the same time.
是的，拜託妳。我無法一次拿所有的箱子。

Jane Okay.
好的。

Bob It would save me a trip if you help me carry them.
如果妳幫我拿一些，我可以省得再跑一趟。

Jane No problem.
沒問題。

Bob Dick is now letting me work on accounts receivable things.
迪克現在讓我做應收帳款。

Jane That's good.
那很好。

Bob It is good. He watches over me to make sure that I do okay.
是很好。他會看著我，確定我做得對。

Jane Good.
很好。

Bob He always checks everything to see that I do it right. I'd hate to make a mistake.
他總是查看每件事，看我做對了沒有。我不喜歡犯錯。

Jane It's good that you're doing work by yourself and that Dick checks your work.
你自己能獨力自己做事，又有迪克幫你檢查，那很好。

Bob It is.
是的。

He hands her two boxes for her to carry.
他給她兩箱讓她拿。

Jane Tell me what you know about accounts receivables.
告訴我，關於應收帳款，你知道些什麼？

Bob Accounts receivables are accounts that owe you money.
應收帳款是欠你錢的帳戶。

Jane Yes.
是的。

Bob These are bills that you have sent out that need to be paid.
這些是你已寄出帳單，需要收到付款。

Jane What else?
還有別的嗎？

Bob When you let people pay you later, that's also called accounts receivables.
當你讓別人晚些付款，那也稱為應收帳款。

Jane Businesses send invoices that say how much is owed.
商家寄發發票，告訴顧客他們欠了多少錢。

Bob When the customer gets an invoice, they write a cheque and send it to the business.
當顧客拿到發票，就會開支票，寄回給商家。

Jane Most people do. Some people don't.
大多數人會這麼做，但是有些人不會。

Bob That's right. Can you put that box down on the floor by Dick's desk, please?
對的。可以請妳把那箱子放在迪克桌旁的地上嗎？

Jane Do you want it here?
要放在這裏嗎？

Bob
Yes. That's perfect.
是的，那再好不過了。

Jane sets down the box.
珍放下那個箱子。

Bob
Thank you.
謝謝妳。

Jane
I can open it for you.
我可以幫你把它打開。

Bob
Okay, if you have time.
好的，如果妳有時間的話。

Jane
So are you doing collections?
那麼你在作收款嗎？

Bob
Yes. I'm phoning clients who haven't paid their invoices.
是的。我打電話給還沒有支付發票金額的客戶。

Jane
Really?
真的嗎？

Bob
Yes. I phone to remind them to send in their payment.
是的。我打電話提醒他們把款項寄回來。

Jane
I hate having to do that.
我討厭必須要做那樣的事。

Bob
I don't. I think doing collections is easy.
我倒不會。我想收款這件事很簡單。

Jane What do you do if they still don't send payment?

如果他們仍然不付款，你會怎麼做？

Bob The people who don't pay after I phone them get a letter and then I call again.

在我打了電話後，仍不付款的人會收到一封信，然後我會再打一次電話。

Jane I see!

這樣子啊！

Bob I just keep phoning them and mailing letters to them until they pay.

我只是不斷地打電話、寄信給他們，直到他們付款為止。

Jane Don't you find that hard?

你有沒有覺得那很難？

Bob Not at all. It is the people who owe money find it hard when I call.

一點也不。當我打電話去時，欠錢的人會覺得很不好過。

Jane Really?

真的嗎？

Bob They are embarrassed that I have to call them.

他們覺得很難為情，因為我必須打電話給他們。

Jane You are good at collections.

你很擅長收款。

Bob It's better to give the money that you owe than to receive a phone call from me.

付你所欠的錢總比接到我的電話好過。

Jane You are not mean. You don't embarrass them.

你態度不惡劣，不會讓他們很難堪。

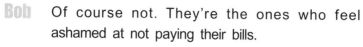

Bob Of course not. They're the ones who feel ashamed at not paying their bills.
當然不會。他們是感到羞恥的一方，因為沒有付帳單。

Jane I should get you to do my collections.
我該讓你去幫我收款。

Bob Help me hook up this computer and I'll think about it.
幫我把這台電腦裝好，我會考慮看看。

Comprehension Questions 理解測驗

____ (1) Who does not like to do collections?

A) Bob

B) Jane

C) Dick

D) Ann

____ (2) What is collections a part of?

A) Accounts

B) Receiving

C) Accounts receivable

D) Receivable accounts

____ (3) When will Bob do collections for Jane?

A) He won't.

B) She didn't ask.

C) He said he would think about it.

D) Bob does not do collections.

_____ (4) Where is Dick?

    A) He is getting the new computer.

    B) He is talking with Jane.

    C) He is walking clients to the door.

    D) None of the above

Vocabulary 字彙

set up		組裝
accounts receivable		應收帳款
check	*v.*	檢查
invoice	*n.*	發票
customer	*n.*	顧客
collection	*n.*	收款
remind	*v.*	提醒
payment	*n.*	支付的款項
mean	*adj.*	卑鄙的
shame	*v.*	使羞愧
hook up		組裝

Answers 解答

(1)B (2)C (3)C (4)C

Unit 2 Payback
回報
MP3-45

Jane walks by Dick's office. She sees that he is in and she stops to talk.

珍經過迪克的辦公室。她看見他在，於是進去和他講話。

Jane How do you like your new computer, Dick?

你喜歡你的新電腦嗎？迪克。

Dick It is great, Jane. It was a long four days waiting for it.

太棒了，珍。等待它的這四天有夠漫長。

Jane I can't believe you were without a computer for that long.

我不敢相信你等了那麼久沒有電腦可以用。

Dick I have Ann to thank for getting it here that fast.

我要謝謝安，讓電腦那麼快送來。

Jane How's that?

怎麼回事？

Dick The computer store was being really unfriendly to me.

那家電腦店對我很不友善。

Jane Really?

真的嗎？

Dick They said we had an outstanding invoice. It hadn't been paid in five months.

他們說我們有張拖了很久、而尚未付清的發票。已經遲了五個月了還沒付。

Jane That's crazy. How does an accounting firm not pay invoices?

那是不可能的事。一家會計師事務所怎麼會不付款？

Dick They weren't going to give me the computer until this invoice was paid.

他們本來不打算給我電腦，除非我們先付款。

Jane What did you do?
然後你怎麼做？

Dick I talked to Ann. She looked for this invoice everywhere. No one had seen it.
我告訴安。她到處找這張發票。沒有人見過它。

Jane How odd!
多奇怪的事啊！

Dick She told the computer store that.
她告訴電腦店這件事。

Jane What did they do?
他們怎麼說？

Dick They were angry. They said they wouldn't do business with us again.
他們很生氣，還說再不跟我們做生意了。

Jane This is terrible.
這真是太糟了。

Dick Just wait. It got better. Ann asked them to fax over the invoice right away.
等一下，後面更精采了，安叫他們把發票馬上傳真過來。

Jane Yes.
然後呢？

Dick She told them that all of our accounts are in good standing.
她告訴他們，我們所有的帳戶信譽良好。

Jane Yes.
是的。

Dick She told them that this had never happened before.
她告訴他們這種事以前從未發生過。

Jane Go on.
繼續講。

Dick She said that if they faxed the invoice, she would personally hand deliver a cheque.
她說如果他們傳真發票過來，她會親自送上支票。

Jane Wow. What happened?
哇。然後呢？

Dick They did fax over the outstanding invoice right away. Ann looked at it.
他們真的馬上把未付款的那張發票傳真過來。安看了發票。

Jane And?
然後呢？

Dick And they had the wrong address. We never got it in the first place.
上面的地址是錯的。我們根本從未收到。

Dick and Jane burst out laughing.
迪克和珍大笑。

Jane Oh, my goodness.
我的天啊！

Dick Isn't that funny? Ann walked over there with the invoice and told them to correct our address.
那不是很好笑嗎？安拿著發票過去，告訴他們要更正我們的地址。

Jane　She did?
她真的這樣做？

Dick　She showed them that the address on the invoice was wrong. They were embarrassed.
她把發票上錯誤的地址展示給他們看。他們很糗。

Jane　I bet.
我相信。

Dick　Two people from the store walked back with her carrying my computer for her.
那家店派了兩個人幫她拿著電腦，與她一起回來。

Jane　Ann is my hero.
安是我的英雄。

Dick　Yes. She's very calm under pressure.
是的。她在面臨壓力時，仍很鎮靜。

Jane　How embarrassing for that computer store.
這對電腦店來說是多糗的事啊。

Dick　That's payback for thinking that we wouldn't pay our bills.
那是他們認為我們不付帳的回報。

Jane　I like accounts payable. It's fun sending cheques to people.
我喜歡應付帳款。寄支票給別人很有趣。

Dick　And Bob loves to do accounts receivable.
而鮑伯非常喜歡做應收帳款。

Jane　I know. He and I were talking about that yesterday.
我知道。他和我昨天談論到那個。

Dick He said he might help you with your collections.
他說他也許會幫妳收款。

Jane Yes.
是的。

Dick He would do it as a way to pay you back for helping him hook up my computer.
他如果幫妳做的話，就把它當做是妳幫他組裝我的電腦的回報吧！

Jane I hope he does. That would be great.
我希望他會幫我。那樣就太好了。

Dick Just don't get too attached to him. I want him back.
只是不要太依賴他。我還想要他回來呢！

Jane No problem.
沒問題。

Comprehension Questions 理解測驗

____ (1) What is sending payment a part of?

A) Accounts receivable

B) Accounts payable

C) Collections

D) None of the above

____ (2) When did Dick get his computer?

A) Yesterday

B) The day before

C) Tomorrow

D) The day after that

_____ (3) Where did Ann hand deliver payment to?

    A) A hardware store

    B) A stationery store

    C) An electronics store

    D) None of the above

_____ (4) How did Ann know that they never got the invoice?

    A) It was addressed to the wrong business.

    B) It was addressed to the wrong person.

    C) It was for the wrong amount.

    D) It was addressed to the wrong address.

Vocabulary 字彙

outstanding	*adj.*	未付款的
firm	*n.*	公司
odd	*adj.*	奇怪的
fax	*v.*	傳真
standing	*n.*	名聲
deliver	*v.*	遞送；運送
calm	*adj.*	沈著；鎮靜
I bet		我確信；我敢打賭
pressure	*n.*	壓力
payback	*n.*	回報
attach	*v.*	依賴；附著

Answers 解答   (1)B (2)A (3)D (4)D

Unit 3 Go with the Flow

跟著潮流走

MP3-46

Jane is walking past Ann's office just as Ann gets off the phone. Ann calls to her.

珍經過安辦公室時，剛好安講完電話。安叫住她。

Ann   Jane, can you come in here, please?
珍，可以請妳進來一下嗎？

Jane   Sure. What can I do for you, Ann?
當然。有什麼事嗎，安？

Ann   I am sorry to call you in like that. I just saw you walking by my office.
我很抱歉這樣把妳叫進來。我剛好看到妳經過我辦公室。

Jane   No problem.
沒問題的。

Ann   I need to talk to you. Is that okay with you? Are you in a hurry?
我需要與妳談談。方便嗎？趕不趕時間？

Jane   I was just going to grab a coffee. What do you need to talk to me about?
我只是要去喝杯咖啡。妳想要和我談什麼呢？

Ann   I need to do a cash flow statement for my superiors.
我需要為我的上司做一份現金流量表。

Jane	You mean the partners? 你指的是那些合夥人們？
Ann	Yes. The school just called. My son cut himself while chopping vegetables. 是的。但是學校剛打電話來說，我兒子在切蔬菜時，切到自己。
Jane	Oh, dear. I hope he's okay. 哎呀！我希望他沒事。
Ann	It's not too bad. The big problem is my son can't stand the sight of blood. 情況不是太糟。問題是我兒子看到血會受不了。
Jane	I have heard of people like that. 我聽過像這樣子的人。
Ann	Yes. He passed out. They took him to the hospital. He has no car. 是的，他昏倒了。他們送他去醫院，而他沒有車回家。
Jane	I wouldn't want him driving right now anyway. 無論如何，我不會想要讓他馬上開車。
Ann	He doesn't have any money for a taxi because his wallet at the school. 他沒有錢搭計程車，因為皮夾留在學校了。
Jane	I wonder why no one from the school stayed with him. 我好奇為什麼學校沒有派人留下來陪他。
Ann	That's probably best. I need to go to get him and take him home. 也許那樣最好。我需要去看他，然後帶他回家。

Jane	So you don't have time to do the cash flow statement.
	所以妳沒時間做現金流量報表。

Ann	Exactly. Can I ask you to do it for me?
	正是如此。我可以拜託妳幫我做嗎？

Jane	It's been a long time since I did one. Will you please go over it quickly with me?
	我上次做這個表是很久以前的事了。請妳很快地和我複習一遍好嗎？

Ann	Of course.
	當然。

Ann starts to gather her things to get ready to leave.
安開始收拾她的東西，準備離開。

Ann	A balance sheet tells you what your business is worth.
	資產負債表告訴妳公司的價值。

Jane	Right.
	對。

Ann	An income statement tells you if you are making a profit.
	收益表告訴你公司是否賺錢。

Jane	Right.
	好的。

Ann	A cash flow statement tells you how to run your business. A business runs on cash.

現金流量表告訴你如何經營公司。公司是用現金在經營。

Jane Okay.

好的。

Ann A cash flow statement helps you look at the past to plan for the future.

現金流量表幫助你觀察過去，以便計畫未來。

Jane That's a nice way of putting it.

那是描述這個表格不錯的方式。

Ann It shows the partners what cash is available and when more is coming.

它顯示給合夥人，讓他們看手頭可用的現金有多少，何時會有更多現金進帳。

Jane What do I do?

我要做什麼呢？

Ann You need to show the sources of cash and the cash outlays.

妳需要顯示出現金的來源和支出。

Jane Okay.

好的。

Ann The difference between those two shows what cash there is that is left over.

從這兩者的差異就可以看出哪裏有多餘的現金。

Jane When you say sources of cash you mean all money that is coming in.

當妳提到現金的來源，妳是指所有進帳的錢。

Ann Yes.

是的。

Jane	And when you say cash outlays, you mean all the money that needs to go out. 當妳提到現金支出，指的是所有出帳的錢。
Ann	You got it. 妳說對了。
Jane	That is easy. I can do that for you. No problem. 那很簡單。我可以幫妳做。沒問題的。
Ann	Thanks, Jane. I am going to go now. 謝謝妳，珍。我現在要走了。
Jane	Don't worry about it. Drive safely. 不要擔心。小心開車，注意安全。
Ann	Bye, Jane. 再見，珍。

Comprehension Questions 理解測驗

____ (1) When did Ann's son have an accident?

    A) This afternoon

    B) This evening

    C) This morning

    D) All of the above

____ (2) Where is Ann going?

    A) To pick her son up from the hospital.

    B) To take him home

    C) To drive him home

    D) All of the above

_____ (3) How can Jane help Ann?

A) She can do an income statement.

B) She can do a balance sheet.

C) She can sit at Ann's desk.

D) She can do a cash flow statement.

_____ (4) Why does Ann need to pick up her son?

A) He cut himself while chopping vegetables.

B) He does not have money for a taxi.

C) He does not have his car.

D) All of the above

Vocabulary 字彙

grab	v.	抓取
cash flow		現金流量
chop	v.	切；砍
pass out		昏倒
wallet	n.	皮夾
profit	n.	盈利
available	adj.	可用的
outlay	n.	支出；花費
source	n.	來源

Answers 解答 (1)C (2)D (3)D (4)A

Chapter 8

Choices
選擇

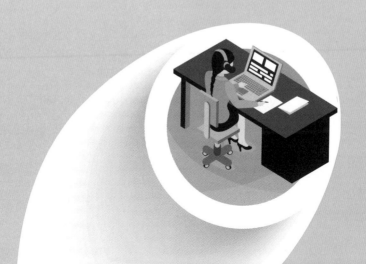

Unit 1　Pick and Choose
挑和選

MP3-47

Dick is working in his office. Bob comes in with two coffees.

迪克在他辦公室工作。鮑伯拿著兩杯咖啡進來。

Dick Bob, I need to speak to an organization tonight. Do you want to come?

鮑伯，我今晚需要對一機構發表演說。你想來嗎？

Bob I don't know, Dick. It depends what you will be speaking about.

我不知道，迪克。要視你演講的內容而定。

Dick What do you mean?

此話怎說？

Bob If you are talking about cats, I don't want to come. I am allergic to cats.

如果你要講關於貓的事，我才不要去。我對貓過敏。

Dick What?

什麼？

Bob They make me sneeze. My face turns all red.

牠們會讓我打噴？。我的臉會變成紅色。

Dick Why on earth would you think I would be talking about cats?

為什麼你會認為我要講關於貓的事？

Bob I am joking, Dick.

我在開玩笑，迪克。

Dick Oh! You're so funny. I was wondering what was wrong with you.

哦！你真的很有趣。我還在奇怪你是哪裡有問題。

Bob I love cats. I was just being funny.

我喜歡貓。我剛才只是說著玩的。

Dick You got me.

你讓我當真了。

Bob I would like to come to hear your speech. Are you nervous?

我想要來聽你的演講。你會緊張嗎？

Dick Yes. Will you listen to my speech? I want to practice.

是的，你可以聽一下我的演講嗎？我要練習一下。

Bob Okay. Go ahead.

好的。請說。

Dick Thank you. I will not do the whole speech for you right now.

謝謝你。我現在不會發表全部的演說給你聽。

Bob Okay.

好的。

Dick First, I will introduce myself and talk a little about our accounting firm.

首先，我會介紹一下我自已和我們的會計師事務所。

Bob Of course.

當然。

Dick After that is the part I need to practice.

之後就是我需要練習的部份。

Bob Go ahead, Dick.

請繼續，迪克。

Dick Okay. If you don't have an accountant, you should shop for one. Ask other people about their accountants. Find out what they like about them.

好的。如果你沒有會計師的話，就應該去找一位。問問其他人的會計師，去了解為什麼有些人會喜歡他們的會計師。

Bob Yes.

是的。

Dick Another good thing to do is to go to meet with several accountants. Interview them as though you had a job position to fill.

另一個好方法是與幾個會計師見個面。去和他們面談，假裝你需要一個會計師。

Bob Good idea.

這是個好主意。

Dick Here are some good questions to ask accountants when you meet with them. Ask the accountant if they have worked with your size of business before.

這裏有一些好問題，你可以在和他們見面問。問問會計師他們以前是否做過與你公司大小差不多的的公司帳。

Bob Yes.

是的。

Dick If they've worked with businesses bigger or smaller than yours, that's not good.

如果他們的客戶公司規模大或小於你的公司，那就不太適合。

Bob	Dick?
	迪克？

Dick	Yes?
	怎麼了？

Bob	The zipper on your pants is down.
	你褲子的拉鏈是開的。

Dick looks down and sees that his fly is open. His face turns red. He zips his pants.

迪克往下看，看到他的拉鏈是開著的。他臉紅了。他把褲子的拉鏈拉好。

Dick	I am so embarrassed. These pants do that.
	我很糗。這件褲子會這樣子。

Bob	Yep. It was all the way down.
	耶！它整個都開了。

Dick	The zipper on them slowly falls down. Most times I remember to check.
	褲子的拉鏈會慢慢滑下。大多數的時候，我都會記得檢查。

Bob	You better not wear those pants to your speech tonight.
	晚上你最好不要穿這件褲子去演講。

Dick	Right. I'll go home and change.
	對。我會回家換褲子。

Bob	Okay. Go on with your speech.
	好的。繼續你的演說。

Dick   Ask each accountant about the cost. It's good to know what they will charge you.

問每一個會計師的費用，知道他們將和你收費多少是比較妥當的做法。

Bob   Dick?

迪克？

Dick   Now what?

又怎麼了？

Bob   You will have to change your shirt, too.

你上衣也該換。

Dick   Why?

為什麼？

Bob   You have a big stain on the front of it.

你上衣的前面有一大片污漬。

Dick   I do? Darn it.

真的嗎？該死。

Bob   Did you have pizza for lunch?

你午餐是不是吃了披薩？

Dick   Yes. How did you know?

是的。你怎麼知道？

Bob   Your shirt is telling me. I think you're wearing pizza sauce.

你上衣告訴我的。我想你沾到了披薩醬汁。

Dick   Thanks a lot.

非常謝謝你。

Bob   Would you prefer that I didn't tell you?

你會不會比較喜歡我不告訴你？

Dick No. You are a good coworker and a good friend. I just feel silly. That's all.

不。你是我的好同事和好朋友。我只是覺得自己很可笑而已。

Bob Don't worry about it. Finish your speech.

別為那個擔心。講完你的演說。

Dick Ask your accountant if he/she has a client that you could talk to.

問問你的會計師，你可不可以和他客戶談談。

Bob Good advice.

好建議。

Dick You want to know what other clients think of this accountant.

你想要知道別的客戶對這個會計師有什麼看法。

Bob Yes.

是的。

Dick Ask yourself if you feel comfortable with this person. Does he/she seem smart?

問你自己，與這人在一起時，你是否感到自在？他／她看起來聰明嗎？

Bob Good question.

好問題。

Dick Is he/she polite? Do you feel that you can trust him/her?

這個人有禮貌嗎？你覺得可以信任這個人嗎？

Bob Good.

很好。

Dick And then I'll thank them for letting me speak to them. What do you think?

然後我會向他們道謝，謝謝他們請我來演說。你認為如何？

Bob Do you really want to know?

你真的想知道嗎？

Dick Yes.

是的。

Bob I think your shoelace is untied.

我想你的鞋帶沒綁好。

Comprehension Questions 理解測驗

____ (1) When does Dick have to give this speech?

    A) Tomorrow

    B) This afternoon

    C) Tonight

    D) Tuesday night

____ (2) Where does he have a stain?

    A) On his pants.

    B) On the front of his shirt.

    C) On his tie.

    D) On his face.

____ (3) How is Dick feeling about giving a speech?

    A) He loves it.

B) He is nervous.

C) He is angry about it.

D) None of the above

_____ (4) Why is Dick embarrassed?

A) He has a bad speech.

B) He has bad breath.

C) There is something stuck in his teeth.

D) His zipper was open.

Vocabulary 字彙

organization	n.	機構
allergic	adj.	過敏的
sneeze	v.	打噴嚏
interview	v.	面談
position	n.	位置
zipper	n.	拉鏈
fly	n.	西裝褲前部的拉鏈
zip	v.	拉拉鏈
stain	n.	污漬
darn it		該死（damn it）
coworker	n.	同事
silly	adj.	愚蠢的
advice	n.	勸告
smart	adj.	機敏的
shoelace	n.	鞋帶
tie	v.	綁；繫

| untie | v. | 沒有綁；沒有繫 |

Answers 解答 (1)C (2)B (3)B (4)D

Unit 2 It's the Season
季節到了
`MP3-48`

Bob is walking past Jane's office.
She sees him and calls him in.
鮑伯經過珍的辦公室。她看到他，於是叫他進去。

Jane Bob, can you come help me?
鮑伯，你可以進來幫我嗎？

Bob Yes, Jane. What do you need help with?
是的，珍。妳需要我幫什麼忙？

Jane I need help with a speech I need to give.
我需要幫忙，關於一個我必須要做的演講。

Bob Why is everybody doing speeches all of a sudden?
為什麼突然每個人都要發表演說？

Jane It's the season.
因為季節到了。

Bob What does that mean?
那是什麼意思？

Jane You know that Christmas carol that says 'tis the season to be jolly'?
你知道有一首聖誕頌歌裏面說：「這是該喜樂的季節」？

Bob　Yes.
我知道。

Jane　It's that time of year. It is year-end for a lot of people.
現在是一年中的那個時節，這個時節對很多人來說是年終。

Bob　Right.
對了。

Jane　People need to get their personal income taxes in.
人們需要準備報他們的個人所得稅。

Bob　Of course.
當然。

Jane　Businesses will need to have their taxes ready soon.
公司很快也需要準備好他們的稅。

Bob　Yes.
是的。

Jane　Everyone needs an accountant. They phone and ask us to come speak to a group.
每個人都需要會計師。於是他們打電話來邀請我們，進行團體演說。

Bob　Okay.
噢。

Jane　We do it free of charge. It's our way of helping others. We share our information.
我們做這件事不收費。這是我們幫助別人的方式。我們和他人分享我們的資訊。

Bob Just as you have shared it with me.
就像你和我分享資訊一樣。

Jane In a way, yes. Now, will you listen to this speech?
可以這麼說。現在，你準備好要聽這個演說了嗎？

Bob Yes. Go ahead. I'm becoming an expert on listening to speeches.
是的，開始吧。我快成為聽演講的專家了。

Jane Thanks. You can do a lot of your own financial records by using your computer.
謝謝。你可以用自己的電腦，來為做很多自己的財務記錄。

Bob Good.
很好。

Jane Some things that you can do yourself are recording daily transactions.
你自已可以做到的是登錄每天的交易。

Bob Right.
對。

Jane And the maintaining of the general ledger.
和總分類帳的維護。

Bob Right.
對。

Jane You can also do your own accounts receivable and your own accounts payable.
同時，你也可以幫自己做應收帳款和應付帳款。

Bob Right.
對。

Jane How does that sound so far, Bob?

到目前為止，聽起來如何，鮑伯？

Bob It sounds good so far. And I'm happy to see that you aren't wearing any food.

到目前為止聽起來很好。並且我很高興看到妳沒有沾到什麼食物醬類。

Jane What?

你在講什麼啊？

Bob shakes his head and smiles.
鮑伯搖搖頭笑著。

Bob Never mind. Go on with your speech. You're doing great.

別在意。繼續妳的演說。妳表現得很好。

Jane You'll need an accountant to help with adjusting entries if you make a mistake. They can prepare financial statements, close entries, and do income tax returns. They can even help you make your budget for the next year.

如果你做錯了，你將需要一個會計師幫你調整登錄。他們可以準備財務報表，總結登錄和申報所得稅，甚至可以幫你做明年的預算。

Bob What's the matter?

怎麼了？

Jane I forgot what I was going to say next. Oh, yes. Now I remember.

我忘了接下來我要說什麼。噢，現在我想起來了。

Bob Pick up where you left off.
回到妳剛才沒講完的。

Jane You'll need an accountant at least once a year. They'll close the books at year-end.
一年你至少需要會計師一次，他們在年終時會結算帳目。

Bob Yes.
是的。

Jane They'll file your income tax and prepare your financial statements.
他們會申報你的所得稅、準備你的財務報表。

Bob Right.
對。

Jane The more often you get financial statements, the better.
你越常拿到財務報表，越好。

Bob It's the best way to know how your business is doing.
它是讓你了解公司營運情形的最好方式。

Jane That's part of my speech.
是我演說的一部份。

Bob Good job.
妳表現得很好。

Jane Thank you. This is Ann's speech but she can't go. She asked me to do it instead.
謝謝你。這是安的演說，但她無法去，她要我代替她去。

Bob Are you nervous?
妳會緊張嗎？

Jane Not at all. Ann and Dick always give the speeches. I'm glad to have the chance.

一點也不。安和迪克常常演說。我很高興有這個機會。

Bob I would tell you good luck but you will not need it. You're very good.

我本來要祝妳好運的，但妳不需要它。妳表現得非常好。

Jane Thanks.

謝謝。

Comprehension Questions 理解測驗

____ (1) How come Jane is giving this speech?

A) Dick doesn't want to do it.

B) Dick can't do it.

C) Ann doesn't want to do it.

D) Ann can't do it.

____ (2) Why doesn't Jane do more speeches?

A) Dick does all the speeches.

B) Ann does all the speeches.

C) Dick and Ann do all the speeches.

D) None of the above

____ (3) Who wrote this speech?

A) Jane

B) Bob

C) Dick

D) Ann

____ (4) What is Jane speaking about?

A) What you can do without your accountant

B) What you will need your accountant to do

C) Not getting food on your shirt

D) Listening to a speech

Vocabulary 字彙

speech	*n.*	演講
carol	*n.*	頌歌
charge	*n.*	索取費用
expert	*n.*	專家
transaction	*n.*	交易
maintain	*v.*	維護
adjust	*v.*	調整
prepare	*v.*	準備

Answers 解答   (1)D   (2)C   (3)D   (4)B

Unit 3 Can We Keep Him?

我們可以留下他嗎？   MP3-49

Dick sees Ann leaving the staff room.
He joins her in the hallway.

迪克看見安離開員工休息室。他加入她一起在走廊上
走著。

Dick   Hi, Ann. What are you doing right now?

嗨，安。妳現在要做什麼？

Ann I am going back to my office. I just finished having a break.

我要回去我的辦公室。我剛休息完。

Dick I see.

是這樣子的啊！

Ann There are donuts in the staff room. My son made them.

員工休息室有甜甜圈，是我兒子做的。

Dick How nice.

真好。

Ann You can have one if you want. There should still be some left.

如果你要的話，你可以吃。應該還有些剩下的。

Dick I'll get one later. I would like to talk to you if you have a minute.

我等一下再去拿一個。如果妳有時間的話，我想和妳談一下話。

Ann Is there something wrong?

有什麼事不對勁嗎？

Dick No. Everything is okay. I would just like to talk to you.

不，一切都很好。我只是想要妳談談。

Ann Okay. Come on in.

好的。進來吧！

Dick and Ann go into her office.
迪克和安進去她的辦公室。

Ann　Have a seat. I'll shut the door. Now tell me. What is bothering you?

請坐。我來關門。現在告訴我，有什麼事在困擾你嗎？

Dick　It is not as serious as you seem to think. It's about Bob.

沒有像你想的那樣嚴重，是關於鮑伯。

Ann　Yes?

是嗎？

Dick　You haven't talked to me since I suggested that you hire him.

自從我向妳建議雇用他，妳還沒和我談過。

Ann　Right.

是的。

Dick　I just wanted to ask you if you had a chance to think about it yet.

我只想要問妳，是否有機會考慮這件事了？

Ann　You really think Bob is that good?

你真的認為鮑伯有那麼好？

Dick　Yes. Can we keep him?

是的。我們可以留下他嗎？

Ann　You sound like you are talking about a puppy dog.

你講話的語氣好像是在講一隻小狗。

Dick No.
不是這樣的。

Ann My concern is that Bob does not have any training.
我的顧慮是鮑伯沒有受過任何訓練。

Dick What? What have I been doing with him these last nine weeks?
什麼？那過去九個星期我和他一起做了些什麼呢？

Ann You make a good point. What I meant was that he has no accounting course.
你說的話有道理。我的意思是他沒有上過會計課程。

Dick And?
然後呢？

Ann He has not been through an accounting program.
他也沒完成任何會計訓練計畫。

Dick I've worked with him for over two months. That should be worth something.
我與他一起工作了兩個月，應該有些價值吧？

Ann I suppose.
我想也是。

Dick He has been trained for our firm by our firm. He would be a perfect fit.
他被我們的事務所訓練，來為我們做事。他會是完美人選的。

Ann I guess you're right.
我想你是對的。

Dick He already knows everything that we need him to know.

他已經知道所有我們需要他知道的一切。

Ann My problem is this. The partners want all of our staff to be educated.

我的問題是合夥人想要所有我們的員工都有專業教育背景。

Dick Do you think it's fair to tell him he has to go to school before we give him a job?

你認為告訴他在我們給他工作之前，他必須先去上學，這樣公平嗎？

Ann Not really.

不盡然。

Dick What does that say about what we taught him? What does that say about us?

那樣子的話，我們教他的又算什麼呢？那樣子我們又算什麼呢？

Ann I hadn't thought about it like that. I'll talk to the partners about this.

我沒有用那個角度想過這件事。我會與合夥人們談談這件事。

Dick You will?

妳會嗎？

Ann I'll do it this afternoon. I don't know if they will have time for me but I'll try.

我今天下午會做這件事。我不知道他們是否有時間給我，但我會試試看。

Dick　Okay.

好的。

Ann　I'll come to see you as soon as they make a decision. I promise. You have my word.

我答應你，只要他們做了決定，我會盡快和你碰面。你有我的承諾。

Dick　Okay. Thank you, Ann.

好的。謝謝妳，安。

Ann　By the way, between you and me, I hope we get to keep him, too.

順便告訴你，就你知我知喔！我也希望我們能留下他。

Comprehension Questions 理解測驗

____ (1) Who will decide if Bob gets hired?

A) Ann

B) Dick

C) The partners

D) Jane

____ (2) Why does Dick think that Bob should get hired?

A) He is already trained.

B) He is a nice guy.

C) Bob deserves a break.

D) Both (B) and (C) are correct.

____ (3) When will Ann give Dick an answer?

A) Once she decides

B) Once the partners decide

C) Once Bob decides

D) Both (B) and (C) are correct.

___ (4) How many weeks has Bob been volunteering?

A) Eight

B) Nine

C) Ten

D) None of the above

Vocabulary 字彙

donut	*n.*	甜甜圈
puppy	*n.*	幼犬；小狗
perfect	*adj.*	完美的；最佳的
fit	*n.*	合適
educate	*v.*	教育
fair	*adj.*	公平的
promise	*v.*	答應；允諾

Answers 解答 (1)C (2)A 3)B (4)B

Chapter 9

Learning More
多學一點

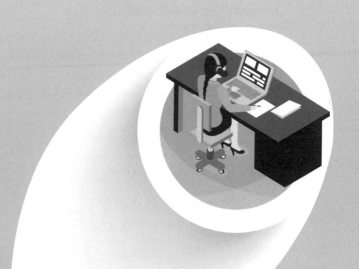

Unit 1 **One or the Other**
這個或是那個

MP3-50

Bob walks into Dick's office carrying two coffees. He gives one to Dick.

鮑伯帶著兩杯咖啡走進迪克的辦公室。他拿一杯給迪克。

Bob How are things going today, Dick?
今天一切都好嗎,迪克?

Dick Not bad. What about you, Bob? How are you this morning?
還不錯。你呢,鮑伯?今天早上好嗎?

Bob I am good. You look different today. Why do you look different?
我很好。你今天看起來不一樣。為什麼會這樣呢?

Dick I have glasses on.
我戴了眼鏡。

Bob But you don't wear glasses.
但你不戴眼鏡的。

Dick That used to be true. I need glasses now. I had my eyes tested three weeks ago.
以前那是真的。我現在需要眼鏡。三星期前我去檢查眼睛。

Bob I see.
我懂了。

Dick Today is my first day wearing my new glasses.
今天是我第一天戴新眼鏡。

Bob　They look good on you. Do you like them?
你戴起來很好看。你喜歡你的眼鏡嗎？

Dick　I don't know how I'll ever get used to having them on my face. They feel funny.
我不知道要怎樣習慣把眼鏡戴在臉上，感覺很滑稽。

Bob　You'll get used to them. So what are we doing today?
你會習慣的。那我們今天要做什麼呢？

Dick　You have really helped me to get caught up in my work.
你真的幫忙我，讓我能趕上進度。

Bob　Good to hear.
很高興聽到你這麼說。

Dick　I no longer take work home with me. My office is organized and tidy.
我不再把工作帶回家。我的辦公室很整齊，很有條理。

Bob　That's good.
那很好。

Dick　I come to work the same hours as everyone else.
我上班的時間和其他人一樣。

Bob　Good.
這很好。

Dick　The company no longer has to pay me overtime.
公司不用再付我加班費。

Bob　That's good for the company.
這對公司很好。

Dick	That's right. Overtime costs them a lot of money. Let's do what you want to do.
	沒錯。加班費讓他們花了不少錢。我們去做一些你想要做的吧！

Bob	Great.
	太好了。

> *Bob thinks for a minute.*
> 鮑伯想了一下。

Bob	I'd like to learn about the two different methods of accounting.
	我想要學習關於會計的兩種不同方法。

Dick	Are you talking about the cash method and the **accrual** method?
	你講的是現金法和應計法嗎？

Bob	Yes.
	是的。

Dick	These are the two different ways of accounting for small business. We will talk about the cash method of accounting first.
	這些是小企業做會計的兩種不同方法。我們先談談會計的現金法吧。

Bob	Okay.
	好的。

Dick	You only record income when you get paid.
	當你收到付款時，才記錄收益。

Bob
Okay.
好的。

Dick
You only record an expense when you pay it.
只有在付款時,才記錄費用。

Bob
You only record income when you receive payment from a customer.
只有在接到客戶付款時,才記錄收益。

Dick
Yes.
好的。

Bob
And you only record expense when you write a cheque to someone else.
只有當你開支票給別人時,才記錄費用。

Dick
The problem is if you do a lot of invoicing, it's hard to know what's in stock.
問題在於如果你開了一大堆的發票,你很難知道庫存有多少。

Bob
I see.
我明白了。

Dick
Stock has left the store but you didn't record the sale because they did not pay you.
貨物已經離開店了,但你沒有記錄銷售額,因為他們還沒付款給你。

Bob
Now what about accrual?
那應計法呢?

Dick
You record the income at the time of sale, not when you get paid.
你在銷售出去時就記錄收益,而不是在收到款項時。

Bob　I see.
　　　我明白了。

Dick　You record the expense when you get your stuff,
　　　not when you pay for it.
　　　當你拿到想要的東西或服務時，就記錄費用，而不是在你
　　　付款時記錄。

Bob　Right.
　　　好。

Dick　This is more work but it is better bookkeeping.
　　　You have better records this way.
　　　這樣比較花工夫，但它是比較好的記帳方式。用這種方式
　　　的記錄會比較好。

Bob　That is easy.
　　　那很容易。

Dick　You are smart.
　　　你很聰明。

Comprehension Questions　理解測驗

____ (1) What is new about Dick?

　　　A) He has a new shirt.

　　　B) He has a new tie.

　　　C) He has new pants.

　　　D) He has new glasses.

____ (2) Why can Bob do whatever he wants
　　　today?

　　　A) He has helped Dick to get caught up.

　　　B) He has new glasses.

C) Dick does not feel like working today.

D) Bob needs to feel special.

___ (3) When does the accrual accounting system record expense?

A) When the company gets paid

B) When the company gets the product or service

C) When the company feels like it

D) None of the above

___ (4) When does the cash method record income?

A) When the company gets paid

B) When the company gets the product or service

C) When the company feels like it

D) All of the above

Vocabulary 字彙

test	v.	檢查
overtime	n.	加班費；加班時間
cash method		現金法
accrual method		應計法
stock	n.	庫存；存貨
stuff	n.	東西

Answers 解答 (1)D (2) A (3)B (4)A

Unit 2 Petty Cash
零用金

MP3-51

Dick enters his office and gets to work. Bob comes in right after him.

迪克進入他的辦公室,開始工作。鮑伯緊跟進去。

Bob Dick, there are no more pens in your office. I don't know where they all went.

迪克,你辦公室沒有筆了。我不知道它們都到哪去了。

Dick Pens come and go, Bob. It's not a problem. Go to the **supply** room.

筆會來來去去,鮑伯。這不是問題。去文具室領吧。

Bob I did.

我去過了。

Dick Get a box of pens and bring them here.

拿一盒筆回來這裏。

Bob I already went to the supply room. There are no pens in there, either.

我已經去過文具室了。那裏也沒有筆。

Dick That's okay. We'll just ask Ann if we can take some money out of petty cash. Then you and I will go down to the store and buy some pens.

那沒關係。我們去問安看看,是否能從零用金拿出一些錢。然後你和我再去店裏買筆。

Bob Great.

太好了。

Dick We'll see if there is anything else that the supply room has run out of. If there is something else, we can get it at the same time.

我們去看看文具室有沒有短 其它東西。如果有的話,我們可以一起買回來。

Bob Petty cash?

什麼是零用金?

Dick All businesses should have a petty cash fund for small day to day expenses.

所有公司都應該有筆支付每日小額費用的零用金。

Bob Sounds good.

聽起來很不錯。

Dick You don't want to have to ask the store to invoice you for some pens.

你不會想要和店家索取筆的發票。

Bob Right.

對。

Dick They want payment when you buy. Besides.

當你買東西時,他們就會要你付款。而且…

Bob Besides what?

而且什麼?

Dick It's too much work to get our accounts payable department to cut a cheque.

讓我們的應付帳款部門開張這樣的支票,實在太大費周章了。

Bob The store doesn't like to take cheques anyway.

再說商店也不喜歡收支票。

Dick Exactly.
正是如此。

Dick stands up and puts on his coat.
迪克站起來穿上外套。

Dick At times like this, it is best to take money out of petty cash.
像這種時候，最好是從零用金拿錢出來。

Bob Where is this petty cash kept?
零用金放在哪裏呢？

Dick We have a petty cash box that we keep locked up in a drawer.
我們有一個零用現金箱，鎖在抽屜裏。

Bob Okay.
好的。

Dick You get the key from Ann. You take out what you think you will need. When you come back, you put any leftover change back in and the receipt.
你從安那裏拿鑰匙。你拿出你認為你需要的金額。當你回來時，把剩下的錢和收據放回去。

Bob Anything else?
還有其它要注意的事嗎？

Dick Just lock it up and give the key back to Ann. That's all there is to it.
只要把箱子鎖好，把鑰匙還給安。這就是所有的步驟了。

Bob   Easy.

這很簡單。

Dick   Yes.

是的。

Bob   What happens when petty cash is empty? When all that's in there is receipts?

當零用金用完了，會怎麼樣呢？當裏面只剩下收據時？

Dick   You add up those receipts. You write a cheque for that amount.

你把收據的金額加起來，再開一張那個金額的支票。

Bob   I see.

我懂了。

Dick   Write the cheque to petty cash and go to cash it.

開一張支票給零用金，然後兌現。

Bob   Of course. It all makes sense to me now.

當然。現在對我來説，一切都很清楚了。

Dick   Then you have all the money back in petty cash. You're back where you started.

然後你把所有的錢放回到零用金裡，這下你又回到原來的起點了。

Bob   How much do you keep in petty cash?

零用金裡該放多少錢？

Dick   It depends on the business. It is best to keep very little. We keep fifty dollars.

要視公司大小而定。最好留很少。我們留五十元。

Bob I will go to see what else we need for the supply room.

我去看看文具室裏還缺些什麼？

Dick I will get the key from Ann.

我去和安拿鑰匙。

Comprehension Questions 理解測驗

____ (1) What have they run out of?

A) Cash

B) Petty cash

C) Pens

D) Receipts

____ (2) Where are all of the supplies kept?

A) In a drawer

B) In a locked drawer

C) Ann keeps them.

D) In the supply room

____ (3) How do you replenish petty cash?

A) Write a cheque to petty cash.

B) Cash a cheque to petty cash.

C) Write a cheque for the total of the receipts.

D) All of the above

____ (4) How much money do they keep in petty cash?

A) Fifty dollars

B) Fifteen dollars

C) Five dollars

D) Fifteen hundred dollars

Vocabulary 字彙

supply	*n.*	供應
run out of		用完
petty	*adj.*	小的
petty cash		零用金
department	*n.*	部門
lock	*v.*	鎖
receipt	*n.*	收據
add up	*n.*	把⋯加起來
amount	*n.*	總額
make sense		有道理
replenish	*v.*	補充

Answers 解答 (1)C (2)D (3)D (4)A

Unit 3 Closing the Books
結帳

MP3-52

Bob and Dick are working in Dick's office.
鮑伯和迪克在迪克的辦公室工作。

Bob I am excited to do this speech, Dick.
我很興奮要進行這個演說，迪克。

Dick That's good, Bob, because I hate speeches. Ann thinks I love them but I don't.

那很好,鮑伯,因為我討厭演説。安以為我喜歡做這個,其實我不喜歡。

Bob Really?

真的嗎?

Dick So if you like doing them, I like having you do them.

那麼如果你喜歡做這個,我就想讓你做。

Bob It is fun. Besides, I am helping people.

這很有趣。而且,我在幫助別人。

Dick Do you want to go through your speech one more time?

你想要把演説從頭到尾再演練一遍嗎?

Bob No, thank you. I am ready.

不用了,謝謝你。我準備好了。

Dick I think you should go through it one more time.

我想你該再全程演練一次。

Bob I think you're more nervous than I am.

我想你比我還緊張。

Dick I know for sure that I'm more nervous than you are. Are you nervous at all?

我很肯定我比你還緊張。你會緊張嗎?

Bob Not really.

不盡然。

Dick I thought so. Okay. Pretend I'm the audience. Say your speech.

我也這麼認為。好的。假裝我是聽眾，進行你的演説吧。

Bob If I have to.
如果我必須要這樣做的話。

Dick Yes.
是的。

Bob Okay. Here goes.
好的。我要開始了。

Bob stands up.
鮑伯站了起來。

Bob At the end of an accounting period, you need to close the books. Accounting periods are one year long. At year-end, you need to close the books. You will file your income tax return at the same time. You want your financial statements done at least one time a year. To keep an eye on your business, it's best to have the statements made more often. Some people like to get them every six months or every three months. Some people even have them done every month. Are you bored yet?

在一個會計期間結束時，你需要結帳。會計期間是一年。在年終時，你需要結帳。同時你要申報所得稅。你的財務報表至少一年要做一次。為了檢視你的事業，最好一年做許多次財務報表。有些人喜歡六個月或三個月做一份。有些人甚至每個月做一份。你會覺得很枯燥嗎？

Dick　No. But I really like closing the books. I love to do financial statements.

沒有。但我真的喜歡結帳。我喜歡做財務報表。

Bob sits down.

鮑伯坐了下來。

Bob　I hope they don't get bored. It seems like a long speech.

我希望他們不會感到無聊。這似乎是個很長的演說。

Dick　It isn't that long. You can stop in the middle and ask if they have any questions.

不是那麼長。你可以在中間停下來，問他們有沒有問題。

Bob　I was going to ask if there were questions at the end.

我準備在最後再問他們有沒有問題。

Dick　Do both. That will break up the speech. It won't seem so long to you.

兩者都做。那樣會把演説分成兩部份。對你來說就不會太長。

Bob　That makes sense. Okay.

那很有道理。好的。

Dick　Keep going.

繼續下去。

Bob　If you don't get statements every month, you still close the books every month. This helps you to keep your books well organized. It helps you to send out invoices and to pay your invoices. It also helps you to check your bank statements and send in sales taxes. How was it?

如果你沒有每月拿到報表，還是可以每月結帳。這樣可以幫助你保持帳目井然有序。它幫助你寄出發票和支付發票款項。它也幫助你檢查你的銀行報表和繳交營業稅。我講的怎麼樣？

Dick Good.

很好。

Bob How do I tell them it is the end of the speech?

我該怎麼告訴他們，這是演說的終了。

Dick I don't know.

我不知道。

Bob I can say thank you.

我可以說「謝謝」。

Dick Sounds good.

聽起來很好。

Bob By the way, Dick. I'm going to be closing the books on my time with you.

順便說一下，迪克。我將要結算我和你的時間了。

Dick What do you mean?

你這話是什麼意思？

Bob Another accounting firm has offered me a job.

另外一家會計師事務所提供我一份工作。

Comprehension Questions 理解測驗

____ (1) Why is Bob giving this speech?

    A) Dick can't be there.

    B) Dick hates giving speeches.

    C) Bob asked to do it.

    D) Ann said he has to.

____ (2) What is the speech about?

    A) How to open the books

    B) How to prepare statements

    C) How to close the books

    D) How to close statements

____ (3) How often do people get financial statements?

    A) Once a month

    B) Twice a year

    C) Four times a year

    D) All of the above

____ (4) Why is Bob leaving Dick's firm?

    A) They won't give him a job.

    B) He doesn't like it there.

    C) He has a part time job at another firm.

    D) All of the above

Vocabulary 字彙

go through		經歷
pretend	v.	假裝
audience	n.	聽眾
close the book		結帳
period	n.	期間
file	v.	申請
keep an eye on		檢視
check	v.	檢查
offer	v.	提供

Answers 解答 (1)B (2)C (3)D (4)C

Chapter 10

A Perfect Fit

最佳人選

Unit 1 Accounting Programs
會計課程

MP3-53

Jane comes into the staff room. She is reading a book. Dick is eating an apple.
珍進去員工休息室。她正在讀一本書。迪克在吃蘋果。

Jane　Dick, tell me what is bothering you.
迪克，告訴我什麼事在困擾你。

Dick　Bob is going to be leaving us, Jane.
鮑伯將離開我們，珍。

Jane　What? That is terrible. Why?
什麼？那太糟了。為什麼呢？

Dick　He has been offered a part time job at another accounting firm.
別家會計師事務所給他一份兼職工作。

Jane　That is too bad. He is taking that job because we have not offered him one here.
那太可惜了。他要接那份工作是因為我們這裏沒有提供工作給他。

Dick　If we offered him a job here, he wouldn't leave. He'd take our job and stay.
如果我們給他一份工作，他就不會離開。他會接受我們的工作而留下來。

Jane　Does Ann know?
安知道這件事嗎？

Dick I'm not sure.
我不確定。

Jane You must tell her.
你應該告訴她。

Dick I will. I will go to see her this afternoon when she comes in.
我會的。今天下午當她進辦公室時,我會去見她。

Jane Why don't you go to see her now?
為什麼你不現在去見她呢?

Dick She's out of the office this morning. What are you doing?
她今早不在辦公室。妳在做什麼?

Jane I am looking at programs that you can take in accounting.
我在看會計方面可以上的課程。

Dick What have you found?
妳找到了什麼?

Jane You can take programs at different kinds of schools. There are career colleges.
不同的學校提供不同的課程。他們是職業學院。

Dick Career colleges?
職業學院?

Jane The programs they offer are entry level. They won't give you a high-level job.
他們提供的課程只是初級的。他們不會給你高層工作。

Dick Oh.
喔。

Jane　They'll get you in on the ground floor. They are certificate or diploma programs.

他們會幫你打下基礎。這些是證書或文憑課程。

Dick　That's what I took. I took a diploma program from a career college.

那就是我上過的課程。我在職業學院修了文憑課程。

Dick throws the apple core away in the garbage can.

迪克把蘋果核丟在垃圾桶裏。

Jane　Yes?

是嗎？

Dick　It was called an accounting technician diploma.

它叫作會計專員文憑。

Jane　A diploma takes less than a year. A university program gives you a degree.

拿張文憑花不到一年。大學課程可以給你一個學位。

Dick　Yes.

是的。

Jane　It usually takes about four years to get a degree.

一般要花四年才能拿到一個學位。

Dick　That's what you did, right? You got a degree from the university.

妳就是那樣做的，對吧？妳有大學的學位。

Jane　Yes. I was in the College of Commerce. I got a commerce degree.

是的。我讀商學院。我有商業學位。

Dick When I started, the partners were happy with me having a diploma.

當我剛來時，合夥人很樂於見到我有一張文憑。

Jane That was a long time ago.

那是很久以前的事了。

Dick Now they want their employees to have university degrees.

現在他們要員工們有大學學位。

Jane Yes. With a Commerce degree, you have a major. You can specialize in certain areas. Most of my friends specialized in marketing.

是的。有一個商業學位，代表你有主修。你可以專攻某個領域。我大多數的朋友專攻行銷。

Dick There are different titles for accounting degrees.

會計學位有不同的名稱。

Jane It is called designation. You can have different designations.

那叫名稱。你可以有不同的名稱。

Dick What is your designation?

妳的名稱是什麼？

Jane I am a chartered accountant. Some people become certified public accountants.

執照的公共會計師。

Dick Right.

對的。

Jane	Others become certified general accountants.
	其他人成為有執照的一般會計師。

Dick	Do you like being an accountant?
	妳喜歡當會計師嗎？

Jane	I do but I've been thinking about taking another course.
	我喜歡，但我一直在考慮修別的課。

Dick	Interesting.
	真有趣的想法。

Jane	That's why I'm reading this book. I might take a Master in Business Administration.
	那是為什麼我在讀這本書。我也許會修一個企業管理的碩士學位。

Dick	Then you will be like Ann. I hope you do not leave when Bob leaves.
	然後妳會像安一樣。我希望當鮑伯離開時，妳不會離開。

Jane	We'll see.
	到時就知道了。

Comprehension Questions 理解測驗

___ (1) Why is Dick upset?

    A) Ann is not in her office.

    B) He is talking to Jane.

    C) He has too much work to do.

    D) Bob is going to leave.

____ (2) When will Dick talk to Ann?
- A) When he is done talking to Jane in the morning
- B) When Ann gets into the office
- C) In the afternoon
- D) Both (B) and (C) are correct.

____ (3) What course would Jane like to take?
- A) College of Commerce
- B) Master in Business Administration
- C) Accounting technician
- D) Both (B) and (C) are correct.

____ (4) What did most of Jane's friends specialize in?
- A) College of Commerce
- B) Master in Business Administration
- C) Marketing
- D) Accounting Technician

Vocabulary 字彙

career	adj.	職業的
entry level		初級
ground	n.	地面
certificate	n.	証書
diploma	n.	文憑
core	n.	果核
garbage can		垃圾桶

degree	*n.*	學位
commerce	*n.*	商業
specialize	*v.*	專攻
marketing	*n.*	行銷（學）
designation	*n.*	名稱
chartered	*adj.*	有特許執照的
certified	*adj.*	有執照的
take a course		修課程

Answers 解答 (1)D (2)D (3)B (4)C

Unit 2 News
消息

MP3-54

Ann is looking for Dick. She finds him in the staff room.
安在找迪克。她在員工休息室找到他。

Ann Dick, can I see you in my office, please?
迪克，請你來我辦公室好嗎？

Dick Yes, Ann. Do you want me to come with you right now?
是的，安。妳要我現在就跟妳走嗎？

Ann Yes, please.
是的，麻煩你。

Dick　What is this about?
　　　有什麼事嗎？

Ann　Let me just say that you do good work for us here at the firm.
　　　讓我先這麼說，你在我們公司工作表現很好。

Dick　Thank you.
　　　謝謝你。

Ann　Your work has helped us to keep an eye on the business. It has helped us to make sure that the business is successful.
　　　你的工作表現幫助留意公司的經營狀況，幫助我們確定公司經營成功。

Dick　That's good.
　　　那很好。

Ann　Your work has given us the financial information that we need to make decisions. Your information has helped us to budget well. We want to thank you for all the good work that you do on the finances of the firm.
　　　你的工作提供給我們決策時需要的財務資訊。你的資訊幫助我們把預算編列得很好。我們要謝謝你，因為你在公司財務上所有的優秀工作表現。

Dick　You're welcome.
　　　不客氣。

Ann　And I have some news for you.
　　　我有一些消息要告訴你。

Dick looks worried.
迪克面帶憂慮。

Dick　Are you letting me go?
你們要叫我走路嗎？

Ann　No! Why would you think that?
不是的！你為什麼會那樣想？

Dick　I don't know. I do not understand why you are thanking me for the work I do.
我不知道。我不明白為什麼妳要為我做的工作謝我。

Ann　Because the work you do has helped us to budget well.
因為你的工作幫助我們把預算編得很好。

Dick　You said that.
這話妳剛剛講過了。

Ann　Because we can make a good budget, we can now offer Bob a job here.
因為我們把預算編得很好，現在才可以提供鮑伯一份工作。

Dick　Oh! That is great! Oh, no.
喔！太棒了！喔，糟了。

Ann　What is the matter? Aren't you happy?
怎麼了？你不開心嗎？

Dick　Bob has been offered a job at another firm.
別家公司已經給鮑伯一份工作了。

Ann　What?
什麼？

Dick Yes. I was going to tell you yesterday but you didn't come in.

是的，我本來昨天要告訴妳的，但妳昨天沒有回來。

Ann My meeting went over time. It went all afternoon.

我的會議一直延長到下午。

Dick Yes. Bob got a job.

是的，鮑伯有工作了。

Ann Well. That's not good news.

那不是個好消息。

Dick No. It isn't. He is a good worker. He's also already perfectly trained.

對，那不是。他是一個好員工，也已經受過完善的訓練。

Ann Yes.

是的。

Dick He would have been perfect for this job.

他是這工作最適合的人選了。

Ann Well. I don't know what to say. I guess I am sad. Bob is a good worker.

我不知該說些什麼。我想我很難過。鮑伯是好員工。

Dick Yes.

是的。

Ann I need some time to think about this, Dick. Will you please excuse me?

我需要時間想想這件事情，迪克，我得先離開一會兒？

Dick Sure, see you later.

當然。再見。

Comprehension Questions 理解測驗

___ (1) Where was Ann yesterday afternoon?

A) She was in a meeting

B) She was at home

C) She was with her son

D) She was at work

___ (2) Where did Ann and Dick meet?

A) They met in her office.

B) They met in his office.

C) They met in Bob's office.

D) They met in Jane's office.

___ (3) Where is Dick?

A) He is in the washroom.

B) He is in Jane's office.

C) He is in his office.

D) He is in the staff room.

(4) Where is Jane?

A) She is in her office.

B) She is in Bob's office.

C) She is in Dick's office.

D) It does not say.

Vocabulary 字彙

keep an eye on		注意;檢視
information	*n.*	資訊

budget	*v.*	編列預算
over time		超過規定時間
perfectly	*adv.*	完全地
excuse	*v.*	原諒

Answers 解答 (1)A (2)A (3)D (4)D

Unit 3 Good News All Around

到處都是好消息   MP3-55

Dick sits alone in his office. Jane knocks on his open door and then enters.

迪克在辦公室獨自坐著。珍敲敲打開著的門，然後進來。

Jane Dick, come to the staff room with me.
迪克，跟我來員工休息室一下。

Dick Why, Jane?
為什麼呢，珍？

Jane There is cake in there.
那邊有蛋糕。

Dick Why is there cake?
為什麼那邊會有蛋糕？

Jane We are celebrating.
我們在慶祝。

Dick I don't feel like celebrating. I am going to stay here and work.

我不想慶祝。我想待在這裏工作。

Jane Why don't you feel like celebrating?
為什麼你不想慶祝？

Dick What's to celebrate? That Bob is leaving? That this is his last day with us?
慶祝什麼呢？慶祝鮑伯要離開了？今天是他與我們的最後一天？

Jane You don't know?
你還不知道嗎？

Dick Know what?
知道什麼？

Jane Dick, Bob isn't leaving.
迪克，鮑伯不離開了。

Dick He's not? What? Are you sure? You had better not be joking.
他不離開了？什麼？妳確定嗎？妳最好不要開玩笑。

Jane I'm not. Ann talked to Bob. She offered him a job. He starts in three weeks.
我沒有。安和鮑伯談過。她提供他一份工作。他將在三星期後開始。

Dick He is? That is great news. I'm so happy. He'll be the perfect assistant for me.
是這樣子嗎？那是太棒的消息了。我好開心。對我來説，他是最理想的助理。

Jane He is not going to be your assistant, Dick.
他將不會是你的助理，迪克。

Dick He's not? What is he going to be doing then?
他不會？那他要做什麼工作？

Jane My job.
我的工作。

Dick looks surprised. Jane smiles.
迪克看起來很驚訝。珍笑著。

Dick What? What are you talking about?
什麼？妳在講什麼？

Jane I am leaving.
我要離開了。

Dick You are? Are you joking?
妳？妳在開玩笑嗎？

Jane No, I am not. I am going back to school. I want to get my masters in business administration.
不，我不是在開玩笑。我要回去唸書。我想要拿企業管理碩士。

Dick I don't know what to say. I'm glad that Bob will be here. I don't want you to go.
我不知道該說什麼。我很高興鮑伯會留下來，但我不想要妳走。

Jane I know. I'm sorry.
我知道。我很抱歉。

Dick I'm happy for you. But I will miss you.
我為妳高興。但我會想念妳。

Jane No, you won't.
不，你不會。

Dick Of course, I will. All these changes and I still don't have a part time assistant.

我當然會。在經歷這一切的改變後，我還是沒有一個兼職助理。

Jane Yes, you do.
你有的。

Dick I do? Who?
我有？誰呢？

Jane Me!
我！

Dick You? Really?
妳？真的嗎？

Jane Yes. I can't afford to go to school full time. I'm only going part time.
是的。我無法支付全職學生的學費，所以要半工半讀。

Dick What does that mean?
這是什麼意思？

Jane Ann gave me a job as your part time assistant.
安給我一份工作，要我當你的兼職助理。

Dick This is amazing. I am so happy. Everybody wins.
這實在是令人吃驚。我很高興。每個人都是贏家。

Jane There's more.
還有更多的。

Dick More good news? I can't believe it. What else could you possibly tell me?
更多好消息？我不敢相信。還有什麼是妳可能告訴我的呢？

Jane Ann has been promoted.
安獲得擢升了。

Dick Promoted? She can't go any higher.
擢升？她不可能升到更高的職位。

Jane Yes, she can. She has been asked to become a partner in the firm.
她可以的。她被邀請成為公司的合夥人之一。

Dick Wow! I can't believe it. That's great.
哇！我不敢相信。那太棒了。

Jane She's very happy.
她很開心。

Dick But that will leave a vacancy in the manager's position.
但經理的職位將會有空 。

Jane Not for long. She will keep doing the manager's duties until I'm done school.
不會太久的。她會繼續做經理的工作，直到我唸完書。

Dick Oh?
哦？

Jane The firm has asked me to be their manager as soon as I am done school.
公司已經叫我當經理，一旦我唸完書。

Dick That's terrific. What a happy day. I'm in shock, so many changes.
那太好了。多快樂的一天啊。我很震驚，有這麼多的改變。

Jane All of them good.
但所有改變都是好的。

Dick Yes, all of it good. You don't have any more news for me, do you?

是的，都是好的。妳沒有更多消息要給我吧？

Jane No. That's it.
不。那是全部了。

Dick That's good because I don't think I could take any more of this good news.
那好，因為我不認為我可以再接受更多好消息了。

Jane Now will you come for cake?
現在你會來吃蛋糕了嗎？

Dick Is it chocolate cake?
是巧克力蛋糕嗎？

Jane No. We know you don't like chocolate.
不。我們知道你不喜歡巧克力。

Dick Good news all around. Everybody wins.
到處都是好消息。每個人都是贏家。

Comprehension Questions 理解測驗

____(1) Why was Dick upset?

    A) He thought that there was no cake.

    B) He had to work while everyone else got a break.

    C) He was going to miss Bob.

    D) All of the above

____(2) Why is Bob taking Jane's job?

    A) She is going to school.

    B) He needed part time work.

    C) Jane has been let go.

D) None of the above

___(3) Why will Jane take Ann's job?

    A) She is going to school.

    B) She needed full time work.

    C) Ann has been let go.

    D) None of the above

___(4) Why is it good news all around?

    A) Bob is staying and Dick has a part time assistant.

    B) Jane and Ann will both get promotions.

    C) The cake is not chocolate.

    D) All of the above

Vocabulary 字彙

celebrate	v.	慶祝
offer	v.	提供
miss	v.	想念
afford	v.	有足夠的金錢(財力)
amazing	adj.	令人驚訝的
win	v.	贏
promote	v.	升
vacancy	n.	空缺

Answers 解答 1)C (2)A (3)D (4)D

國家圖書館出版品預行編目資料

財務會計英語 看這本就夠了(增訂1版) / 張瑪麗編著.
-- 新北市：哈福企業, 2023.12
　面 ；　公分. -- (英語系列；84)
ISBN 978-626-97850-1-8 (平裝)

1.CST: 商業英文　2.CST: 讀本

805.18　　　　　　　　　　　　112017563

免費下載QR Code音檔
行動學習，即刷即聽

財務會計英語 看這本就夠了
(附QR碼線上音檔)

作者／張瑪麗
責任編輯／Vivian Chen
封面設計／李秀英
內文排版／林樂娟
出版者／哈福企業有限公司
地址／新北市淡水區民族路 110 巷 38 弄 7 號
電話／(02) 2808-4587
傳真／(02) 2808-6545
郵政劃撥／ 31598840
戶名／哈福企業有限公司
出版日期／ 2023 年 12 月
台幣定價／ 399 元 (附線上 MP3)
港幣定價／ 133 元 (附線上 MP3)
封面內文圖 / 取材自 Shutterstock

全球華文國際市場總代理／采舍國際有限公司
地址／新北市中和區中山路 2 段 366 巷 10 號 3 樓
電話／(02) 8245-8786 傳真／(02) 8245-8718
網址／ www.silkbook.com 新絲路華文網

香港澳門總經銷／和平圖書有限公司
地址／香港柴灣嘉業街 12 號百樂門大廈 17 樓
電話／(852) 2804-6687
傳真／(852) 2804-6409

email ／ welike8686@Gmail.com
facebook ／ Haa-net 哈福網路商城

哈福

哈福